Out of Time

Brand of Justice
Book 10

Lisa Phillips

TWO DOGS PUBLISHING, LLC

eBook ISBN:979-8-88552-260-1

Paperback ISBN: 979-8-88552-261-8

Library of Congress Control Number: 2024952624

Published by: Two Dogs Publishing, LLC. Idaho, USA

Cover Design by: Sasha Almazan and Gene Mollica, GS Cover Design Studio, LLC

Edited by: Meghan Kleinschmidt, Literary Pearl Editing

Out of Time

Chapter One

In the fight to safeguard her family, Kenna Banbury had one weapon—and it wasn't a gun. Right now, she couldn't even hold one, let alone pull the trigger, so that was out. Knives. Stun gun. Pepper spray. She usually carried those things on any given day, but bad guys didn't need to be annoyed, they needed to be eliminated.

Kind of like the nuisance currently following her through New York City, late on a Wednesday evening. If that *was* who had been behind her for the last half dozen blocks. Her friend. Her associate.

Could be anyone, really. But she was pretty sure she knew who it was.

Kenna kept walking while the icy January breeze cut against her cheeks. Cars passed her on the street, going in both directions. Black SUVs and a silver Mercedes. The steady buzz of traffic alongside her was like a drone that seemed to occupy the city of New York. Every second of the day, the sound hovered in the air relentlessly, except for the occasional siren in the distance.

A guy on a bicycle cut in front of her, coming down 121st from her right and crossing to bump off the curb. She slowed her pace for a second, stepped aside, and continued down Broadway all the way to 116th street, where it seemed the person behind her, following her, was prepared to make his move.

Up at the restaurant a few buildings ahead, a group spilled out and headed away from her. The light and music from the buzz of humanity inside tipped onto the sidewalk every time the door swung open. She could go inside the restaurant, walk all the way up to the bar, and force a confrontation with her pursuer. In public, where she would have witnesses. But the type of person behind her wasn't the kind to want a big public spectacle.

He was, however, gaining on her.

Kenna spotted an alcove and kept walking toward it, waiting until she could practically feel him breathing on the back of her neck. She stepped to the right at the last second. He grabbed for her elbow as she spun onto the step and turned, kicking out with her leg, using the momentum of the turn and the step to give her the force she needed to cut one lower limb out from under him.

Unless, of course, he was expecting that. Which he must have been, because he didn't go down.

Ramon yelped. He hopped a couple of times on one foot, clutching the side of his leg just above his knee. "Yeouch. Dead leg. Dead leg. I've got a cramp. Aahhhh. That hurts. You're mean."

Kenna stared at her colleague. She wanted to stand there staring at him and cross her arms in front of her, but that wasn't something currently in her wheelhouse. Not with braces on both wrists. The injuries to her forearms didn't have much to do with her wrists, but immobilizing the whole thing—on both arms—kept her from making the strain on her forearms worse.

Her physical therapist actually had the audacity to tell her that she was the kind of person who would happily make things worse before she allowed them to get better. As if. For some reason, Jax had found that hilarious, but she didn't want to get into thinking about her FBI agent boyfriend right now.

She'd spent six weeks in Phoenix at his house. Recovering. Resting. Now it was back to work.

Kenna said, "If you didn't want a dead leg, maybe you shouldn't have been following me."

Ramon lifted his head, still rubbing the side of his leg. "Where did you clock me, 116th?"

Kenna smirked. "How about 129th." He'd definitely been following her walking south down Broadway for more than a mile.

"You lie." He narrowed a suspicious gaze on her.

"Would I?" Sure, they hadn't seen each other in a couple of months, except at Christmas, but Ramon knew her. They'd been at Quantico together. He'd gone undercover with a cartel, been burned, and when Kenna discovered him in Mexico, she had helped right that wrong. They'd taken down the dirty FBI agent who'd destroyed his career.

As a thanks for her help—although sometimes it felt more like a punishment—Ramon had decided she should train him to be a private investigator. Which was great, mostly. She was helping keep him on the straight and narrow.

Kenna had spent the holidays with Jax and his sister's family in Colorado, where her friends Stairns, Elizabeth and Maizie lived. She hadn't seen Ramon since Christmas.

"Okay, fine." He huffed. "You wouldn't lie. But I want to know how you figured out I was following you." He tested putting weight on his leg, then swung an arm around her shoulders. "But first tell me about this place where we're going."

"I regret asking you to be my backup."

"No, you don't." Ramon gave her shoulder a squeeze. "You're just mad that your boyfriend didn't want to take the weekend off to do a B&E with you."

"I didn't even ask."

"Good call." Another squeeze. "The Boy Scout doesn't need a black mark on his record. Can you even imagine what the media would do with news of an FBI Special-Agent-in-Charge from Phoenix breaking into an office building in New York City? There would be rumors flying all over the internet that he's up to all kinds of fun stuff."

"Fun stuff, like the kind that gets you put in jail for fifteen years?"

"Exactly." He let go of her to hit the button for the crosswalk.

Kenna had been in New York City just long enough that she'd figured out locals looked at the opposing direction of traffic and waited for their light to turn red, which always happened a second before the crosswalk turned green. She clocked the shift in the traffic and set off, stepping from the curb a second before the crosswalk light changed.

Ramon caught up. "Okay, you need to tell me how you do that."

She smiled to herself and said over her shoulder, "I've developed extra sensory perception. It happens when one of your physical abilities is nonexistent. You develop other special skills."

"So because you sprained both your injured forearms to the point that they're barely even usable, you've suddenly developed psychic powers?"

"It's definitely a more interesting turn of events."

Ramon caught up to her on the opposite sidewalk. "How far are we going, anyway?"

"95th."

"Is there a reason we need to walk from 130th all the way down to 95th? We could have just parked around the corner."

"True, but you need the steps."

He muttered something about Maizie under his breath.

Kenna's teenage friend, the girl who ran tech support for her business, had given them all smart watches at Christmas. It had only taken them a couple of days to realize she now had access to all their health data and could track their location at any time. No doubt these weren't your average smartwatches. The almost-adult had probably rewritten the software entirely, making it so they could never be tracked by anyone—but her.

She said, "It isn't as if she has no reason to be worried about us."

Kenna and Ramon had gotten into plenty of trouble since meeting again in Mexico, and they'd been in more than one hair-raising situation together. In comparison, the last month or two had been relatively calm.

Ramon said, "Did you decide if you're going to London?"

"What's to decide? Preston is looking for someone who

can run his protection detail. And a bodyguard without the full use of all four limbs isn't exactly anyone's first pick. His life is in danger, and I'm not going to be able to protect him if something happens." She glanced over at him, wondering if she should mention that things with Preston's request didn't quite add up. She just hadn't figured out why she was dragging her feet.

She said, "Which is why you're the one who needs to go."

"No go." Ramon shrugged. "He said it has to be you."

"Well, who knows. If we can shut down the threat tonight by convincing Wilson Sandhurst to quit coming after him, then no one will need to go to London with Preston. Because he won't be in any danger since his brother-in-law won't be trying to kill him."

Preston Lightwood had served twenty years for his wife's murder—and claimed even now to not be guilty. Still, his wife's brother had put out an invitation online looking for anyone willing to kill Preston for money.

Ramon said, "Maybe he just likes your company, so he wants you to go."

She wasn't going to touch that one. Preston had been friends with her father, and she figured he had stories he wanted to tell. Or for old times' sake, nostalgic reasons. He could simply want to spend time with her as a way to remember her father.

But it wasn't like there was any point in him paying her to protect him when her arms barely functioned. She couldn't even hold her phone up for that long. And it was taking way too much time for her to not wake up realizing how useless she was. Right now, she needed to feel like she could do *something*. Like this job.

Not that achieving what they'd come here to do would convince her she could keep people safe.

Jax.

Maizie.

Ramon.

Even Stairns and Elizabeth.

There were more in a wider circle, but the core was right there. And if she couldn't get the muscles in her arms to work, what good was she to any of them?

"Let's just get this done. I want to know why Wilson Sandhurst won't drop the issue of his sister's death. Preston can't live the rest of his life looking over his shoulder for an assassin after a payday." She realized they'd walked to the right cross streets and pointed west. "This way."

"You have the package from Maizie?"

"Delivered to my hotel room this morning." Kenna found the side door of the office building, where a small lobby would lead to the stairwell. They would have to climb fourteen floors to get to Sandhurst's office, but if Maizie's gadgets worked correctly, they wouldn't be seen entering. "How about you?"

Ramon patted his front right pocket.

Kenna looked up at the outside of the tall building, pretty sure she wasn't supposed to pray for favor when she was technically breaking the law. So she avoided asking for help —or permission—and she wasn't going to broach the subject with Ramon when she knew his stance on issues of faith.

Just because she believed didn't mean he had to in order for them to work together. He knew that if he wanted to ask about it, he only had to voice the question aloud, and she would be happy to talk about the change of heart she'd had in Mexico.

She hoped he would one day, but she wasn't going to push him if he wasn't ready.

Kenna slid the phone from her pocket and opened the app Maizie had remotely installed. She activated the signal jammer that would prevent any security system from alerting the owner to their presence here tonight. The small panel beside the door where anyone could use a key fob and gain entry clicked and the light turned green.

"Want me to go first? I brought my gun."

"Why don't we hold off on weapons until we know what the situation is inside."

"If the situation is people shooting at us, just get behind me, copy?"

Kenna didn't want to, but she said, "Copy."

She stepped inside the darkened lobby, where a cream-colored waiting area sat empty of people or much light. Turning on a flashlight would only let someone passing by outside know they were snooping around in here, so she walked from memory, using the map in her mind of the schematics Maizie had sent to her. "The stairs should be to the right, past the elevators."

"Great." Ramon huffed out the word and kept huffing all the way up the stairs. "If you make any cracks about my floors target, I'm going to push you back down these stairs."

Kenna grinned to herself. No way was she going to admit that, even she was feeling the burn of walking up more than a dozen flights of stairs. And that was after spending the last eight weeks working on her lower body strength.

"You're not even winded." Ramon frowned at her.

"I haven't been sitting around being miserable about my arms. I've been working out."

Jax had come up with a training plan she could do

without using her arms, attaching kettle bells to a belt so that she could move around with weights and develop her leg muscles. She'd asked him how many people he expected her to be kicking—or was it doors she was supposed to be opening with a stiff boot? He'd only laughed and told her to do two more sets of squats. The guy might be a tough taskmaster in the gym, but she had to admit, she felt better than she had in a long time. Strong. Capable—as much as was possible with her arm injuries. Almost as if Jax knew what she needed, and he'd figured out how to give it to her. Her favorite workout was when she swam laps of the pool with her arms secured to her waist to keep them from flopping around.

"Pretty elaborate plan to get me to work all your cases while you've been recuperating."

She glanced over at him. Did he mean hurting her arms in New Orleans? He knew that what'd happened hadn't been planned, but enough time had passed she could find his comment amusing.

Kenna snorted. "And yet it's been working. Haven't you been working my open cases?" She motioned to the door with a tip of her head. "Heavy door. If you don't mind."

"Right." Ramon pulled his gun and stepped first into the carpeted hallway of the office belonging to Wilson Sandhurst.

She stepped in, and her nose wrinkled right away.

What was...

The guy had some kind of consulting business, working with financial firms and investment corporations. Sandhurst and his small group of employees had occupied this space for nearly four years.

Kenna stepped into the hallway. "So why does it smell like fresh paint...and something else?"

Chapter Two

Ramon lifted his chin. "Bleach? Maybe they recently renovated and did a bunch of cleaning."

Sure. And maybe someone had been murdered in here, and the crime scene was cleaned up.

Kenna moved past him into the office and tapped the flashlight on her phone. They were unlikely to be seen from the fourteenth floor. Her previous surveillance from the neighboring building had given her enough intel to know it was likely the blinds would be all pulled down—and tonight was no exception.

She turned around, looking at the walls and the floor. "Fixing things up and cleaning doesn't usually smell like someone is trying to cover up a crime."

"Hopefully, something good happened in here, and this isn't just a boring office," Ramon muttered.

Something good...as in, a crime? Boy, he was an interesting guy.

He said, "I hate paperwork."

"I have actually noticed that." She tried to keep her tone mild, not like it irritated her that he failed to turn in paperwork after an investigation. And never did until she threatened him bodily harm.

She continued to scan the floor and walls with her phone but didn't see anything except new-looking carpet and fresh paint.

Ramon said, "If my sister's husband had killed her, I would just walk up to him and put a bullet in his head. I wouldn't wait twenty years for him to serve his sentence and then get out, only to go online and ask for people to kill him. Meanwhile, Preston is writing an autobiography to try and convince everyone he's innocent. As if that will help after he's dead."

"Get to the point."

"All this without an agreement and money up front like a contract kill. It's just a request for murder." He let out a noise of frustration. "If Wilson was actually trying to kill Preston, then Preston should be dead already. Failure is a lack of effort."

And Ramon was mad about it? "Is this because Wilson Sandhurst refused to let you take the contract to kill Preston?"

"It was a good plan. Even Jax thought it was a good plan, and your boyfriend and I don't always see eye to eye."

Kenna figured that was because Jax lived on the right side of the law. Ramon seemed to pick and choose what laws he wanted to follow. But given his instinct was to protect innocent people, she usually didn't argue with his methodology.

"Here." Kenna stopped walking, shining her light on the floor. The slight difference between the existing paint and the patch of fresh color reflected on the wall.

"Shame we have no Luminol to see if there's blood residue."

"Maybe Maizie can build us a gadget we can carry that will show biological material left behind." Kenna didn't usually work crime scenes, but this was definitely the aftermath of a cleanup attempt. "Let's keep looking."

Ramon sighed, loud enough she frowned.

Kenna said, "You can go look in the rooms behind us, you know. If we split up, it'll take half the time."

"I'm good with you."

Kenna kept walking along the hall, frowning because she knew he wasn't going to be able to see it. "I don't need a babysitter."

"I have a gun."

She kept her lips pressed together and blew a long breath out her nose. "How long were you behind me on the street?"

"Longer than 129th."

"How long?"

"Albuquerque."

She spun around. "Seriously?"

He shrugged. "Jax hired me. Your boyfriend pays well."

"This is unbelievable." She turned back and kept walking. "You know, the longer we stay here, the greater the chance we'll get caught. If that happens, it'll be your fault because we didn't split up."

"You're not mad Jax hired me to protect you?"

"You should go walk through those offices behind us. Make this go faster. But no, I'm not mad. He's worried about me, and I appreciate the fact someone cares about me enough to lay down money to make sure I'm protected."

"A *lot* of money."

"I think it's sweet."

Ramon snorted. He probably didn't agree, which considering his lack of romantic entanglements—at least as far as she knew—it wasn't super surprising.

Kenna stopped at the midpoint in the hall. "Huh." She looked around.

"More paint?"

"The schematics for the office had a different layout." She turned back.

"Please tell me there's a secret lair. Please, please." He touched his hands together, the gun sandwiched between them. Prayer and a weapon, one and the same to him. All his hopes wrapped up in his ability to resolve a situation.

His way.

"Find a sledgehammer. I'll tell you which wall to bust."

"Fire axe." Ramon turned, looking around. "No, no, no, a chair. I'll throw an office chair at the wall."

Kenna snorted. "Or we could find a door. There probably isn't anything, and I'm just remembering wrong."

"Point the way. I'll find out."

She stepped into a side room. A smaller office than what should be here. "Let me check my map." Kenna navigated to the different open app on her phone and the open pdf Maizie had sent her. She looked at the walls, then the map, then the walls again. "This room should be bigger."

"I love a good secret passage. Like that guy in Chicago who kept people in his house, tortured them in different rooms, and watched from the walls."

That was at least a century ago. "You mean H. H. Holmes?"

"Yeah, that guy."

Kenna didn't agree. There had been far too many secret passages in her life lately. Like the room in Vegas where she'd killed the man who had held and tortured Maizie for years. Or the hallway in that house in Scottsdale where she'd seen a disturbed young girl. One she wasn't sure she could've saved. More likely she'd be hunting the girl in a few years. She couldn't have gone up against that family, so she'd done what she could. God would take care of the rest.

"You're gearing up to argue." Ramon chuckled. "I watched a murder documentary on the plane, that's all. It was about killings from the 1800s and early 20th century. Jack the Ripper. Holmes."

Kenna shook her head. "I did a lot of reading in Phoenix. Thrillers. Sci-fi novels. Ancient history."

She'd spent nearly two months at Jax's house, give or take the trip to Colorado for Christmas. He'd slept in her RV in the garage he had on the side of his house. Despite the fact he didn't have a leisure vehicle, she did. Kenna didn't think too much about what it meant that he'd purposely bought a house with an RV garage, and neither of them had commented on how he'd chosen it so she could be there.

She'd spent that time recuperating after the nearly devastating injury she'd suffered in New Orleans. But considering a friend had lost one of his colleagues, her pain was nothing to what others had gone through.

Because of her.

"You held up a book?"

Kenna said, "Maizie got me an e-reader, and a stand that holds it up above my face while I'm lying in bed, and a remote to click to turn the page."

"Humanity is doomed."

Kenna laughed out loud. "That wall." She pointed for a second, then let her arm relax. "There should be more of this room behind it."

"Sit tight. I'll look." Ramon strode from the room, probably in search of an axe or a chair to throw.

Kenna perched on the edge of a desk. No papers. No computer. Not even a pen and some sticky notes.

The whole place was like *after* crime scene cleanup had visited. After the gore had been washed away and things were put back to rights. As if no one who worked here intended on coming back. But staff had been moving behind the blinds just yesterday.

What had happened here?

Kenna heard a tiny snick. She extinguished the flashlight beam on her phone camera, and the room plunged into darkness.

A door panel slid back from the wall, creating an opening where before there hadn't been one—just a stretch of wall. Someone stepped through. She couldn't make out anything about the person, but they walked with light feet. Kenna caught the faint scent of perfume. A woman?

She kept still while the woman crept to the door.

Until Ramon filled it, light from a flashlight in his hand illuminating the woman. Petite. Hair tied back. "Going somewhere?"

The woman screamed and launched herself at him. Scratching and biting. The two of them tumbled back into the hall with a thud, and she could hear them fighting.

Kenna went to the wall and felt around the join where the door had separated away. She leaned on the door. Shoved with her shoulder.

Nothing.

She went to the hall. "Hey, see if she has a key."

The door frame was an inviting place to lean. Listening to the grunting and the soft thuds of a fist or elbow on flesh.

Ramon cursed.

"You really should do something about your language, you know. It's a bad example for Maizie." Kenna tapped the flashlight button on her phone and illuminated the two of them, each grappling for supremacy over the other on the new carpet. Rolling around. Punching. Looked like the woman bit his arm. *Ouch.* "Anytime, bro."

Ramon flipped his assailant.

The woman twisted. Kenna spotted a flash of something silver in the light.

Before she could say "knife" and waste time with Ramon having to figure out a solution, Kenna took two running steps over to them and kicked out with her foot.

Kenna caught the woman's head and knocked her to the side. Ramon grabbed her wrist and immobilized the knife, discarding it. The woman slumped to the carpet, out cold.

Ramon said, "I had it handled."

"Check if she has a key on her for the secret room. We need to get in there. They don't even have a computer out here." Kenna kicked the knife away from the woman.

Ramon checked her pockets. "Key fob."

"Let's give it a try." She took it and went back into the room, running the fob over the wall on the seam.

A dull click sounded inside the wall, and the panel popped out toward her. "Now we're talking."

Chapter Three

Kenna palmed her phone and dialed Maizie before she even stepped into the secret room. It rang a couple of times. She hit the speaker button, and her teenage friend said, "Banbury Investigations."

"Just me and Ramon. We found a secret office behind a hidden door."

"Cool. Shame they're using it for evil, not good."

"Objection," Kenna said. "Speculation."

Maizie said, "Find proof I'm wrong, then."

Kenna felt the pull of humor on her lips, curling up the ends. With everything she'd gone through, Maizie had every right to need a barrage of mental health medications just so she could get through a day. Some people would've just opted for full-time medical care at an institution. No one would've blamed her for needing that or never wanting to function in society.

A lifetime of being tortured before she found her freedom.

What Kenna had been through didn't even compare.

Miraculously, Maizie seemed to have settled into life as a young woman. She had help whenever she needed it, thanks to Elizabeth who lived in the cabin nearby. She had her own space in the Airstream. She had a hobby that she'd turned into a job, doing tech work for Kenna, and she was even studying for her GED so she could start college classes in the fall. The young woman was carving a life for herself, one with a support system and healthy habits.

Kenna wanted to get down on her knees every day and thank God this girl had a future. That the monster who'd raised her didn't have the final say on how her life went. He'd tried to take everything from her—and Kenna had killed him for it.

Every day Maizie lived, she got to take a piece of her life back.

"Lot of stuff in here." Ramon wandered around the room, shining his flashlight so Kenna could see the dimensions.

"It's not a big space. Looks like ten by ten, or thereabouts." She looked over her shoulder and found a light. Flipped it on. "Whoa."

"What is it?" Maizie said through the phone speaker.

"Images and papers, stuff all over the walls."

"Crazy conspiracy stuff?"

Kenna spotted a picture she recognized. "More like surveillance, and it looks like Preston is the target." She looked at the PC, a computer tower down on the floor, monitor and keyboard on the desk. "Want me to pull the hard drive and send it to you?"

"Let's see if I can copy it now, if you have time."

Kenna looked at Ramon, but he was studying the images. She spotted a familiar face and frowned. "Ramon, is that a picture of Jax?"

"And you." Ramon sidestepped.

"Great." They were all under surveillance. Kenna shook the mouse awake and said, "If this thing has a password, how are we going to access it?"

"Just insert the thumb drive I sent you."

Ramon came over and handed her what had been in his pocket.

"Thanks." She bent and inserted it in the slot. "This tower has a tab; I can pull the hard drive if we need to run."

It wasn't only Maizie who had been learning things. Kenna had picked up some choice stuff from her young friend. Assuming that movie they'd buddy watched was accurate. Maizie had deconstructed what worked and didn't work from the whole thing. Kenna's wish for the girl was that she went and did any job she wanted, but gaining notoriety wouldn't be a good thing. Someone like Maizie needed to live a quiet life under the radar.

The teen said, "Okay, I'm in."

On the desk, the monitor flashed on. The mouse moved on the screen—Maizie connected remotely—and things started to move fast. Windows opened and closed, text filled boxes faster than Kenna could think, let alone type.

She watched Maizie run several simultaneous searches.

A file popped onto the screen, and she clicked to open it. Video format. The screen showed what looked like a video conference, a meeting between Wilson Sandhurst and a group of suited individuals. Maybe investors or partners.

The screen flickered and changed. The image was still visible, but beside it popped up a window where someone typed. A second later, Wilson said what had been typed.

"Is that you?" Kenna leaned down to look closer.

"It's not me. I'm watching like you are."

"Someone was feeding him what to say?"

Maizie said, "Actually...one sec." She clicked something, and another window popped up, with Wilson Sandhurst's image in it. "It's an avatar. He isn't really in this meeting. He, or someone else, is typing in the words in real time, and Sandhurst, the image, says whatever it is."

"Like Artificial Intelligence?"

"More like a computer program someone wrote, and they're controlling it. So I don't think it uses AI. It's a talking head."

"So more like ventriloquism."

Maizie said, "Sure, maybe... After I look up what that is."

Maybe it was better she didn't know. "Wait until later," Kenna said. "You'll end up going down a rabbit trail of comedy routines."

"Good to know."

At least it wouldn't be terrifying for her—hopefully. "So Sandhurst isn't attending his own meetings. Someone is putting words in his mouth."

"Why would they do that? Where is he?"

Kenna said, "It explains why we haven't been able to track the man down. Just his office. Maybe he's locked down somewhere."

"Or dead," Ramon said from across the room. "That would be helpful."

"Except the call has already gone out for Preston's death. If he's dead, there's no one to retract the hit." She glanced over at Ramon, who had turned to her. "Unless we use the avatar."

He put a finger to his lips.

She frowned and mouthed, *What?*

Was the woman who'd attacked him in the room?

Kenna glanced at the door, but no one stood there.

Ramon crooked his finger, a dark look on his face. One she'd seen before when a newborn baby had been in danger of being kidnapped to repay the parents' debt. Thankfully, the mother and child were safe and thriving now.

Kenna angled her face to the phone. "Keep looking at the computer, Maze. I need to check something." She wandered over to Ramon. "What is..." Kenna nearly choked. Or threw up.

Ramon shifted and put his hand over her mouth. She blew her cheeks out and breathed through it, then nudged him away with her hip. He let go of her face and stood staring at her.

She looked from the wall to him.

He whispered, "They have pictures of all of us. You. Me. Jax, even. Preston and the Miami team, since New Orleans. Nora and Ellie. Even the Rysons and their kids. What do they want with kids?"

Kenna looked at the wall.

Half a dozen pictures of Maizie. One had her in a gown, standing beside a very much older man. A completely blank expression on her face. She couldn't be more than twelve.

Kenna wanted to tear the photo off the wall.

Rip it to pieces.

Burn this whole place down.

I killed that guy.

She couldn't even think his name. Not now. Not ever. Nothing would touch Maizie. Not ever again. Kenna was going to make sure of it. The girl had gotten herself free, and it would stay that way.

She clenched her teeth and took a few deep breaths. She lifted her foot and kicked her boot into the wall. It embedded in the drywall, and, small mercies, she didn't injure herself.

"Are you guys okay?"

Kenna turned back to the phone and called out, "Yeah, Maze. We're good." She turned back to Ramon and lowered her voice. "All this gets destroyed."

He said nothing, just lifted a hand and pointed at one of the pictures. "That's the Airstream. Stairns' place."

Where Maizie lived.

"They know where she is." Who she was. Where she came from.

They knew everything about her.

Kenna turned and faced him, everything in her going solid. Every muscle, tendon and joint in her body felt like concrete.

Wilson Sandhurst knew about Maizie.

They'd done their homework on Kenna's entire operation, every person she worked with and was connected to.

Forrest Crosby, an author in Wisconsin who she emailed occasionally and had remained friends with since they met.

Sheriff Melinda Bracken, who worked in Arizona not far from where Jax lived. They'd had coffee a couple of times the past few months. In fact, there was a picture of the two of them at a wrought iron table, chatting.

Sheriff Omar Samuels, getting sworn in to the position a few months ago in Bishopsville, California.

Senator Avery Masonridge from Florida, on a street in Georgetown with a couple of security guards as she greeted a taller man.

It was a who's who of nearly everyone she'd met or worked with the past couple of years. The Rysons. Elizabeth and Craig Stairns.

And Maizie.

"I'm gonna kill Sandhurst. And whoever he's working with."

Ramon said, "You don't think he could be this informed on his own?"

"It feels bigger. It feels like...something. How do they have all this? It's insane. It's like they've been watching us for months. Years even."

"It doesn't feel like one person is the target." Ramon folded his arms across his chest. "It feels like information gathering. And it's time to gather some more." He turned and strode out of the room.

Kenna went back to the computer, and her phone still beside it. "Maizie, did you copy everything? We need to get out of here before we overstay our welcome."

Maybe Ramon would agree to bringing the woman with them.

Maizie said, "I copied everything. This looks like his computer, but it's going to take time to go through everything and figure out what we can learn from it."

"Ask Stairns to help. I'll give him a heads-up." On that, and the fact these people had their eyes on Maizie. Not only did they know who she was, and that she existed, they knew where to find her.

It made Kenna want to grab everything and run. Just sprint out the door downstairs and run as far and as fast as she could—all the way to Colorado.

She needed to hire a protection team of her own. Anything to keep her family safe.

Wilson Sandhurst shouldn't have even found Maizie. He should never have known the teen even existed. The fact he had…

It seemed like he had serious help.

Funding.

Resources.

"She's gone. Made a run for it." Ramon darkened the doorway. "And I hear sirens outside."

"Help me pull all this down." She waved at the room and went to one side, where she started tearing papers off the wall. Ramon moved twice as fast, clearing two walls in the time she took to clear one. He gathered it all off the floor into a pile, leaving nothing behind.

"Maizie, I need the hard drive, right?" Kenna crouched in front of the tower.

Her teen friend's voice came through the phone speaker. "One…sec…okay. Hit the tab and pull it out. You see it?"

"Yep. It's not a normal household PC. This person made the hard drive so I can eject it." She straightened with it in her hand. "Let's go." She grabbed her phone and the drive. "Bye, Maze."

Before the girl could answer, Kenna ended the call and slid the cell into her back pocket.

Ramon took the lead, folding all the papers and rolling them up, which created a bundle that billowed out one side of his jacket. He braced it with one hand and held his gun with the other. They headed down the stairs.

Four floors down, Kenna heard something. She whispered, "Cops."

Ramon backed up a couple of steps, and they went

through a door on floor ten, standing out of sight while the cops continued up.

"Okay." Ramon pushed off the wall and looked through the little window in the door, a small square with wire criss-crossed in the glass. "Coast is clear."

They headed down and out a side door they hadn't used earlier. It led to a rear parking lot.

Kenna scanned the empty lot, praying the cops who were around here didn't notice them. There was nowhere to duck for cover and hide.

Ramon passed a dumpster and slowed enough she could catch up. He stowed his gun. "We should've tied that woman up."

"I thought she was out cold."

"Guess she woke up and decided to leave."

Kenna frowned, walking faster than her normal pace to stay beside him. She glanced back over her shoulder but didn't see any cops. "She probably called the police as well. Or whoever she works for."

"Did you see the cot behind the desk?"

Kenna glanced at him. "What?"

"She was sleeping in there. Whoever she was."

And the woman had left of her own accord, so it wasn't a case of captivity. She'd come out of the room on her own. But why sleep there? "What is going on?"

"Usually it takes longer into a case before we're asking that."

"I'm going to call Stairns and warn him that Maizie has eyes on her." She didn't know whether to tell him to run or book them all on a six-month cruise under fake names. Nor did she know if they were in any danger at all. Maybe whoever it was had no intention of harming them.

As long as Kenna did what they wanted.

"This way." Ramon had her cross the street. A couple of miles later, they were under a bridge. A collection of tents and people gathered around in ragged clothes. Among them, she could see people in red suit jackets handing out brown paper bags. Sacks of food or other supplies, it looked like.

"Are you meeting someone?"

Ramon shook his head. "We need to burn this stuff. They need fuel to keep warm."

She stopped at the edge of a group. Ramon headed for a barrel, where four or five people gathered around holding their hands out. He tipped the papers, photos and copies of documents into the barrel.

Fuel for the fire.

The one inside Kenna burned far hotter than this. She drew out her phone and called Stairns.

He picked up after the first ring. "Kenna?"

"I'm on my way back to Colorado." She fought to keep her control. "We have a serious problem."

Chapter Four

Colorado
Thursday 7:34am

The door to the Airstream was open, visible through the closed screen. Kenna stepped onto the rug that lay over the grass in front of the screen door and said, "Knock, knock."

Her dog appeared inside, and Cabot's nose flared as she inhaled Kenna's scent.

"Hi, doggy." She smiled as she approached, tugging open the screen door.

Cabot's tail wagged.

Kenna stood on the stool and gave her dog a rubdown, head to tail. Emphasis on behind the ear scratches and a little massage to relieve the tension in her neck muscles. The dog groaned and leaned against her. "You're a good girl. Yes, you are."

Cabot wandered off to lie down on a dog bed beside the double at the bedroom end of the Airstream. The animal had slept on the second twin bed in Kenna's van before it blew up. Before Cabot had surgery. Kenna was glad the dog could be here full time with Maizie, so the teen wasn't so alone. But she missed her rescue. Cabot laid her chin on her paws and stared along the interior of the trailer, watching Kenna. Watching Maizie.

Kenna gave her a hand signal she'd taught Cabot to stand down, and the dog let out an exhale. "Should I take off my shoes?"

Maizie sat at the table, leaning back against the denim-blue cushion. Hands over the keys of her laptop. "Can you?"

"Slip ons." She opened the screen and kicked them out onto the rug. "Much better. Can I sit?"

Maizie didn't take her attention from the laptop screen. "Huh? Uh...yeah, sure."

Kenna had left Ramon on the back porch of the cabin with Stairns. Kenna's former boss might feel the need to make amends for the way her FBI career had ended, but she had given up holding a grudge years ago. Life was far too short to hold wrongdoing over someone's head. Kenna liked the path her life had taken. One that led to her two favorite rescues living in the backyard of his retirement cabin.

She sat with her back to the window, so Maizie could see her profile. Phone on the table. The sound of Maizie typing was soothing. "If I sit here long enough, I'll fall asleep."

"Take a nap, then." Maizie tapped some more.

They often kept the phone line open and went about their business. Resting knowing they were connected even if they were hundreds or thousands of miles from each other.

Maizie said, "Didn't you sleep on the plane?"

"Does anyone ever actually sleep on a plane? I'm not sure." Kenna tucked her arms against her front, making sure she wasn't pulling on her hands. She curled her legs up, feet on the seat. Yeah, five minutes, and she'd be out for the count. "I need to tell you what we found in New York."

"Does it matter?"

Kenna said, "Aren't you curious?"

"Sometimes not knowing is far healthier than knowing and wishing you didn't. I've got enough I wish I could erase."

"I thought about that, too." She'd spent the plane ride from the East Coast to Denver trying to figure out if Maizie maybe didn't want to know. "It's up to you. It's always up to you."

After she'd lived a life where all the choices had been taken from her, now Maizie got to be the one to decide.

"Is knowing going to change what happens next?"

Kenna couldn't quite get past the fact that if it was her, she would want to know. In fact, she was pretty sure that not knowing and wondering would drive her crazy. But the key lay there in the middle. *If it was her.* And right now, it wasn't. It was about Maizie. If the girl didn't worry about what she didn't know, then good for her. Probably far healthier than overthinking.

"I'll run down what's going to happen, and you tell me," Kenna said. "Ramon and I are here. He's working on a schedule with Stairns that makes sure you're covered at all times. I'd like to install trail cams, or some kind of surveillance, around the property and farther out. Just so we can see anyone if they decide to show up."

Did the girl want to know that someone had been close enough to get a photo inside the Airstream? Likely that was past the healthy boundary she wanted to draw.

They'd burned the images, but the pictures had been taken from ground level. So in the trees around the property...with a telephoto lens? What were their other options? A drone, maybe? Surely, they'd have heard the sound of the engine.

Maizie shifted her hands back to her lap. She turned those huge blue eyes to Kenna. Haunted shadows stared at her, a lifetime of pain etched into her features. But she was learning how to smile. How to braid her hair. What clothes she wanted to choose for herself. How to cook what she wanted to eat.

Kenna said, "That color blue looks really good on you."

Maizie looked down. "It's a ratty, secondhand sweater."

"And? Secondhand stores rock." She nearly suggested going shopping together, but that would have to wait until after the threat had been eliminated.

But how would Kenna manage that if she was here on protection detail?

"You can buy me something this color when you're in the UK."

Kenna frowned. "No way I'm going to London now. Not when we know someone found you. They know you're here. They know where you came from."

There was more she wanted to say, things like "they don't know who you are, or where you're going" to try and reassure Maizie. They didn't know the future the teen had to look forward to. They didn't know what was in her heart.

"You *have* to go to London." The teen turned the laptop to show her the screen. "Contents of the hard drive you grabbed. This is a manifest for a flight that landed at

Heathrow Airport in London. The only passenger was Wilson Sandhurst."

Kenna shifted to sit up a little bit. "We need to talk about you being at risk."

"No we don't."

She decided to be stubborn *now?*

"The drive is in my backpack." The need to get here to ensure Maizie was safe had overridden everything. Even good sense, apparently. "What else was on there?"

"All things Wilson Sandhurst."

So now she was ignoring the obvious threat on the horizon—disassociating with work rather than letting the fear swallow her up?

In an odd way, Kenna found she could respect that. "It's Sandhurst's computer, right? Did you find out who he has trying to kill Preston?"

Maizie said, "I'm not convinced it's his, or that he's necessarily even used it. Ever. Seems more like someone keeping up the impression he's at work, miles—or a whole country away—from his brother-in-law that he wants dead."

"An alibi? That's what that woman was?" Kenna asked. "Makes sense then why she's pretending to be him on conference calls."

"That was pretty sophisticated stuff. I understand how it works, but it would take me weeks to write a program that made it look like you on a video call. Even then, it would be buggy."

"You could pretend it's a poor internet connection."

"Only so many times before someone got tired of dealing with it."

Kenna nodded. "True. So Sandhurst is where...in the UK?"

"If Preston is going, then maybe Wilson will try and kill

him personally, and he's crafting an alibi in New York so it looks like he never left the country."

"But you know he's there." Kenna frowned. "If she has this tech, maybe it's to double-cross him and cut him loose after Preston's dead."

"Don't let him get killed." Maizie's face flashed with a desperate expression.

Kenna sat up and turned to face her. "Hey, that thing you're feeling right there? It's why he should go with people who can physically protect him. I can't. It's why I want to stay here. To make sure *you're* safe."

"Your logic makes no sense." Maizie sniffed. "You need to go to London and figure this out. Keep Preston safe."

"Because you care so much about him?" Kenna didn't want to worry that this young woman with little experience of the world had latched onto an older man who could replace the man who controlled her.

Not a good outcome, but it also wouldn't be so surprising. Who knew what ways her captor had twisted her. What neural pathways had been set and would need a lifetime to unwind.

Maizie might never be able to make healthy choices in intimacy. In setting boundaries.

In the people she wanted in her life.

Maizie said, "Well, yeah. Of course I care if he dies. Not that he knows who I am other than 'Ms. Smith' at Banbury Investigations. He sends me updates about Nora and Ellie. Did you see the last set of photos? Ellie is so big!"

"Don't change the subject," Kenna said. "I'll look at them later."

Maizie frowned. "Fine. It's also because he knew your dad. Preston can tell you stories, give you answers you don't have. You lost that sheriff, Joe Don Hunter. We never figured out what that autopsy was in his safe. Preston might be able to tell you more about your parents."

Kenna studied her, wondering if this had to do with Maizie's lack of information about her own background. "I didn't know your mother for long, but I might be able to answer some questions about her...and your half-brother."

Both of them were dead, but Kenna would do what she could to give Maizie answers.

"This isn't about me. This is about *you* getting answers."

Kenna sat back in the chair. "Touché?"

Maize sort of smiled.

This young woman would always seem like an "old soul" or whatever that expression was. With the life she'd had, she'd been forced to mature far too early. Parts of her might always be childlike, and other parts were far too wise beyond her years.

Maizie rolled her eyes, one of the few times she looked and acted like a teenager. It made Kenna want to say *don't you roll your eyes at me, missy.* The entire exchange hung in the air, unspoken. A connection that was more than words. It was about doing what was best for the other person. Something Maizie was apparently as much on board with for Kenna as she was for Maizie.

The laptop dinged quietly, and a message popped up in the corner of the screen.

"Bear?"

Maizie flinched.

Kenna wasn't going to let her hide it. The conversation looked like check ins, not some intimate and completely inappropriate conversation. "He's contacting you?"

Maizie shrugged. "I know he isn't letting anyone else know where he is. I told him I could see him regardless. That I'd know where he was even if he ditched his phone—

which he did. So I told him to check in with me, and that way if anyone asked, then I could confirm he's alive at least. But I said I wouldn't reveal his location if he told me a general area."

"And if he lies about where he is?"

Maizie shrugged. "So far he hasn't—as much as I can tell. I know Bear disappeared after Allie died, but maybe he wants someone to connect with. Even just checking in on his general location."

"It's a nice idea." Kenna gave her a small smile. "I'm glad we know he's safe."

"I'm not going to tell him you know."

Kenna nodded.

"That's why you have to go to London."

She started to argue, but Maizie cut her off.

"Because we keep this family safe. And if you're here watching out for me when Ramon and Stairns are here, then who is watching out for Preston?"

Kenna stared at her.

"And while you're making sure the Miami team protects him adequately, he can tell you what he knows about your parents."

"Not just my father?"

Maizie spoke softly. "Preston met your father years before you were born. Before he was ever married. Before he met your mother."

"He never told me that."

She knew almost nothing about her mom, who had died only a few years after she was born. Kenna said, "It's hard to miss what you don't have."

Maizie stared at her. "No, it isn't. I missed it all, every day. So much it was like a constant ache in my chest. Elizabeth said it's because I knew I wasn't free, but I should be."

"Everyone should be free."

"But I knew I wasn't."

"You think I'm captive to the things I don't know."

Maizie said, "Who you are is a case you need to solve. Maybe it's the most important case you'll ever work."

Chapter Five

Preston Lightwood smirked. Not his usual look, but in this case, hearing her story of what Maizie had said to her, he didn't seem able to hold it back.

The black town car pulled up to the curb at the office of Miami Security International. A glass-walled building reflecting the bright Florida sun.

Kenna unclipped her seatbelt but didn't move. "I'm being hoodwinked into going."

Preston laughed aloud. "You wouldn't be here if you weren't curious."

"You didn't get me to London yet." All she wanted to do was convince him to cancel the whole thing. If Sandhurst was in the UK, it was far too dangerous for Preston to go. He had to see that.

Unless the whole point was to force a confrontation.

She studied the man on the bench seat beside her. The driver and his associate got out of the front and prepared to protect them as they moved from the vehicle to the front door. This was the life he led, one where people watched his every move. Not because they were family, but because he paid them.

Did he feel the need for more family?

Preston wore tailored slacks and a white shirt. He'd rolled up the sleeves to reveal the prison tattoo on his left forearm. Gray hair cut neatly, close to the sides of his head. He smelled faintly of hair products. She was pretty sure he'd gotten himself a manicure, which was maybe just a function of being in Miami.

She tried to measure him up against her father, but her impressions of her dad were of a man larger than life. That air of something superhuman about him, as if he could do anything. Not just the normal little girl impression of who her father had been, but also that of an investigator trying to measure themselves up against their hero. He'd never been a perfect man. He hadn't raised her perfectly, and she wasn't sure that she'd say he did the best he could at all times.

He'd done his job the best he could.

Raising her? She tried to honor the spirit of who he'd been. What was the point of resenting things she couldn't change?

The door opened.

Preston got out, waiting while she did the same by sliding across the seat after him. He said, "You did bring your passport, didn't you?"

"That isn't the point." She'd also packed a few days' worth of stuff. She could stretch it to a week. The bag was one where she could get the strap over her head, across her body, and spread the weight, leaving her hands free.

The Miami sun beat down, and she turned to frown at the blue sky. "Doesn't Florida know it's January?" All she had in her duffel were cold weather clothes she'd packed for New York. Then being back in Colorado, there had been no time to accommodate the weather here. She still had gloves in her bag.

One of the Miami guys said, "It's always summer here. Unless there's a hurricane."

"Don't worry, Kenna." Preston patted her shoulder. "We won't be in town long."

Kenna pressed her lips shut tight and focused on getting inside the building without anyone getting killed. She also had to figure out how to open the door if she was the one left to pull on the handle. Would they leave it to her?

At the last second, she stopped, her hands tucked in the pockets of her jean jacket. If they didn't know her situation, they were going to have to figure it out pretty quick. She wasn't the one to look to for hand-to-hand combat...or opening heavy doors.

Preston hit a button beside the door, which eased forward toward her, sending out a gust of air-conditioned air with it.

Kenna stepped into a lobby, all glass tabletops and white furniture. "This place would make a wicked crime scene." It was so stark she wanted to throw some color on it.

One of the Miami guys snorted. "Check out the painting." He motioned to the wall on the far right side.

A white background. Splashes of red paint in arcs across the canvas. "Spatter patterns?"

He laughed aloud.

Preston groaned.

The driver, standing behind them bringing up the rear. "Maybe it's like an ink blot test. You see what you want to see."

She turned to him. "And you see butterflies or flowers?"

"Or the split second after a bomb goes off in a café in Mogadishu." He shrugged, his expression deadpan.

She glanced aside at the painting one more time. "Double homicide. Chicago. Highrise. No witnesses. The cleaning lady found them. The cops think it's a murder-suicide at first, but when they start to look into it, they realize that his assistant is having an affair with their realtor, and both of them wanted to profit from selling the apartment to a rich couple they know from San Diego."

A tiny flicker of relief entered his expression. He wasn't thinking about bombs anymore. "Do you sleep at night, or do you dream about murder-sueys?"

"You think I sleep?"

The corners of his lips curled up.

Preston nudged her elbow. "If you're here to convince me you're not the person to go with us to London, you're going about it entirely the wrong way."

A suited man walked down the hall toward them, same age as Preston or thereabouts. But he had lived a rough life, so he now limped on one leg and used a cane. He had stark white hair and lines on his tanned face that was just a bit leathery. He wore a suit and had a ring on the index finger of his left hand—the one curled around the head of the cane.

The men beside her straightened to attention in a way that was all about respect.

Preston said, "Earl Jonas, this is Kenna Banbury."

She held out her hand, and the split second of fear that

this would hurt a lot evaporated when he clasped her fingers gently and said, "Ms. Banbury."

"Mr. Jonas. It's nice to meet you."

"And you. I've heard good things from my people, and from Preston."

"I'm sorry I couldn't do more for Allison Moore." She and Allie had been on their way to being friends when she was killed in New Orleans. "I'm sorry for your loss."

He nodded. "Thank you." Jonas glanced at the bomb-in-the-café guy. "Let's settle in the conference room."

The front doors of the building opened behind them, and two men walked in, one carrying her duffel bag.

"This way." Café guy held out one hand, and they all went to a conference room that was barely bigger than the table in the middle.

She wasn't going to offer up the information that Bear, their former teammate who'd gone AWOL after Allie was killed, was in contact with her assistant. Maizie could do what she wanted as long as it was healthy and legal.

If it wasn't legal, they needed to discuss it.

Kenna wasn't even in the communication loop with Bear, so it wasn't her information to share. But she could confirm she knew he was alive if they asked.

Jonas settled at the head of the table. Everyone else took a seat, Kenna beside Preston. "Miami Security International has lost valuable assets recently, but that hasn't diminished our ability to protect assets. Either locally or far afield. That being said, if you wished to travel to a warzone, I might have some misgivings about failing to follow the government's advice about travel safety."

"How do you feel about purposely going somewhere when you know the person trying to kill you is also there?" She asked Jonas the question but shot Preston a glance.

Café guy, across the table, said, "We call that one of those things that make life interesting."

As if Kenna needed these guys to encourage Preston. "Keeping you safe means not letting you willfully put your life in danger. So consider me your travel safety advisor."

Jonas said, "Preston and I have discussed the circumstances and the risk. Both he and I agree the risks can be mitigated with a small team." Sounded almost like he wanted to say *strike team*. But didn't.

"Even when we know for a fact Wilson Sandhurst is in the UK?"

Jonas nodded.

She wasn't ignorant of what Miami Security International did in a lot of places around the world. Working contracts that would require strike teams. Protecting people and furthering the cause of peace in the world by combatting those who sought to threaten the balance of treaties and agreements made by those in power.

She wasn't the kind of person who worked in that field.

Kenna shrugged. "Great, then send your small team with Preston. I'll stay here and make sure the threat doesn't spill over to my family."

Preston shifted in his chair. "If you were so determined not to come, why are you here?"

"To tell you to your face. It's more convincing that way." No one needed to know that Maizie had convinced her to get this far and at least talk to Preston face-to-face.

"Not getting on a plane in the first place would've been convincing enough." He was so smug. Thought he was *so* smart.

Kenna crossed her arms trying to huff but clenched too hard on her forearms. Her breath hitched in her throat.

Eyes started to roll back in her head. Everything went white.

"Easy."

"Yeah." She closed her eyes and let out a breath, waiting for her equilibrium to settle. "I'll be a great asset on a protection team." She sniffed back the burn of unshed tears and blinked against the moisture. Letting some go in physical therapy was one thing. Doing it in a meeting was entirely different. Her physical therapist called it "eyeball sweat." Which was gross, but she got the point.

"I don't need you there to protect me." Preston waved across the table at the two men on the other side. "Hollace and Nielson are here for that. You're not even going to be there to coordinate their efforts—MSI doesn't need that kind of support. They know what they're doing. They're pros."

"And I'm eye candy?"

Preston said, "As amusing as it would be to explain that to a certain Special-Agent-in-Charge, no."

She shrugged. "I think I've waited long enough for you to give me a straight answer."

"How about a book?" Jonas slid a leather-bound book from in front of him, across the table toward her.

Preston snagged it and pulled it the rest of the way so that it was in front of her on the table.

She stared at the embossed MB on the bottom right corner of the cover. "You have one of my father's journals?" She opened the front cover and saw his handwriting. A single word.

London.

"We won't be taking that back," Jonas said. "It's yours, for obvious reasons. However, if you'll permit me before you start reading, I'd like to run down the case as it stands. Then you can decide if London is where you're headed next."

Hollace, who was Mogadishu Café guy, and Nielson pushed their chairs back. Hollace said, "We need to finish packing the gear. Wheels up in two hours."

Preston nodded. "Thank you, gentlemen."

Kenna's phone buzzed on the table. The screen lit up long enough she saw the location app had notified her that Jax completed a flight. Phoenix to London.

She stared at the screen. *I'm being hoodwinked.* This whole thing was a conspiracy. Jax was going to be there to control the Kenna fallout. Preston needed her to go. It had to do with her father.

"You're going to risk getting yourself killed for whatever this is?" She turned to Preston because she wanted to see his face.

"If it convinces you how much this means to me, then yes. I'll tell you this is so important for you—and maybe for the whole world—that I'll die for it." His expression bled with determination.

"The fate of the world?" Kenna shook her head. "I might've gone along with it, but that pushed it a little too far." She nudged her chair back with her legs and stood.

"Believe me. Don't believe me." Preston shrugged.

Jonas pointed a remote over his shoulder and clicked a button. The screen behind him came to life. An image of a woman taken years ago given the graininess and the color. Dark hair, dark features. Slender. Shadows in her eyes, not unlike the ones she'd seen in Maizie. Kenna's mother stared back at her from the wall. Underneath, there was text.

Agent 2387.

"Sit down, Kenna." Jonas set the remote down. "I'm about to change everything you know."

Chapter Six

Malcom Banbury dipped his head against the wind and driving rain. He turned from Charterhouse Street onto Ely Place, and "a few doors down," as the Brits would say, he ducked into an alley between buildings.

The place he was going had been there since 1547, according to the hotel desk clerk. A small measure of security on the off chance his body washed up in the Thames in a few days. The police would know where to start looking for whoever had killed him.

Most likely the person who had asked to meet him here.

Someone who'd gone so far as to break into his hotel room and leave a note under his pillow.

The alley took him to a tiny walkway between two brick buildings that connected with a floor over his head. The opening spat him out into an empty space, open air. The tables and chairs were unoccupied. Barrels and plant pots. A bench. The outdoor seating for the pub was currently unoccupied thanks to the afternoon rain shower that had left puddles in the walkway.

Inside, the pub glowed yellow between the small squares that made up the windows, panes of square glass lined with iron painted black. *Ye Olde Mitre* was a tavern that looked like a doorway into a past that was long gone, swallowed up by technology and "progress." Though, Malcom wasn't sure that's exactly what had happened.

Was life any better these days?

Barely thirty-five, and he already felt like a crusty relic. A throwback to what was and what should've been. He'd served in the military first, now the FBI. He was coming up on eight years as an agent. Who knew what would come next, but he was getting restless wearing a suit. Tired of knocking on doors asking stay-at-home moms if they knew the guy living next door was a deranged sociopath who had killed six people over the past fifteen years.

This assignment wasn't exactly *sanctioned,* but he was going to get real evidence and take it back to D.C. File a case officially. Get the investigation rolling. Which would mean other agencies got involved, and the brass would start mentioning things like "international cooperation."

Maybe, with whatever he got out of this meeting, they could bypass all that. He could close the case with this trip.

No one would ever know he was here, or that he'd taken care of it. Just him.

He pushed the door open and was greeted by a wall of warm air, thanks to the blazing fire at one end of the room. Dark wood dominated the space, which was almost full of patrons. Office types in their suits, having a drink at lunch.

Older men sat at tables, playing checkers. Groups of tourists stood around at the bar, chatting and laughing.

Malcom turned his head away from the flash of a Polaroid, not wanting to be seen in anyone's vacation pictures. He ordered a pint of lager at the bar and took it with him.

He found a half-empty room toward the back, patterned red and black carpet and red walls, with matching drapes that swooped down at the top, tied back with a yellow cord. Two chandeliers. Malcom took a stool in the corner across from an empty one.

He pulled out the file from his briefcase and flipped through the notes he'd already made. Photos. Missing person reports.

He smelled the faint scent of vanilla at first. A second later, a woman eased into the other stool across from him.

Malcom didn't look up from his papers. "I'm meeting someone."

"Who has better information than what you've got in those files...yes, I know." Her alto voice had a throaty tone to it.

This was the person he was meeting?

Malcom lifted his gaze from the paper and looked at her. Dark brown eyes, dark hair. Mediterranean maybe. A tan that suggested she'd been somewhere other than England recently, and she'd spent time in the sun.

He said, "I guess you already know who I am."

"You are American. I wondered if I'd heard wrong." Her lips were full, her cheekbones high.

What did she see when she looked at him?

Three days' growth of stubble. The scar above his eyebrow from when that child molester in Boston came at him with a broken beer bottle. Hair that needed cutting and was already threaded with gray, the relentless passage of time whether he liked it or not.

Pretty much characterized his life.

Whether you like it or not. He had to make a choice where he could.

Right now, the choice was to put the papers away and just look at her. Sure, he needed to find out the reason she'd wanted to meet. Now that he'd seen her, it was more than that.

Malcom interlaced his fingers on the file. "Is my being American a problem?"

Her cheeks flushed. She had to be at least thirty, but he couldn't nail it down more specifically than that. White blouse. Gray trench coat. Simple gold chain with a tiny cross around her neck. "It's just that most Americans aren't experts at...quietly blending in." She actually looked impressed.

A couple of older men in suits took a table on the other side of the room.

Malcom did a split-second assessment and decided they weren't here to listen in or watch this conversation. She didn't even look their way, but it wasn't because she was unaware of the potential threat.

"The question is..." She eyed him. "Do you know about Scotch eggs?"

Malcom frowned. "What-eggs?"

She chuckled, shifted off the stool, and stood. At least five-eleven, tall enough she was probably self-conscious about her height. The skirt that was probably meant to hang to her knees only came down to several inches above it. Flat black shoes, so she didn't tower over her superiors.

He stood as well, not just because she needed to know

she would fit under his shoulder, but also because being a gentleman wasn't that much extra effort. Not after the way he was raised, anyway. His whiskey-soaked father had beaten him every day of his life. His mother had hidden in the corner, knitting. Crochet. Anything that gave her something to focus on other than the reality happening around her.

"I'll be back." She touched his arm, then glanced at his beer. "Another one?"

He nodded. "Thanks."

She eyed him, a curious look on her face, and wandered through the room to the bar. Chatted with the bartender and came back not long after he'd settled into the chair again. Malcom wasn't going to disguise the fact he watched her go and come back. Some might call it operational security—keeping the target in sight at all times. Turned out, for him, it was just so he could take her in.

The two guys across the room didn't even look.

She set a plate on the table and eased onto the stool, taking a sip of his beer. "I like the taste, but a whole glass of it?" She shook her head. "Even half a pint is too much."

He took the glass and used it to indicate the plate. "These are Scotch eggs?"

"Okay." She rubbed her hands together in front of her. "Hard-boiled egg, wrapped in a thick layer of pork sausage, covered in breadcrumbs. Baked or fried, but if they know what they're doing, they're fried."

"This is why you broke into my hotel room? So you could introduce me to food I've never had before?"

She grinned, and it changed the landscape of her face. Years of stress disappeared, clouds parted, and the sun shone through for a second. "Trust me."

So this was a test.

Malcom took a sip of the beer, then picked up one of the eggs and bit off half of it.

"Sometimes they're a bit dry, but you can dip them in mustard. That's the best way."

He smiled, and chewed, and kept smiling. No way would he admit to a living soul that he was completely enamored with her. Probably it was the whole point. Get him hooked. Dangle a beautiful woman in front of him, one who wasn't flashy like some high-society wife on the arm of a power monger. No, this woman would blend in. She would assimilate into any situation and go unnoticed.

If she wanted, that was.

He noticed her now—which was likely the point.

She picked up the second egg and took her time enjoying it.

"Are you going to tell me your name?"

She wiped a tiny crumb of egg yolk from the corner of her mouth. "You go first."

"You don't know?"

"Did you use your real name to check into that hotel?"

"Fine." He washed down the egg with a sip of beer the way God intended—room temperature. "I'm Malcom Banbury."

She stuck her hand out. "Hi, Malcom Banbury. I'm Amara Clarke."

He held her hand. "It's nice to meet you. Unless you're here to kill me and these egg things are poisoned, in which case it *isn't* nice to meet you."

Amara chuckled, a lighter sound than her normal tone of voice. A contradiction in terms, like the woman herself. A little bit exotic, a little bit standard British. A whole lot of mystery he wanted to unravel. She said, "I'm not here to kill you."

"Right." He nodded. "Too public. People have seen us together."

"I'm here to help you."

If she wanted to kill him, he would probably have been stabbed in some back alley, or poisoned with something that made it look like he drank too much or had a heart attack. That was how these people worked. He had two murder cases to prove it. Another one here in London just weeks ago. Fourteen missing persons cases that dated back over thirty years—the most recent just two months ago.

"I would like help." He didn't need to lie all the time. "I don't like feeling as if I can't get a handle on a case. This one is...complex."

"The intrepid special agent from America is stumped."

"Met Police aren't being too helpful."

She let out a little snort. "Shocking."

He smiled. "I'm assuming you have something for me, Amara?"

Otherwise, why meet in person? She could have assessed him simply by following him as he went about his investigation. It probably wasn't just so she could feed him a snack. "Those eggs are good, by the way."

"Better with mustard."

"Most things are." Malcom wanted to say her name again. To feel it, so he didn't wonder if he would ever get to say it again.

A tiny flicker of humor lit her gaze, but it was gone so fast he wondered if he saw it. She reached into her pocket, to the inside of her trench coat. She drew out a folded paper.

No, a photo.

"This was taken three weeks ago. It's all the intelligence we've managed to gain in years of investigating."

"They're connected?"

She handed him the photo.

He had to point out the obvious. "You fit the profile."

"I'm too tall." She sipped his beer again. "I'm surprised you haven't been thorough enough in your inquiries to realize that."

"I meant your coloring. Your build."

"It goes deeper than that."

Did it? He looked at the photo in his hand, mostly to give himself a second to absorb the idea. She knew a lot about the case. That could mean she was involved or personally connected. She wasn't a cop. He could tell that much. Police in England just had an...edge to them. There weren't many women officers—sorry, *constables*. Even if the prime minister was a woman, that didn't mean "progress" wasn't a hard-won race.

The grainy image was the color of a British sky—gray and cloudy.

Amara said, "If he's not in charge, then he's at least deeply involved."

But she wasn't going to tell him who this was?

"My hands are being tied. I won't be able to help you after this." She shifted on the stool. "I'm afraid I've done all I can."

Maybe she didn't want him to know how nervous she was. So Malcom studied the photo. "What if I need to reach you?"

"I'm sorry."

He looked up, frowning. "Why are you sorry?"

"You'll never see me again." She slid from the stool and walked out of the room.

Malcom gathered his things and followed her. She wasn't in the alley. He rushed to the street but couldn't see her.

She was gone.

Chapter Seven

The airplane wheels touched down on the tarmac. Rain pattered against the window beside her. She wasn't sure she'd looked out once. Instead, she'd spent the last eight or so hours napping intermittently, between reading a handful of pages of her father's journal. Absorbing moments, snatches of his life—and how he'd met her mother—until she couldn't take in anymore.

Rubber buffeted the tarmac under them, and the plane slowed to a stop. Lights came on. Belts unbuckled, and Kenna got the latch of hers open. Her arms were stiff, and she needed to take more pain meds before she got off this swanky private plane.

Preston shifted in his seat, then pushed the sleep mask up his face and off his head. He'd changed into jeans and added a casual jacket over his button-down shirt. Like a corporate guy traveling internationally.

The two Miami guys, Hollace and Nielson stood. Hollace stretched, and Nielson went to the closet at the back where they'd stowed their gear. A flight attendant in uniform eased down the aisle and took Preston's sleep mask. The slender woman came with the plane, working for MSI along with the two pilots. She'd taken one look at Kenna the second she came aboard and told her to feel free to take her shoes off.

Maybe she saw the wealth of life-shattering things she'd had to absorb in the last few days, the thread of worry for Maizie running through it all. But she'd kept her distance and not tried to chat them up with endless small talk.

Kenna could barely compartmentalize everything Mr. Jonas had told her. It was insane—like something out of a movie.

Now she was in England. Not on the road, in her RV, where she needed to be. That was the only place she'd ever found the peace she needed to handle the direction her life had gone—until she found Jesus. But she couldn't even drive it right now. The rig was parked in Jax's garage still, and it would stay there until someone moved it.

How she was supposed to find the space to deal with... Oh, right.

I feel like I got knocked off my axis, but You know that. Why hadn't she thought to pray yet? Shock, probably. As if that justification was an excuse. *Help me find my equilibrium, make sense of all this, and work out what I'm supposed to do with it.*

She felt as if the reaction wanted to spill out of her. Emotion bubbled up like water boiling, about to tip over the edge. Willpower, or self-control, was the only thing that stuffed it down. Later, when she was by herself, she could have a true reaction. Somewhere no one would see it.

She was closer to her parents now than she'd ever been. And more aware of how far from her they were.

"Here." Hollace dumped her duffel on the seat beside her.

"Thanks." It was the first thing she'd said to any of them the whole plane ride. No one had really been in the mood to chat. Now she said, "You guys are really okay being here?"

"I like my job. I get paid well."

Nielson stepped into view beside him. "I've never been to England. It's dark. Should it be this dark?"

Preston stretched in his seat and lifted his hands above his head. "Rain like this is called *drizzle*. And yes, it's almost always gray outside. Dreary. Overcast. Good luck finding blue sky and sunshine. Especially this time of year."

Kenna dipped her head and slid the strap of her duffel over her shoulders so she could stand with it across her body and not have to lift it with her hands. She tucked the journal into the inside of her jacket so she could keep it close, and it wouldn't get rained on. The hood of her sweater would keep rain from frizzing her hair until she could get an umbrella.

"Here." Hollace held out something small in his palm.

Kenna took it, unfolding the knife with a blade she'd guess was just shy of three inches. "What's this for?"

"It's not a weapon. If anyone asks. It's for a hobby, like rope cutting or something like that. You're a Girl Scout."

Kenna blinked. "What?"

Nielson made a face like he understood her confusion. "Exactly. Welcome to the UK. Unless it's a rifle or shotgun for hunting, it's illegal. Handguns–illegal. Knives–illegal. Pepper spray–illegal. Mace. Batons. Anything you could use as a weapon? Don't even think about it. So you've gotta get creative."

"Turns out," Hollace said, "you don't have the right to carry any kind of weapon. Nor do you have the right to take a life under any circumstances whatsoever. You are able to reasonably defend yourself until such time as the police show up to arrest your assailant."

"Right." She glanced at Preston.

He shrugged. "I guess it works for them."

Nielson's expression deadpanned, and he recited, "I look forward to the assistance of local law enforcement."

"I'd rather stay off their radar." Kenna didn't want to get tangled up in something she had no explanation for. Nor did she want to end up in a foreign prison, even one in a country that had a good relationship with the US.

"As would I." Preston stood. "Let's try and keep our presence here as quiet as we can."

The flight attendant opened the door, already wearing a knee length dark blue rain jacket with a hood. All that was visible were pantyhose and a pair of plain, black, low heels. A uniformed black man stepped onto the plane, and Hollace handed over their passports. The representative of British customs and immigration wore a blue uniform and a wide-brimmed police hat with black and white squares on the front, and *Border Force* on his shirt beside the dark blue tie. He reached into the inside pocket of his jacket and pulled out a pen. Made some notations on a pad.

Asked a couple of questions about the purpose of their visit, referring to Kenna and Preston as Mr. and Mrs. McBannon.

Kenna gave the rehearsed answers, and after he left, she stood. She jogged the duffel to sit behind her hips and headed for the door, where the flight attendant handed her a paper cup with a plastic lid.

"Coffee?"

Kenna could've hugged her. "It's official, you're my new favorite person."

The attendant chuckled. "See you in a few days for your return trip."

"Thanks." Kenna tugged the hood over her hair and stepped out into the chilly morning. Gray cloud cover. Drizzling rain.

A plane took off behind them, a huge double decker 747 with *British Airways* across the side.

Wind swirled around them. She glanced back to see Hollace come out in front of Preston, Nielson behind. Kenna descended the plane steps to where a car had been parked not far away.

The back door opened, and a familiar man unfolded himself from the back.

She took the next two steps faster, until she was jogging down the steps to where he met her at the bottom. It didn't matter the circumstances, meeting someone at the airport after a long flight meant smiles and hugs.

Jax wrapped his arms around her, smiling right back. "Don't spill your coffee."

She leaned back in his hold and took a sip, hiding under his chin from the rain. "Nearly forgot."

"That would be a travesty." He shifted her slightly and gave her a chaste kiss before he looked over her shoulder and said, "Jax."

"Hollace." After a second's pause, he said, "Is it bring your boyfriend to work day?"

She grinned into Jax's shirt, still not willing to let go. She felt the motion of their handshake but ignored it. With everything that'd happened in the past two days, there was no way she could handle this by herself. She needed time with Jax to shore up her defenses. To withstand what happened next. She needed to nap, read her Bible, and spend time with her boyfriend.

She also needed to not be needy.

The strength this was going to require might not come from her, but she wanted to know she had it. That meant a balance between standing firm so this storm didn't blow her over entirely and knowing she couldn't do it alone.

"Nielson."

"Jax. Nice to meet you guys." He paused. "Preston."

"Fancy meeting you here," Preston said, a chuckle in his tone. "Isn't that what the Brits say?"

Kenna had no idea. But she had coffee. "Can we get out of the rain?"

She wanted a second to ask Jax exactly how much he'd known before he suddenly decided to fly here, even before she'd made her decision to come to England.

The sound of car engines revving had them all shifting around, on edge. Except Kenna, who didn't even know what it might be. She handed Jax her coffee and turned to face him. Close enough it would still only look like a hug, while she slid the journal from inside her jacket and tucked it into the side of his open suit jacket, sliding it to rest behind his belt.

She stepped back, as if reacting to the entrance of several black vehicles, and he stuck his hand in his pocket. Probably holding the journal where it was.

He took a drink of *her* coffee.

"Hey—"

"Nothing is free, babe."

She didn't have time to glare at him. The vehicles stopped, blocking their exit.

Jax said, "State department," loud enough for them all to hear.

Preston glanced at him. "Americans?"

Jax nodded.

A crowd of men and a few women climbed out of every door, of all four vehicles. She counted twenty people. Half of them spread out, making a perimeter. A man in the center took point, striding over to them, opening a black umbrella so he could walk over under cover and protected from the rain. Gray suit, black wool coat. Brown shoes. Military haircut, but an older guy. Probably in his sixties.

He walked all the way to her, which caused Hollace and Nielson to contract around Preston. Jax moved to shift in front of her. She touched his back and stayed by his side.

"Kenna Banbury?"

She said, "Depends who's asking."

Because if it was the Brits who wanted to know or look at the fake passport MSI had given her, then that was not her name for the purposes of this trip. They didn't want Wilson Sandhurst knowing they were here. But then, with the resources he had at his disposal there was no reason to believe they'd remain under the radar.

The man pulled out a leather wallet a lot like Jax's and flashed a badge, along with his photo ID. "Assistant Director Carlton, State Department." He took a step back, motioning to the car. "If you'd come with us."

"Why am I going to do that?"

"Because the alternative is that we put you in the car by force."

She glanced at Jax. "What do you think? Such an intriguing offer. How can we refuse?"

"Maybe he has more coffee. This one is empty." He didn't look happy.

Jax knew more than the rest of them that they were being railroaded here, and there wasn't much they could do about it. If anything at all. The state department could make their lives, and their job here, extremely difficult.

The agent said, "Just you."

Kenna shook her head. "No deal. Special-Agent-in-Charge Jaxton comes with me."

Hollace caught her glance and nodded. Which she took to mean they were good, they'd protect Preston. "We'll see you at the hotel."

Assistant Director Carlton didn't seem overly pleased. Finally, he realized he had no choice and said, "Very well. Come with me."

Preston was the one who said, "Where are you taking them?"

"The US embassy," Carlton said. "Don't worry, they won't be harmed." He turned away, and his people returned to the vehicles. One door remained open at the rear of the closest car.

Jax took her hand, and they headed for it.

Kenna had to break the tension somehow. "Fancy meeting you here?"

He smiled over at her. "I'm in London attending a conference on the future of international law enforcement."

"Of course you are."

"Don't worry, I blocked out plenty of time for whatever mischief you get up to."

She lifted one eyebrow. "I can handle whatever this is. I know what I'm doing."

"I know." He kissed her once. "That's why I'm here."

Chapter Eight

Kenna stared out the window. "Looks like the rain is tapering off."

Jax came to stand close behind her, sliding an arm around her waist. "Do you want this back?" He patted the front of her hip, but she caught his meaning—the journal she'd slipped into his hands.

"It's my father's." She didn't even know where to start explaining being here, or the fact Miami Security International had been in possession of one of her father's missing journals. Specifically, the one that detailed how he'd met her mother. And that, along with that, they'd shown her information that confirmed Amara Clarke had been a British secret agent.

Jax said, "I haven't been here long, but I've made a discovery."

She caught the lightness in his tone and turned her head, asking, "What's that?"

"Bacon sandwiches." He tipped his head to the side. "Though, it's not bacon like you're thinking. It's back bacon, so it's more like a thin ham kind of thing, but I figure bacon—"

"Is bacon."

"Exactly." He gave her a squeeze.

Kenna let out a long sigh. "Thanks for coming... assuming there isn't something you haven't told me about this whole deal and why I'm here. Or what's going on with Sandhurst, or that woman at his office. Because if you do, you should probably tell me now."

"That sounds like a lot, and I'll need you to brief me. I actually *am* attending a conference next week that I managed to jump on before registration closed. Just in case you need help. I figured why not come here a couple of days early and adjust to the time change. Rest, maybe do some sightseeing—if the weather clears up."

"Solve a case. Escape mostly unscathed from some terrifying situation." She eyed him. He didn't know all of what was going on, but he'd kept in touch with Preston—or Preston had kept in touch with him.

She turned from the window to him and lifted onto her toes to touch her lips to his. "Thanks for not having some keeping-secrets-from-me part in this."

"It's just support. You know that."

"Backup?" Maybe he could carry a gun here. That might come in handy.

"Back. Front. I like the view from all angles."

Kenna rolled her eyes, making sure it was extra dramatic.

He laughed and kissed her forehead. "I'm glad it worked out that I could be here."

"Me, too."

The door started to open. She slid her arms from around his waist and stepped away a fraction. They weren't two entities—they were a team. She knew he intended to present it that way when he shifted closer to her.

Whatever this meeting was, Jax didn't have a problem with the state department knowing they were together.

A man entered. Short, maybe five-seven, max. He had kind of a weaselly face, with a hook nose and hair that billowed out from a side part, long enough that it curled under his ears. He looked like an aging musician, his hair light brown with no gray, even though he had to be at least in his fifties. The athletic pants, running shoes, and zip-up track jacket gave him a casual feel. He looked like a parent-coach.

"You caught me in my Saturday clothes, I'm afraid." He grinned and came over. "Not my normal weekday three-piece suit." He stuck his hand out to Jax. "SAC Jaxton."

"Sir." Jax shook his hand. "This is Kenna Banbury."

"Exciting." He flicked his eyebrows up and nodded. "Ma'am."

Kenna shook his hand.

"This is the Ambassador, Ronald Mattheus."

"Sir." Kenna let go of his hand. "How are you?"

"Oh, well. Better now that we can finally solve this mystery."

"Excuse me?" Kenna tried to figure out if it was only jet lag, or if she was missing something. Sure, it was mid-morning, but it felt like it should be evening, and she was due to crash any moment. Sleep sounded like a good idea, even if she would adjust to the time change better if she could stay up while it was light outside.

He turned to the door, which opened again. A younger man Kenna recognized from the airport came in with a dark blue canvas bag, flat like a file folder but with one zippered end. A diplomatic pouch.

The ambassador said, "Thank you, Thomas."

"Sir." The man nodded, then left as quickly as he entered.

"The US Embassy in London has had in its possession a letter. Addressed to you. It's been here for nearly thirty years, Kenna. And today, I get to deliver it to you." He unzipped the pouch and pulled out a small, yellowed envelope.

Jax touched the small of her back.

Kenna couldn't take her eyes from it. Couldn't move. Was there going to be an end to these sudden deliveries of key pieces of information at some point? She was still reeling from the journal and needed a few days to read it all. Absorb it. Find her equilibrium again.

She managed to say, "What is it?"

"I'm sure you know that opening someone else's correspondence amounts to mail fraud, Ms. Banbury."

"Right."

The ambassador smiled. "That being said, the office pool would like to know what's inside. It will solve a lot of the rumors that have been flying around this place for decades. Someone could win a lot of money."

"And if I don't tell you what's inside?"

"I'll instruct my staff to donate the money to charity and get back to work."

She couldn't smile but would have at any other time.

Instead, she stared at the envelope in her hand, familiar with that handwriting—she'd been reading it all night on the plane. "It's a letter from my father."

Ambassador Mattheus nodded.

Her dad hadn't added a return address, nor had he paid for postage. He'd really left it here? "How long did you say it had been here?"

"On the back, there's an intake stamp. It was logged as received many years ago by the mailroom, along with instructions that it was only to be given to you on the event of your arrival here in the UK—the first time you were to come after your father's death."

"And the fact I traveled under a fake name?"

"I'm afraid not much gets past us, Ms. Banbury."

She said, "Worth a try."

He chuckled. "Special-Agent-in-Charge Jaxton, it was nice to meet you. I'll see you at dinner on Wednesday, unless you're otherwise engaged. And perhaps, if Ms. Banbury is free, she might like to join us?"

Jax said, "Thank you. I'll let you know ahead of time."

"Have a good trip, you two." Mattheus went to the door. "I've got a kickoff to get to. My son is the team captain."

She said, "Nice to meet you."

"Thomas will see you two out but take your time."

Jax nodded. "Thanks."

As soon as the door shut, Kenna turned to him. "I'm scared to open it. I don't know if I want to do it here."

He held the back of her hand, looking at the front of the envelope. "I don't have a car. We should take the train to your hotel."

"Where are you staying?"

"Same place."

"How efficient."

Jax chuckled under his breath. "As if I was going to let you get that far when I'm supposed to be your backup."

"Right. Exactly what I was thinking." She shook her head. "Can we get out of here now?"

Instead of standing there staring at the envelope for a year, which was how much time she would need to process it, Kenna just wanted to get out of that building.

Jax led her to the door, made small talk with Thomas as they rode down in the elevator, and held her hand through the quiet lobby and out the main doors. "The rain stopped."

She didn't let go of his hand. He lifted it and pointed to the right. "Let's go that way and walk along the river. Figure out where we're going."

She squeezed his hand, the letter tucked in her pocket now. Yet another piece of her history. Of who she was. Given to her like a gift she could hold close and savor. "I should thank Maizie. I don't think I'd have come if it wasn't for her. I'd have stayed and pretended I can protect her."

"You *can* protect her, Kenna. That's what you're doing here."

"Is it?" The trip was off the rails, and it had barely started. "It's supposed to be about Sandhurst and finding whoever has Maizie and the rest of us under surveillance."

As they stepped onto the sidewalk that ran parallel to the river, the clouds parted, and the sun shone through. The day was still dreary, and everything was damp—even her. But that little swatch of light brightened everything. "I need fourteen cups of coffee."

Jax chuckled. "Let's see if we find a coffee shop before we find a tube station. One of the lines runs in a circle so we could just go around and around all day if you want. Ignore everything."

"Tempting." She chuckled. "We need to find out where Ye Olde Mitre is. Go there. It's the pub where my parents met."

Jax glanced over at her. "Definitely."

"I want to open it. But I also don't."

"The unknown is scary. You've taken a lot of hits lately."

He would open it for her if she asked him to. He'd take the hit, which made her wonder how to balance their relationship. She didn't want to be the weak, needy one. She wanted to be strong enough that she could help him stay standing when he took a hit.

They walked all the way to a bridge. She would have to get her phone out and check the maps app to find out which one. But Kenna didn't want to break the peaceful silence between them. Jax led her to the brick wall that lined the side of the river.

She looked out at the brown-ish water, then downriver at the buildings on either side. "I need to work this case. I'm getting sidetracked by personal stuff."

"Maybe you should get sidetracked. It could be important."

"But it doesn't save lives. It doesn't bring justice where there wasn't any before. It's just me-stuff."

Jax stood close, also staring at the water. "You haven't worked a case since New Orleans. Now that you have a shot at one, it's going to feel odd to be dealing with so much personal stuff at the same time. But it's not selfish to take the time to learn what you need to learn. It's who you are, and all of it is *why* you feel such a need to save lives and bring justice."

"That is it, exactly." She leaned against him. "It feels selfish."

"Would it still feel selfish if it wasn't scarier than any case? Scarier than the things you face in the dark—because this time the dark is in you."

"You think I'm a coward."

Jax stiffened. "The strongest person I know is not a coward. Everyone has something they're afraid of. Whatever is in that envelope doesn't change who you are."

"I guess it's time to turn on the light."

He wasn't wrong that solving other people's cases was easier than dealing with what was in her. She would always rather avoid her own issues than have to face them. Who wanted to be that self-aware, anyway? She didn't need to deconstruct her whole life right now and why she was the way she was. Kenna was a darn good investigator, and she cared about people. That was all it needed to be.

If there was a case here in the UK, she was going to solve it.

After she opened this letter.

She caught a flap on the back and peeled back the envelope as carefully as she could. Jax shifted, glancing around them—covering her. Protecting her. This man God had given her to keep her safe, to help her be strong when she didn't feel it. "Love you."

He whipped back around, no longer focused on what was around them. Several expressions shifted across his face. Finally, with his lips curled up slightly in a smile, he settled on, "Just open it."

Kenna tugged out a single piece of paper. An old photo.

A woman sitting on a low brick wall, the beach and an ocean behind her, wearing a sundress. Long dark hair drifted to the right, tangling on the breeze. On her lap was a chunky toddler wrapped in a beach towel. Both smiled at the camera.

She turned the photo over.
I love you, my darling. I always will.
Don't believe anything they say,
Mum.

Chapter Nine

Nelson Hotel, London
Saturday 5:47pm

Kenna wandered around the living room area of the fancy hotel room, because it was safer than lying down—which would have her asleep in minutes. She'd showered and opted for sweatpants and a tank top, over which she'd pulled a thin sweater. She'd left her hair wet and loose. Earbuds in so she didn't have to hold her phone.

The phone rang until Maizie finally answered with a breathy, "Banbury—oh, it's you."

Kenna smiled. "It's me."

"How is the hotel?"

"It looks like a grandma's apartment. Or her *flat* as they call them here. All flowery upholstery, white net material doilies, and a chandelier. I'll take pictures. There's crown molding on the ceiling. Tassels on the lampshades."

"Send them." Maizie sounded like she was smiling. "I

want to see. Meanwhile, I'll send you the photo I found online of Wilson Sandhurst getting off his plane in Barcelona." She barely paused before she said, "Where is everyone?"

Sandhurst was in Spain, not in the UK? That was interesting.

"Preston and the MSI guys are down in the restaurant eating dinner. Jax and I got fish and chips on the way here at this outside market type place." People everywhere, which meant it was easy to get lost in the crowd. She was still a bit disoriented, so she had no idea where they'd been or what it was called.

"Was it good?"

"It was...greasy. I did not need an entire serving. We should've shared." Next time, she wanted to try something called a "battered sausage." Not because it would be less greasy, but because fried foods all over the world should be tried. "Now Jax is taking a shower in his room, checking in with his office, and then coming over."

His room had two twin beds in it. If things got crowded in here, she was going to crash at his place. Between the two rooms in the suite, there were beds for three. No sharing, thank you. The fourth person got the couch.

Kenna was more worried about the floor-to-ceiling windows. She'd pulled the sheer curtain across so no one could see inside, but it wasn't a foolproof solution.

"How are you feeling?"

She probably meant jetlag, but still... "Completely off balance. People keep handing me random pieces to a puzzle I didn't know I was working on trying to solve."

"You knew Preston had a reason for wanting you to come with him to London."

"Not that he told me what that reason was. I had to

meet with MSI to find out from Earl Jonas that my mother worked for British Intelligence."

"I looked for the name you gave me, but there was nothing. If I dig any deeper, someone will notice, and I'll get flagged."

"And they already know you're part of it." Not worth the risk.

A knock on the door brought her attention around. She wandered over and checked the peephole. Jax.

She opened the door, and he touched his lips to hers, wandering in the room. She pointed to her earbuds. "One sec, Maizie."

She put the earbuds back in the case and tapped the Speaker button on her phone on the coffee table. Kenna slumped onto the couch.

Jax sat beside her and tugged her legs onto his lap. "Hi, Maze."

"Hi, Jax." The teen paused. "Kenna, what did they tell you about her?"

"They had files that said *redacted* across them. Lots of stuff blacked out. Mission names like *Operation Sunflower* and *The Frankfurt Initiative*. Which was completely unhelpful, unless we can find someone who was part of the work she did."

"Maybe that's what Preston knows."

Kenna looked at Jax, who shrugged. She said, "I wish he'd just tell me. I feel like I'm being managed."

Jax squeezed her shin.

"It seems like she worked for the British government. I barely know in what capacity. She met my father—I need to read more of his journal to find out how that went." Kenna hoped it didn't get romantic, because as much as she was curious about where she came from, she didn't want to hear about *everything* they got up to. "I need to figure out some discrepancies."

"What do you mean?" Jax asked.

"I was told...or I always thought...she died when I was little. Like two, or three maybe. My dad never wanted to talk about her, so I didn't ask. I never found any paperwork or anything that mentioned her after he died, in the things he'd kept."

"Which is why we looked into that autopsy Joe Don Hunter had in his safe," Maizie said. "The one everyone seems to conveniently have forgotten about when it could be relevant."

Jax glanced at her.

Kenna shrugged it off and said, "Right. But I think I know who that was. Because my dad's journal starts with talking about how he and Joe Don liked the same woman. I think my dad was about to give her up to his buddy, take a step back, and let Joe Don go for it with her. But then she was killed."

The sheriff she'd met had never married. Maybe he'd carried a torch for that woman for years.

"Maybe he just assumed I knew who my mother was, or how my dad met her." She couldn't ask now because he'd died tragically. "My dad went to London on this case not long after Joe Don's friend died. He was here investigating something, and that's when he met my mother. She gave him information that must've helped. I need to keep reading, but I at least know she worked for MI5. But I don't think they're going to release any information to me."

Maizie said, "I thought that double-oh-seven stuff was MI6?"

Kenna said, "MI5 is domestic intelligence, like Homeland Security."

"Huh. Some of the classes Jax's conference has listed for this week make more sense now."

She smiled. "Glad I could help."

Jax glanced at her. "You should be going to the conference with me."

"I don't think I need any more things to do. I barely know where to start." She winced, but there was a smile in it.

He was here with her. She'd met his sister, brother-in-law, and their kids and loved their family. When his mom and dad were able to meet Kenna, she was going to do it. They'd been busy with their California high society lives and unable to carve out time to meet, so Jax hadn't seen his parents over the holidays, though he had spoken to his dad on the phone.

Maybe his mom had a problem with her? Kenna didn't have time for any more personal things to drop in her lap so she was staying away from it. Making sure they had a solid foundation before she finally met his mom and dad.

One thing at a time.

She was just having trouble getting to the point where it was just one thing.

Maizie said, "I have something if you need answers to at least part of it."

She sounded so unsure of herself. "Hit me with what you've got, Maze."

"Okay." More confidence in her tone now. "I looked into Earl Jonas, the guy who runs Miami Security International. I was hoping they wouldn't be around when I told you."

"Coast is clear." She shifted closer to Jax, curling her legs up so she could lean against his shoulder. "Go for it."

"He was military for years, Marine Corps Intelligence.

All over the world. As far as I can tell, he never met your father."

"Maybe he met my mom, and that's the connection." Her mind filled with the image of that photo. She wanted to draw it out again and just stare at her mother. A faceless, absent presence in her life—a void where Amara Clarke should have been but wasn't. Kenna had put the photo and the journal in the hotel room safe with a combination only she knew.

Maizie said, "Could be. He did spy stuff during the Cold War. At least as far as I can tell. Stairns looked at his record and confirmed what they *weren't* saying. That he worked counterintelligence."

Yeah, he had to be connected to this. "I'd like to know how they got my dad's journal. I need the chance to ask Preston if he had it, or if Jonas is the one who did."

Maizie said, "It wouldn't surprise any of us if it's Jonas. He's super connected in that world, according to Stairns. MSI doesn't seem to have a vested interest in you digging up the case your father worked on there, but it's possible it's related to something going on now. I'm still working on that part. What I found out was that the last couple of bids MSI did for government contracts? They weren't successful."

"So they're trying to get back into someone's good graces, proving themselves," Jax said. "Or getting their own back on whoever is stonewalling them, maybe. If they know they're in the doghouse this could be about doing an end-run around whoever has it in for them."

She didn't like the sound of either of those. "Messing with my life in the process."

"I asked Bear what he knows about any connection between MSI and your family."

Kenna said, "Thanks, Maze."

The lock on the door clicked, and Preston came back in with Hollace and Nielson.

She lifted the phone, said, "Call me back if you find something," and ended the call. "Hey, guys."

"Kenna. Jax." Preston wandered over and sat in a salmon-colored armchair, making the spindly, wood legs creak.

"You on duty, Kenna?" Hollace said. "I need a shower."

"I'm gonna call my girlfriend." Nielson had his phone out already.

"I'm good."

Jax said, "Me, too."

The MSI guys disappeared to the bathroom and another bedroom, respectively. Preston shifted in the seat a little more and said, "I don't like babysitters."

"Then don't be a baby." Kenna stared at him. She spotted the small twitch of his lips. Then she hit him with, "You knew my father's connection to this country. My connection. That's why you wanted me to come here."

He didn't waste a beat saying, "Partially."

Jax said, "So what's the other part."

Preston looked at the window, as if he could see outside. As if he could take a minute for himself because they had all the time in the world.

She wasn't here to be part of his protection detail. She might be here because this was the source of the threat against Maizie, but was that only wishful thinking because it would be convenient? She would prefer to go to the conference with Jax, but not if there was work to be done.

"I have a friend who is a retired Metropolitan police officer. Guy was a chief inspector in his prime." Preston looked at her. "He knew your father. Worked with him on his case, making it all official between the FBI and the Brits. Until the whole thing was squashed."

"You know the case?"

"Some of it. Not enough to be helpful."

"What do you know?" Kenna asked, fully cognizant of the fact he wasn't telling her something.

"That it connects to my wife."

Jax said, "And her death?"

Kenna shook her head. "How can this connect you, me, my parents, your wife, and the murder you were accused of?"

Preston's expression flashed with grief. "You mean the one I was convicted of?" He laughed, but there was no humor in it.

"What's going on, Preston?"

She was glad Jax asked, because Kenna wanted an answer to that same question. "What did you bring me here to do? Because I'm guessing it's not so I can take a trip down memory lane."

Preston's eyes reddened, and she saw moisture there. Finally, he said, "I need you to find out what really happened. I need you to end it."

Chapter Ten

The knock came on her door early the next morning. Or she thought it was early. Then she glanced at the clock and realized it was nearly eight.

Kenna kicked the sheet and comforter back on her bed and headed for the door. Through the peephole, she saw Hollace, so she opened the door, even though she had on her sweats and tank from the day before. "Hey."

He strategically didn't look at her arms, just kept her attention with a level gaze. "Preston wants to go for a walk. He said there's a coffee shop on the way."

"Give me ten."

"All right. Come to our room."

She made a cup of coffee in her room anyway. Even though it would be terrible. They also had a couple of different types of tea, but each was a black tea variety. Milk was apparently available on request.

Kenna washed her face, tied her hair back the fastest way she knew how, and pulled on some clothes that would work in varying kinds of weather. Thinner layers. She might even buy a rain jacket if it kept pouring today like it had yesterday. She should check the forecast.

When she looked at her phone, she saw the text from Jax that he'd left for his breakfast meeting with FBI buddies who worked in the London office. That was hours ago now. Ramon had sent a link she clicked. It led her to a site for the security system he'd set up around Stairns' cabin, where Maizie had the Airstream. Heat sensors by the look of them, so he'd know if anyone was creeping around. It all looked quiet, which reassured her. If someone was going to sneak in, they'd likely do it right about this time of night—in the early hours of the morning, mountain time zone.

She'd been awake half the night. Jet lag and a mix of trying to figure out what fresh mess she'd landed herself in. Jax had been fast asleep in the other twin bed, out almost as soon as his head hit the pillow. She'd had a harder time finding rest.

Trying to regain her sense of peace.

The first thing she'd tried—reading her Bible—should've been the thing that solved the problem. But it hadn't seemed like an end to it in the moment, just a reassurance that whatever was going on wasn't outside of God's hands. He was in control. Sovereign—a word she'd had to look up. Kenna knew it had to do with monarchies but not what it meant in Christianity. Now she understood the reference to an all-powerful ruler who could do whatever they wanted. God was good, and He was in control. The ultimate authority.

Not something she could ignore if she wanted to figure out answers to her questions.

She stuck her feet in her shoes and slid the pen knife Hollace had given her into a pocket. Phone. Sunglasses. She'd opted for black pants that had hidden pockets into which she stowed a couple of incidentals like ID and a credit card. Another tank top, over which she pulled a long sleeve checkered shirt to hide her scarred forearms and the braces she put on her wrists.

Kenna got to the door, reached for the handle, and paused.

Fatigue weighed her down. She hadn't even started her day yet or finished that first cup of coffee before she'd brushed her teeth. They were waiting for her outside. She was part of a team, not in charge of her own schedule.

She muttered, "Not my favorite thing," at the same time she opened the door.

"What isn't?" Preston wandered over to her, followed by the two MSI guys.

"Nothing. Sorry I took too long."

Preston shrugged. "I'm eager to stretch my legs. Get some coffee. Talk with you."

They'd left things pretty loose the night before. After he'd dropped another puzzle piece that she had to absorb, it had occurred to her that he might be attempting to save her sanity by only giving her bits at a time. As frustrating as it was that he didn't simply tell her the whole thing from start to finish in one go, it might actually be for the best to go slower.

Who knew what he had to say to her?

She'd read some more of her dad's journal, but the next few days after that first meeting with her mother, Malcom Banbury had knocked on some doors to ask about Amara

Clarke and got nothing. Shut down. Kicked out. Dismissed and told no—or told that she didn't exist.

Any questions he asked hadn't been answered.

Her dad had decided she gave him a fake name because she didn't want anything to do with him. Or she believed she was in danger, so she was actively lying low. He'd leaned more toward that one, because he'd had that protector instinct in him that he'd ingrained in Kenna.

She wasn't sure it helped her to keep reading just on the off chance she would discover a little bit of peace in the middle of this. But it allowed her to feel close to him.

Kenna followed them to the stairs, down to the ground floor and across the lobby with its wingback armchairs and the dining room off to the side. The smell of sausage made her stomach flip a little—probably because it was empty.

Preston walked to a hostess stand, and the older woman behind the podium bent, retrieved a white paper bag, and said, "Here you go, dearie."

"You're a doll. She'll love it."

The older woman flushed, then patted a hand on her straight gray hair to smooth it down. "Enjoy. High tea is at three."

"Thanks." Kenna didn't know what she was thanking the woman for, but she figured it was in that bag. And wasn't "high tea" sandwiches and little cakes? That could be good. Maybe Jax would want to go.

Then again, considering their names on the reservation indicated she and Preston were the couple, she might have to go with him and not Jax.

They headed for the door, while Preston dug in the white paper bag.

Hollace said, "One second, please."

Preston nodded absently. Hollace stepped outside, probably to ensure it was clear.

Kenna looked around the lobby, doing a visual sweep, just to see who was hanging around. No one paid them much attention, if any.

Most folks within view were enjoying their breakfast. A guy in the lobby read from a newspaper called the *Daily Mail*. The receptionist typed on the computer, a phone tucked between his ear and shoulder. The guy had dark skin and a turban holding his hair up.

"Here. It's supposed to be amazing, and you can eat it while we walk." Preston had a white-wrapped sandwich in one hand, butcher paper covering what smelled like sausage.

"What is it?"

"Apparently, they put sausages in sandwiches. With ketchup, which is called *tomato sauce*."

Kenna frowned.

"Try it." He handed her a napkin as well.

"Let's get walking. Then I'll try it." Because Hollace was headed back in already. He waved to them, and she said, "Let's go."

Outside, the air seemed to hang thick, which surprised her. She hadn't thought it would be humid here. She unwrapped the sandwich. "Don't forget you promised me coffee."

Preston grinned around a mouthful of sandwich, then said, "This is really good."

She took a bite of hers. Stopped. Looked at him.

Preston grinned. "Right?"

"This is supposed to be a sausage." But it didn't taste like any sausage she'd ever had.

"I told you it would be good." He motioned with a tip of his head. "Come on."

She walked beside him, Hollace a few feet ahead as if he wasn't even with them. Nielson was behind them, but anyone watching for long enough would probably realize they were both with her and Preston.

She wondered if they'd purposely drawn her out. So she didn't spend all of her Sunday in a dark depression. To keep her from wondering all day what her father had gotten into that ended with her mother dead and his FBI career on shaky footing.

Fine, she'd skipped to the end and read a *little* of the end of the journal. Just to put her out of her misery. Anything to get a little resolution. But it hadn't worked any more than anything else did, except wallowing in the Psalms, being all miserable with David.

It was your own fault, bro. She hadn't done anything to land herself in this situation that she knew of. Not that she hadn't made any mistakes.

Church bells rang through the city from somewhere she couldn't pinpoint. Traffic seemed like rush hour congestion, but maybe that was normal here in the center of London even if it was Sunday.

A couple of young women wearing tiny dresses, probably in their early twenties, walked on bare feet down the sidewalk, holding high heels in one hand. Makeup smudged on their faces. Hair in need of a comb. They glanced at each other and erupted into giggles, both of them laughing at something on one of their phones. Coming home from a night out that lasted all night.

"This way." Preston waved to a corner, and as they rounded it, she saw a stretch of grass.

"There's a park?"

"There are little ones tucked all over. If the weather's nice, there will be a lot of people out later. Relaxing on blankets, enjoying the sunshine." He led her to a stone bench, and she sat strategically to avoid a bird deposit.

Kenna finished her sandwich, thick slices of bread that had to be homemade. Sausages cut horizontally and laid between the slices. Butter. *Tomato sauce.* "Fine, you were right about the sandwich."

"But it isn't why I had you get up." He stared at the grass, where a toddler ran after a pug wearing a red harness, the mother standing nearby with the stroller. "I wanted to tell you more of the story."

Kenna folded the paper her sandwich had been wrapped in on her lap, smoothing down the creases with her thumbnail. The ever-present burn in her arms reminded her she had no idea when to take meds. Her body clock was so off. "About my dad?"

"Talking about it all yesterday made me have a dream about Julia. My wife."

"I'm sorry it's bringing up painful things."

Preston stared at the ground. "I'd rather lay it all to rest, that's true. But I can't do that if it isn't over."

She remembered something Avery Masonridge had told her, about her father the former president—about her mother having an affair with Preston. Was that even true? She wondered if this was all far more connected than she'd realized. Maybe another piece of this puzzle Preston was going to drop one bit at a time.

She'd joked it couldn't all be connected, but maybe she'd been wrong.

Didn't mean she had to like it.

"If you want it to be over, then why not tell me the whole story," Kenna said. "All of it. The entire thing. No holding back information." She wasn't going to ever be okay with being spoon fed pieces of it even if he insisted. "Just tell me."

"It's hard to know where to start. I don't know the beginning. It's not over so there isn't an end. At least, there hasn't been one yet."

"So you want me to finish it." She turned on the stone bench to look at him. "But you won't tell me what *it is*."

"My brother-in-law. The woman you saw at his office in New York. My wife's death. Your mother's death. It's all connected."

"And I'm supposed to take your word for that?"

Preston said, "Proving it to you won't change the fact it's true."

"And you think it's what my dad was investigating?"

"I know it is." He nodded. "That's how we met. You weren't born yet. That's how long this has been going on. I was here on business. I had access to places he couldn't get to, so he approached me, and we made a deal. He had me go in."

"What was the case?"

A police vehicle with an odd-sounding siren passed on the street. When it had driven down a nearby road, Preston said, "Kidnappings. Young women. Healthy, upper class, successful and athletic. There was a profile, physical and otherwise."

"And you think it's happening again? That women are going missing."

Preston slid his phone from inside his jacket pocket. He unlocked it with his thumb and showed her a headline on the screen.

Another local woman gone missing.

"I know it's happening again. It's why I asked you to

come here." He let out a heavy exhale. "We found the place they were being held. We ended it. I mean, I helped in the beginning, but *he* ended it—your dad. He killed the guy who took them. The guy who was 'keeping' them."

Kenna scrolled down the news article on his phone and absorbed some preliminary details. "You think you guys missed something, like an accomplice?"

"Maybe they just let us believe we'd ended it, rescuing them and killing him. I'd already gone back to the US. When your dad left, maybe they never stopped." He shrugged. "I have no idea what went wrong, but it isn't over."

She handed him his phone back and then paced away from him, across the path to the grass beyond it before she turned back. A handful of pigeons pecked at the remains of a sandwich on the grass to her left beside the thick trunk of an English oak tree.

She tucked her hands in her pockets. "You're telling me you were sitting on this the whole time? You never said anything."

Preston set his forearms on his knees, wringing his hands together. "You were in the middle of that thing with the Rosenbergs. But it's done now, and I know you have it in you to face a powerful foe because I've seen you do it."

Kenna ducked her head, trusting Hollace and Nielson to have their backs.

Going up against the Rosenberg family, even just the fringes of who they'd been in US society, had been one of the scariest times of her life. Even so, she'd done what she could, and Jax helped. God took care of the rest.

They'd rooted out corruption in the FBI and got Jax a promotion because he'd been instrumental in taking down the Rosenbergs. Ended their stronghold grip on the things that shaped American culture and the policies of the government.

No one wanted to believe a shadowy organization subverted basic democracy, but when presented with the evidence, it was hard to deny.

"Your father wouldn't let this go. Are you going to?"

She lifted her head and stared at him. "You think I'm about to go up against people I know nothing about?"

"I'll tell you everything I know."

Would he? Seemed like there was still something he hadn't said. Did it have to do with how cagey Jonas got when she mentioned how her mother had died or something else?

Kenna knew who had killed her. She just didn't know who ordered the hit.

Was she about to find out?

Chapter Eleven

"Thanks for skipping lunch."

Jax shot her a look. "You're meeting with a retired British cop? I'm coming. You're meeting with a retired British cop who knew your father..?"

"I get it." She tucked her arm into his as they walked along the sidewalk. A breeze brushed back strands of her hair, the chill cutting into her sweater, over which she'd pulled a denim jacket.

Jax had a suit on but had a wool coat over it. He needed a hat because the tips of his ears were red. "What?"

Did she want to admit she was a *girl* right now, one who couldn't help wondering if they fit together. At least in appearance, they looked off balance. Her casual. Him professional. She lived her life the way she wanted, which meant being happy with her own choices. That was all.

It didn't mean she had to prove herself to anyone. Least of all people she would likely never see again.

"Nothing," she said. "Don't worry about it."

He shook his head. "Sure."

"So what class did you attend this morning at your conference?"

Given the tug of a smile on his lips, he wasn't fooled by her changing the subject. What woman wanted to actually own her insecurity? Why not just live life instead and not worry about it?

He said, "Criminal Ideology: Eugenics in History."

"Wow. That's a mouthful."

"It was taught by a psychologist from California. His father was a psychologist as well, and he actually supported the Nazis with research he'd done into sterilization."

"Seriously?"

"Apparently, some of the things the Nazis did were ideas they got from the state of California. One of those dark parts of history no one wants to admit, but then later, someone has to publicly apologize for it so that the people who inherited that trademark, or company name, can confirm to everyone that they strongly disagree with what the people who came before them did."

Kenna sidestepped a group of young men in suits, chattering loudly, headed the opposite direction on the sidewalk. Jax stopped at a crosswalk in the center of a group of locals and tourists. They waited for the light to change from a lit red image of a man standing, to a green man walking.

She said, "I don't think I knew that the idea came from the US."

"Easier to blame Hitler for what he did, as if he came up with all those ideas himself," Jax said. "Harder to see the darkness inside ourselves. That the same poison of sin is in all of us, at least the potential for it, even if we're taught morality and how to learn from history."

She nodded, and they set off with the crowd to the center island, where the crosswalk was offset in the middle. Raised the way she had been, the daughter of a famous investigator, Kenna knew right from wrong because she lived on the shadowy side of the line. She traversed the darkness to rescue those who had been sucked into it and couldn't get out on their own.

"I'm so used to facing down one bad guy at a time." She bit her lip. "How am I supposed to go up against something like the Rosenbergs again? Preston made it sound like these people are worse, a bigger threat. Longer standing if you can believe that. Maybe they all knew each other."

"Sounds like it's all the more worth it to end their reign of terror."

"Why does it sound like that's the last thing you want to do?" She tugged him toward the side of a building and stepped out of the flow of pedestrian traffic on the sidewalk.

"We're going to be late for your meeting."

Kenna shook her head. "Talk."

He winced, wrinkling his nose. "You want me to say out loud that the idea of you going up against someone like this again is *terrifying*?"

"Yes," she said. "I want you to say it. I need to hear it, because the alternative is that I'm alone, and no one cares if I live or die."

Jax touched her cheeks, sliding his hands back into her hair. She wanted to grab his waist, but with her arms feeling achy today, she just hooked her thumbs into his belt by his hips. She touched her front to his, closing the space between them.

"Say it," she whispered against his lips.

"You terrify me."

Kenna smiled. "You love me."

"Fine, you don't terrify me. Everyone *else* terrifies me."

He was afraid for her.

She let the thought settle into her heart, where a fragile plant grew out of the scorched earth. It blossomed now, growing stronger when Jax said those Jax things. When they shared a moment, even just a look. All of it added to the foundation of what was being cultivated between them.

She said, "You think I don't feel the same way every time you put that badge on and go to work?"

"I work behind a desk now, and it's all your fault I got promoted."

She ignored that because she knew he wasn't really mad about his current position. "Maybe to avoid this problem, we should both quit our jobs. We can find a cabin off the grid, and we don't leave. That way, we'll be safe, and we won't have to worry about bad guys."

"Agreed. It's called a honeymoon, and it happens after you say, 'I do' on a beach in Florida with you wearing a white sundress and me in linen pants and a white shirt—no shoes. My sister and her family. Your family. We'll send my mother an announcement after."

Yet again, something he said had left her speechless and in need of a moment to process.

Kenna kissed him, enjoying the time. Being close to each other. Knowing where they were headed. That sense of contentment with her life wasn't something she would ever take for granted.

Even with all she'd lost, Kenna couldn't rush into this. The last thing she wanted was to make a gut-reaction decision and always wonder if she'd gone too fast.

Jax seemed content to let her set the pace.

Or he *had*. Was this her sign that he'd been itching to move things along?

When he pulled back, she said, "You want to get married."

"I rolled over last night and fell off that bed onto the floor. I'm surprised you didn't hear the thud."

Kenna ducked her head and touched her forehead to the front of his shirt, trying to hide the smile.

"It wasn't funny at the time, but I can see the humor."

"Poor guy." She patted his chest and stepped back. They really would be late if they didn't get walking again.

"Put me out of my misery, Kenna."

She grinned, laced her fingers in his, and tugged on his arm. Just enough to get her point across without hurting herself. He walked beside her, matching her pace the way he had with so many things.

"I'm not going to make excuses or state my case, because I don't have any good ones, and this isn't about pushing it off as long as I can."

He squeezed her hand gently. "Winter was amazing. Having you nearby, even if you were in a lot of pain and recovering. I don't resent it when you leave to work a case. I leave to go to work, so what's the difference? We both have dangerous jobs."

"But you'd like that honeymoon."

"No pain. No cases. No danger. No cell signal."

Kenna smiled to herself. "Cool weather, moody, rainy mornings, and mist."

"So...Washington state? Or the Oregon coast?"

"I love the Oregon coast." She sighed. "We'll need plenty of coffee, and maybe some books that we'll say we'll get to reading, but we're too busy being lazy."

Jax chuckled, and it dissipated into a groan. "Maybe we

should set a date, and then steer clear of each other until the day. That way we won't get into trouble before the wedding."

"Mmm." She recalled the moment they'd had in Arizona, when they'd shared a hotel suite and had separate rooms. Just a look, and it seemed like it sparked a wildfire between them. "That's why work is good."

"It pays the bills."

"And it'll keep us out of trouble."

Jax said, "As long as the trouble you get into with the case doesn't end up getting you hurt...or dead."

"Isn't that why you're here?"

"If my job is to keep you *out* of trouble, we might need a neutral third party."

She chuckled. "Like a chaperone?"

"On second thought...never mind. That would be weird."

"Weirder than wanting to go somewhere just because it's a place my dad met my mom? Knowing I'll be distracted the whole time we're meeting with this guy, wondering what they looked like. Wishing I could've seen them together."

Instead, they were both gone. And the people responsible for her mom's death were still out there. She knew that's what this was. To her soul, she knew whatever was going on here involved her mother's death.

"I'll ask the questions and make notes. You just worry about you. Sound good?"

She said, "You're the best."

"I'd like that framed and signed." He smiled. "That way, when I do something only an idiot would do, I can remind you what you really think of me." He scanned the cross streets and looked for the alley they'd found on the map.

The tiny, walled pathway ducked between two modern office buildings, hiding the pub that had been in this spot since medieval times set back behind them. Kenna couldn't fathom that much history. Just a generation or two had twisted her around, trying to untangle it all.

Like the fact she was about to enter the place where her mom met her dad.

Jax led the way down the alley to the walkway in front of the long side of the pub. The crowd hanging around outside was a rowdy mix of professionals in suits enjoying their Monday lunch and tourists taking selfies. He held the door for her, and she ducked inside.

They were supposed to meet this guy in the back room, but she wanted to do something first. She eased up to the bar, between two ladies on her left and a big guy in an Arsenal football shirt on her right.

The bartender had bleached blonde curls cut close to his head and an earring in his left ear. He wore leather cuffs and a Van Halen shirt.

"Do you have any Scotch eggs?"

He shook his head. "All out, Luv." And proceeded to pull down on the lever that dispensed beer into the glass he had angled under the spout. "Anything to drink?"

She ordered a soda, and Jax did the same—but asked for a roast beef sandwich with it. Then he glanced at her. "Make it two." He handed over British money and got change back.

"I wasn't hungry, but now I am."

"Right." He winked at her. "Let's go see if he's here."

She took her glass and sipped from the rim so it didn't spill as she weaved through people to the back room. It was decorated in a salmon, kind of orangey-red color. Just like her dad had described it in his journal.

In the corner, an older man in a wool sweater and jeans had hung his dark green canvas jacket over the back of his chair. A wool cap sat on the table beside a nearly empty beer glass and a plate with a fork and some crumbs. He didn't look like a retired officer in the police here. He looked like he belonged on a fishing boat in the icy rain.

"Ian Birch?"

He looked up at her, a craggy face with gray stubble on his jaw, but the warmth in his eyes put her at ease. His wife's profile on social media was full of pictures of their grandchildren, and in a lot of them, he was playing with the kids in the garden. Taking them to feed his horses. "That's me." He leaned back in his chair. "You look like him."

"I've never thought that." She set her glass down opposite him and introduced Jax. They shook hands, and she settled into the chair.

Ian said, "It's subtle, but it's there. The resemblance between you."

She wasn't even sure that was true. "Did you ever meet my mother?"

He shook his head and glanced at Jax who dragged a chair over and sat. Ian said, "Above my pay grade, that one. Your dad didn't have any problem going for it, though. Always had more guts than brains, Malc did."

Kenna leaned back in her seat, trying to reconcile that with the man she knew. Maybe he'd dated other women after her mother died and maybe he hadn't. She honestly had no idea, though he'd certainly embellished in the books he wrote. The ones that had been turned into movies. She didn't know what to believe.

"We're here because we've been led to believe that whatever you worked on with my father might be happening again."

Ian shrugged. "Of course it is."

Over by the bar, someone yelled out, "Two roast beef!"

Jax jumped up and went to grab their sandwiches, returning with two plates. As he settled back down, Kenna said, "What do you mean, *of course it is?*"

"I told him that cutting off the head of the snake, as it were, wasn't going to change anything. They're bigger than one man. It didn't end. They just went dormant for a while."

"And now?"

Ian shrugged. "New generation. Some relative, a son or a nephew. Someone's crazy cousin. Isn't that how it usually goes?"

"This is all new to me. But I have my father's journal."

Ian shook his head. "You won't find much in there."

"Can we get copies of the police report?" Those were usually public record, right?

"I tried. Years ago." Ian lifted his beer glass, realized it was empty, and set it back down with a sigh. "They told me the place where they stored the files burned down. Nothing left, all of it—paperwork and evidence—it's gone. There's no way to dig it up."

"They wanted it buried?"

Ian shrugged. "Whether they did or not, the result is the same. You have nothing to dig up that you can use to accuse the remaining family members of being involved in anything. They got smart. Figured out how to cover their tracks."

"We've dealt with a family like this before, in the US."

"Not like these." Ian sniffed. "I say 'family,' but it's bigger than that. It has to be."

Kenna said, "You came all the way to London from your home. Why meet with us if there's nothing to say?"

"Curiosity?" He eyed her. "An old man's need to relive the glory days, remember good times. All that."

"Is it true, though?"

Ian chuckled. "I don't mind coming uptown sometimes. London has changed, and I like to remind myself I don't belong here anymore. It's a young man's game now. The old guard gets put out to pasture."

Jax swallowed a bite of his sandwich. "How about one last case?"

Ian's expression shifted, and a note of interest flashed in his eyes before it extinguished. "I like my retirement. I just finished renovating the bathroom, and you want me to risk my life by going after them all over again? It nearly destroyed my career before. I had to stay out of it, and your dad took the brunt of the responsibility." He pointed at her. "Are you sure *you* want to dig it all up? Best to let sleeping dogs lie."

He really thought that was best, when he'd straight up told her it was happening again?

"I've never been good at letting things go." Kenna folded her arms as best she could, refusing to let this guy know her physical limitations. He didn't know the kind of person she was, but she didn't want him to think she would back down. "These people killed my mother, didn't they?"

"So you're on a one-woman mission to fight corruption? Is that it?"

Kenna shrugged one shoulder. "Why not? It's the right thing to do."

"The right thing to do is eat that sandwich. Wasting it would be a travesty."

Chapter Twelve

"I didn't come all this way to leave a victim to suffer. That's not what I do." Kenna stared at the older man across the table. She'd paused the conversation long enough to get Maizie on the phone. Muted so she could record everything they said.

Jax sat still beside her. He felt the same way, she knew that. Even if it wasn't technically why he was in England, and he probably had no intention of creating an incident with law enforcement here, he wouldn't walk away and do nothing, knowing someone's life was in danger.

She said, "You think we're just going to walk away?"

Ian leveled a steady gaze on her. "Then they already know your weakness."

Too bad Kenna no longer considered it a weakness to care about people and do what it took to save them. But being predictable was a little riskier. If whoever they were going up against knew her—if they'd done their homework on Kenna Banbury—they'd know that, like her father, she wasn't about to back down.

Walk away.

Give up.

It just wasn't in her nature.

You look like him.

Kenna didn't want to admit what it meant to her to hear those words, even if she didn't believe they were true in the slightest. Then again, given she might be entirely predictable, maybe anyone would guess she'd react exactly like that, and she'd only played into his hands.

Someone who wanted to target her might assume that the lack of family she'd had for years might translate into an innate need to soak up information like that. As if she was a cracked, dry riverbed on the first day of spring rain. Just a throwaway comment, but it turned out it meant *everything* to her.

As many people as she collected over the years since, or the ones to come, no matter how much she filled her heart with hope in the love that God had for her, she still wanted her dad back. She always would.

Jax reached over and squeezed her knee as if he sensed the shift in her. She covered his hand with hers and held on. Kenna said, "I don't consider it a weakness to want to save people. It's what I do, because I care about those victims."

Jax shifted in his seat but didn't let go of her hand. "Can you tell us what the case was that you investigated with Malcom Banbury, and who the two of you took down?"

"Can't say we took down anyone." Ian cleared his throat. "According to the report, I found the house destroyed and the homeowner the only victim of a terrible fire. Anyone else there had cleared out. After that, the case went cold, and there were no new leads."

"That's how you reported it?" She shook her head, unable to believe what she was hearing. "Why not just tell the truth?"

"And have my career destroyed over one case? Do you know how many others I worked over the years?" His expression shifted. "'It's what I do.' Isn't that what you said? You want me to prioritize one case so high it costs me everything. What about all the other good I've done?"

Kenna didn't know how she felt about that. She worked one case at a time and tried to save one victim at a time. He took a long view. Maybe he was wrong, or maybe she was wrong—or they simply had differing opinions.

Ian reached for his coat pocket and tugged out a letter-sized, white envelope. He lifted the flap and drew out a stack of folded papers. Newspaper cuttings that left inky smears on his fingers as he laid them on the table and spread them out between the cups and plates.

Kenna moved the salt and pepper out of the way. "Missing persons reports?"

"The families went to the papers back then, when the correlations between the victims started to become apparent." Ian tapped one page with his index finger. "They weren't officially seen as connected until the parents put it together with the help of a reporter. He was killed in a traffic accident, blamed for driving drunk. But by then, it was too late to squash the report."

"So they were connected in some way, only someone didn't want that getting out?" Kenna skim read a couple of the articles, one an L-shaped cutting of the newspaper detailing a woman who had gone missing one night after ice skating practice. She was supposed to have taken the city bus home but never arrived.

"Each of the four was between five-four and five-seven and they were within a ten-pound weight range of one another. They were an Olympic athlete, a mathematician at the top of her class getting her PhD. Two solicitors, I believe you'd call them lawyers, each one just a few years out of university. No connection between the law firms they worked for. They were promising women. The kind with high-IQs or high ambitions. Women with bright futures."

Kenna said, "So he was after high achievers?"

"Some killers have a type rather than purely looking for an opportunity." Jax leaned forward and read one of the articles. "Instead of just the right *time*, they wait for the right moment with the right person. There is the one they have chosen, and no other will do."

"He went so far as to stalk them for weeks." Ian nodded toward her. "Your father ascertained that through his interviews. We believed the suspect learned their habits. And when he found one of the...locations...we discovered files and files on the missing girls. All kinds of documentation, as well as extensive medical histories. We even found information on other women."

"Future targets? Or women he considered and discarded for some reason?" Kenna couldn't imagine what it would feel like to discover you were a target, unaware a trap was about to snap shut. Even though nothing had happened to them, those women would look over their shoulders forever.

Ian glanced at the main bar area of the pub, distracting himself with the bustle of humanity. Or reminding himself good people existed. Not everyone was in danger. The world wasn't simply a mess of killers and victims, perpetrators and those they committed crimes against.

On occasion, when Kenna was overwhelmed with the darkness in the world, she had to remind herself to overcome the evil with good. To shine a light. To believe in hope, because without that, what point was there in fighting so hard for what was right?

She wanted to know who her mom had been. But if there were victims who were currently captives, trapped and scared to death, she could wait on answers while she fought for justice.

Finally, Ian said, "Malc had a theory about why they were being chosen. And it wasn't just so this guy could have impressive trophies. He thought it might've been some kind of organ harvesting scheme."

Jax pinned him with a stare. "You don't seem convinced he was right."

"He's dead." Ian glanced at her. "Sorry. But he isn't here, and he just grabbed this theory like a dog with a steak. He wouldn't let it go."

"What do you think it was?" Kenna bit the inside of her lip.

A tendon in Ian's jaw flexed. "Two of the victims he found in the lower level of a hospital. They were dead before I got there, given a drug that killed them. The post-mortem the medical examiner did proved it had been a lethal dose. In the report, he also included a note that they'd both given birth in the few weeks prior to their deaths."

"You think he was breeding them, because their organs weren't missing." Kenna winced, knowing Maizie was listening to this. She was a tough girl, but Kenna wasn't going to take for granted her ability to absorb every part of all the cases they worked. Occasionally, one was going to segue into territory that brought up awful memories for the teen. "What did my dad say to that?"

"It would make you blush to hear it."

She figured he was likely right about that.

Her phone buzzed. Maizie had sent a message, even with the open phone line. A question—and a good one. There was no sign she was having a hard time with this conversation.

Kenna lifted her attention from the phone to Ian. "Is there any connection between these people you identified as being victims or possible targets years ago and the women involved in whatever is happening now?"

"Other than them being high achievers?" Ian shrugged his shoulders. "The recent reports are barely discoverable. News gets buried. People are being paid off or silenced. Families are trying to get the word out, but it's written off as the young woman having a drug problem no one knew about. One set of parents had their website taken down—the one dedicated to finding their daughter."

Jax said, "So then, you are investigating?"

"I'm barely making inquiries, son. I'm not connecting myself to this case. Because if I do, I'm on borrowed time. Half the parents are told their girls probably ran off with some young man."

He did seem genuinely worried that whoever was behind this—or whoever was burying it so news didn't get out—would come after him. That his family would pay the price one way or another. They would lose him, or they would be targets themselves.

"How have you found out what you know?"

Ian said, "I don't reveal my sources. I protect their integrity."

"And you keep yourself safe at the same time," Jax said.

Ian shrugged. "I can give you a list of women to look into. I'll recite them, you write it down. Pen and paper. Old school, so there's no paper trail."

Kenna shifted in her seat. "Do you have reason to believe someone has hacked your phone or your home computer?"

"How should I know?" Ian shrugged. "That's why I try not to use either and I have a 'dumb' phone that doesn't even connect to the internet."

Jax dug a pen out of the inside pocket of his suit jacket. "Write the names on the back of this receipt."

Ian took the pen but not the paper. "I'll use the envelope. They won't fit on that eentsy bit of paper." He wrote the list while Kenna ate the rest of her sandwich. Jax got another round of drinks, and Ian asked for strong tea with two sugars.

When Ian was done, he slid the paper over. Six names. Then he took a sip of his tea, which came hot in a mug, something he seemed satisfied by.

"I've got a friend who's a copper who tells me stuff. Don't ask me what constabulary he's with, because even just a general area puts him at risk. We play darts and swap stories. He said a missing person report got squashed. Said it might be happening around the country and even overseas. The Canary Islands. Greece. Places people 'round here go on holiday."

"He put this list together?" Kenna folded the envelope over. What she actually wanted to do was take a photo of it so that it would immediately upload to Maizie. Ian would likely not appreciate that, given he considered electronics a threat—or a vulnerability.

"Brits going missing on holiday isn't necessarily noteworthy, past the obvious problem. But someone should at least be talking about it. These aren't people you can write off as the kind no one will miss, runaways or someone in a mental health crisis. We're talking about a pre-med student. A painter who has been on the map since she was twelve, famous for more than ten years now, and no one noticed she's missing? One of them is the daughter of a Turkish dignitary."

She wanted to look up each one of these women, but when she did, was it going to be what she was currently thinking? That it would be like looking at a buffet menu—of people. A selection. Similar body type, varying genetics.

Kenna said, "Do you know of any connection to the women from years ago?"

Ian shook his head. "It's happening again. I know it."

She saw a flicker there, grounds for someone to say he couldn't let go of that case. He was distraught and traumatized enough to put pieces together with no correlation. "You found them before. You found the place where they were being kept."

"Your father burned it to the ground before I even got there. I've never been back."

"Please give us the address. If you remember it."

Ian said, "As if I could forget." He wrote on the envelope, which she decided to stick in her pocket when he was done. Then he said, "I suppose I should wish you luck, but I'm not sure it will do you any good."

"We appreciate you talking to us." Kenna leaned back in her chair, feeling in a way as if the storm had passed.

Ian sipped his tea. "Always sounds like a good idea until someone gets killed."

"Like my mother?"

"I didn't have nothin' to do with what happened to her.

I was out by then, and your dad didn't ring me again after we parted ways."

Jax asked, "What went down the last time you saw each other?"

"It was all in my report. That I happened to discover the family's country home in flames, and by the time the fire brigade got there, it was too late to save much of the structure. It was a shell of bricks and cement by then, nothing left." Ian's face became impassive, as if he refused to entertain any emotion whatsoever with regard to the events of that night.

She understood the need to compartmentalize that way. The alternative was that she got swallowed up by grief, or the feeling of powerlessness that so often accompanied trying to help people.

"Found a couple of women wandering in the woods if you can believe it." That stoic expression remained. "Got them help. The higher-ups understood that even though I was tasked with accompanying Special Agent Banbury everywhere he went, I unfortunately lost track of him and didn't arrive in time to save the house. We lost track of each other in the confusion of realizing the house was ablaze."

And no one had ever challenged his statement on what happened?

Jax said, "Sounds like a riveting report. What really happened?"

"Malc lost it when he found them, but I'd been held up, so I didn't get there until later." He frowned. "I don't know how the fire started. Maybe it was an accident. Malc came out with a cut in the front of his shirt and blood on his lip. Said the duke was dead."

"The guy was a lord?"

"That's how he got away with it for so long. They're about as untouchable as you can get."

Kenna said, "No one is outside the law."

Ian's expression flashed with something like grief. "Your dad said the same thing." He looked at his watch and took a final slurp of his tea. "Need to go, or I'll miss the next train back."

Kenna nodded.

Jax shook his hand. "Stay vigilant. Just in case."

Ian looked almost sad. "You as well." He slid the jacket off the back of his chair and didn't look back.

Kenna tapped the screen of her phone and put it to her ear. "Maizie, did you get all that?" She could take a photo of the names and the address Ian had given her and get her teenage tech support person on the case, working on gathering information while they made their way back to the hotel.

Or she could go there. Jax probably had to go back to his conference.

"Maizie?"

Jax frowned. "No answer?"

"The line is open." She looked at the phone screen, hung up, and texted Ramon.

WHERE IS MAIZIE?

"I'm gonna make a pit stop before we leave. Too much liquid." She kissed Jax, just a quick touch of her lips to his. Such a normal moment between two people that for a second, it felt as if they had been married for years.

His lips twitched. "I'll wait by the door."

She nodded, passing him without looking at him again. No point letting him know she was flipping out. He already knew she wasn't a normal woman, and theirs was nowhere near a normal relationship.

Kenna found a back hallway and a single occupancy restroom. A few minutes later, she headed back through the bar area and outside, where she didn't see Jax. She turned to look the other direction and nearly slammed into a woman a few inches shorter than her with long, dark hair.

"Sorry."

Even though Kenna had bumped into the woman, she thought it necessary to apologize? Kenna said, "My bad."

The woman's hand collided oddly with hers, and she felt something shoved into her hand.

"What are—"

The woman took a step past her, then darted between two men. They both turned to watch her scurry down the alley.

Kenna had a piece of paper in her hand, whatever the woman had given her. She took a step after the woman, which put her in front of one of the men.

He shot her an irritated look. "Watch it."

"Sorry." She held up her hands, skirted around him, and went after the woman. Jax stood at the end of the alley, where he paced around out of the flow of pedestrian traffic and talked on his phone.

As she approached, he looked over.

"Did you see a woman leaving?"

Jax frowned and hung up his call. "Maybe. But something is wrong. That was Ramon. Apparently, Maizie flipped out and lost it while we were on the phone." He hesitated. "We need to get back to the hotel. He's going to call me back."

"Let's go."

Chapter Thirteen

Finally, Hollace opened the door.

"Took you long enough." Kenna strode past him into Preston's room.

The man himself was on the couch, sitting on the edge of the seat, typing on his laptop, which was on the coffee table. He glanced over and frowned. "What happened?"

Kenna walked over to him. "A woman bumped into me and handed me this."

Preston unfolded the small paper, barely bigger than the one Ian had written on, which was in Kenna's other pocket. "Help me?"

As if she had time to figure out what that meant right now?

Preston started to speak and caught himself. He hesitated and looked between her and Jax. "What else is going on?"

"Nothing with us. Give or take that note." She couldn't even start to work out what they were going to do. Was a woman actually in danger? If so, why didn't she stick around? More likely it was a ruse to draw Kenna out. In which case, she needed to find the woman so they could plan for when the trap snapped shut and use it to their advantage.

She planted her hands on her hips and caught her breath with big inhales. "It's Maizie."

Kenna glanced at the Miami Security guys, but Hollace and Nielson knew the team who had been in New Orleans. Whether or not they knew about her, she still wanted to keep Maizie under wraps as anything other than her support.

The fact she was going through something—or were they under attack?—left Kenna standing there, unable to help and nursing a sick feeling in her stomach.

Jax shut the door behind her. "Everything good with you guys?"

Nielson turned from the window but didn't come over. "Quiet day so far."

Preston shut his laptop. "My meeting was fine. What's going on with Maizie?"

Kenna winced. "I need to call Ramon." They'd given the crew in Colorado this long. Leaving them to focus on Maizie, or whatever was going on. Now it was time to get the rundown. She put her phone on speaker and listened to it ring.

"Hey." Ramon sounded out of breath. "She's...Elizabeth sedated her."

Kenna put the phone on the table and braced both

hands on the edge, hanging her head. "Did you get attacked?"

"No. There's been nothing on the sensors or cameras. The house is secure."

"Okay." Kenna pushed out a breath, relieved to hear that at least. "What happened?"

"I got her laptop. Hang on." He shifted the phone. She pictured him tucking it between his shoulder and his ear. "She was looking at old newspaper articles. A house fire in Nottinghamshire?"

"Okay. We were talking about a fire."

"At a mansion? This place is some kind of historic house. They've rebuilt it. She was on a historical society website with pictures of a big house now open for visits."

Kenna said, "And she flipped out?"

"Maybe something else. She's got tabs on her browser, and a couple of chats open."

"Let's allow Maizie to keep her conversations private," Kenna said. If Hollace and Nielson found out she was talking to Bear, even intermittently, they'd want to know where he was. Hopefully, because they cared.

"Got it."

Jax came over to stand by her. "What exactly happened?"

"She screamed," Ramon said. "I want to say I've never heard anything like it, but you *know* where I've been."

"Torture." Kenna swallowed against a rise of sickness in her throat.

"I thought someone was in the trailer." Ramon paused. "She came tearing out, running as fast as she could, when she rarely leaves the Airstream even on a good day. Cabot was barking behind the screen door. Pretty sure she tore a hole in it trying to get out so she could follow Maizie.

Stairns ran out the back door of the cabin and down the steps. She slammed into him."

Jax laid a hand on Kenna's shoulder. "Did she say anything?"

"Nothing that made any sense. She was mostly screaming. I doubt she'll have a voice left when she wakes up."

"She saw something, and it triggered her." Kenna didn't like being so far away, but if she had been there, would she have a way to help Maizie? "Do what you can. Keep me posted. I want to know the second she wakes up."

"Got it." Ramon paused. "I can't see anything else that sticks out. She was looking at this house. Pictures in their website gallery of the restoration they've done. The other open tabs are searches she's running online for missing persons in the UK and across Europe."

"So it's possible she saw a person's picture. Or their name?"

Ramon said, "It's just search results. Nothing definitive."

"Find out. Call me back when there's an update."

"Got it." Ramon ended the call.

Kenna pushed off the table, walked to the window, and looked out. Below, sidewalks were packed with people walking. Tall-sided buildings on both sides of the street, painted white or left as the color of concrete. High windows that looked out onto the street below with those red buses, black taxis, and fancy cars that paid extra tax to drive in the center of London. People going about their business, most with no idea there was a dark world that lived below the civilized surface. Or if they did know, they chose to avoid it at all costs.

Behind her, Preston said, "She'll be all right, won't she?"

Kenna turned to face him, appreciating the compassion

in his expression. He didn't even really know Maizie. Not like Bear did. Preston hadn't met her, but Kenna had filled him in enough that he was prepared to help them maintain operational security.

"I don't know." Kenna dragged a chair back from the table and sat. It creaked under her, and the pad was pretty thin. Ornamental cut outs in the wood back dug into her shoulder blades. "We knew it was possible at any moment that she could..."

She didn't want to say *have a mental breakdown.* Instead, Kenna said, "Reach a point where she didn't have the tools to handle what was happening."

Jax folded his arms. He looked like a dad about to pummel the boy who'd pushed around his daughter. "Has to be something she saw that triggered a memory."

He and Maizie had spent hours over the holidays playing a card game. Sitting on the floor across from each other, Cabot lying by them. Locked in fierce competition over aces and hearts.

Now they were back to her reliving her trauma.

"Nothing else makes sense."

Kenna said, "We were on a knife-edge as it was. Wondering when something would hit her." She didn't like it, but Maizie had been doing amazingly well. She scrubbed her hands down her face. "We need to figure out what's going on with that note and the case here. Ian told us it's happening again, but he only gave us the names of the missing from thirty years ago."

Jax said, "We can try and contact the cop he knows now. Make an approach, see if we can get intel. It did seem like he doesn't want it buried, even if he isn't the one who can investigate."

"Likely not, if it's across country lines. Jurisdictions.

Citizens involved in crimes abroad. Sounds like a tangled mess." She winced. "The state department isn't going to like it."

Preston sat back on the couch. "What did they tell you when you met with them?"

"Ambassador Mattheus gave me a letter that had been there for years. Maybe since my father was here last, and he mailed it with instructions."

Kenna had come here with him during the summer between freshman and sophomore year of high school—which she'd gone to in person. They'd spent nearly the whole summer in the UK, then down in Paris. A couple of other cities, too. Countries she couldn't recall now.

"A letter?"

She nodded. "It's a photo of me with my mom. When I was a baby."

Jax squeezed her knee.

"Wow."

"I know." But she caught a flash of something in his expression. "Did you know her?"

Preston winced, just a flash of discomfort. Because she was asking or because he'd rather not remember? Finally, he said, "When you look into those women they rescued...the ones not found. The ones who died years ago. Run my wife's history at the same time. Take a look at her family."

Kenna recalled what Ian had said about the two they found deceased recently having given birth. The bodies must not have been too burned if the medical examiner had been able to tell that. Possibly in an area of the house not swallowed up in the blaze. Or there were other bodies aside from ones consumed by fire.

The house had been destroyed. Rebuilt.

If Maizie had been there herself, that meant for sure

that something continued after the "duke" was killed, and after it was restored. Under the noses of whatever organization was currently conducting tours of the house.

Despite having a handful more pieces of this puzzle now, it still didn't make a lot of sense to her.

It almost seemed like her father hadn't stopped anything.

"We need to run everything Ian gave us."

She glanced at Jax, appreciating his ability to be diplomatic. She would rather kick some furniture around to get out her frustration and then go knock on doors. "I need my laptop."

His expression softened. "Can you do without me this afternoon? There's a guy visiting from the Hague who is giving a talk on Criminal Ideology. I'd rather not miss it. Unless you're thinking about following up on anything by yourself. Or standing on a street corner to try and draw that woman out again." He got up and took the paper from the table. Stared at it. Shook his head.

Guess he figured there wasn't much they could do with it. She had other priorities right now, so that worked. Anyone who couldn't give her enough information to move on had to understand that she might not be able to drop everything.

Especially not if it was a trap.

"I'll stay here. Do some research, see what I can come up with."

"Okay." Jax touched his lips to hers. "Maizie?"

"As soon as I know."

He wandered to the door, glanced back at her, and then left. After the door shut, with Hollace and Nielson talking at the other end of the room, Preston said, "You guys seem different than you were in Arizona."

Kenna shrugged. Jax had shown up in New Orleans, but that had been after Preston left.

"Your arms seem way better."

She lifted her hands, held out her arms, and rotated her wrists. "Each set back takes something from the mobility I had. Eventually, I'll get nothing back."

"Or you could stop risking so much using your arms."

"Would you?"

One corner of his mouth shifted up, the lines on his face more pronounced. "Good point."

"Why don't you just tell me what you know about this case?" It was more than a little frustrating knowing he had information and didn't freely give it to her.

"I don't want to cloud the way you work the investigation. My feelings aren't relevant, just the facts. Guilty. Innocent. I've been dragged down enough, kicking and screaming. Trying to get anyone I can to listen to the truth."

"So you don't speak at all? Is silence ever the answer?"

Preston stayed quiet, studying her with a soft expression. "I suppose there's a time to flip tables and a time to stay quiet. At least, that's what I'm trying to put into practice."

Ah, he was referencing the Biblical way. She wanted to read some more, dig into the contexts of both. Find out the circumstances of when Jesus had done each one.

She also had a case to work.

The personal development part might have to wait until the investigation had been completed, but the truth was she might need the information before then. After all, her choices could mean the difference between life and death for her, or for someone else.

"Are you going to help us work this case, or did you get

me here, and now you're done? Working on your business. Observing what I do. Making sure it gets resolved."

"I like your father's tactics better, but I know what I feel like I *should* be doing."

And she wouldn't like it, because it would look like he was doing nothing? She studied him, trying to figure out if that was a question that had an answer.

Kenna said, "Killing an English lord and burning down a registered historical home isn't really my style."

Preston's eyes flashed with the start of a smile. "I've noticed that."

She grabbed her laptop from the backpack by the couch, not really sure when she'd left it there. Before she went to her room last night, probably. Given her jet lag, she was surprised she didn't already feel the need for a nap—and some pain killers for her arms. Soon enough, she would probably feel it. Then in the middle of the night, she would be wide awake for hours.

Kenna used the dresser against the wall, which was tall enough she could stand and type. Ramon had sent her links to the windows Maizie had open on her browser. She sent him a reply, so he'd know she received them, but didn't ask about the teen. If there was news, he'd have told her. Maizie could be out for hours yet, and even then may be unable to explain what had happened. Who knew how long it would be before she could talk about it.

Didn't stop Kenna from wanting to toss this whole case and fly back to Colorado just to sit beside the bed and wait.

She looked at images of the house, trying to imagine a fire. Or horrible scenarios. Instead, it looked like something out of a historical novel. A place to entertain in the parlor or have a ball to show off the house—and the lord's daughters— to the neighbors.

The lord her father had killed, if that was what'd happened...

She still needed to read her dad's journal and see what he said about that night—or what he didn't say about that night. The lord had been interred in his final resting place with a lot of pageantry. A tragedy, at least according to the papers. An *accident*. Survived by one sister and a son who had been seven and away at boarding school at the time.

So there was a son, now in his thirties, who had inherited dad's title and his estate.

And an older sister of the duke who she could possibly interview. She could maybe see if the woman had any clue what her brother had been doing in his house.

People who had no reason to tell her the truth.

A living victim, maybe. Kenna started entering names running them to find out where these women's families were now.

Question was, did she have to investigate the past and what was happening now as one case, or was she here to solve both? And maybe more.

Did her father really make a mistake?

She hadn't wanted to think about that. No investigator wanted to realize they got the wrong man, or only a low level guy not the boss, let alone that they might've killed someone innocent. It was enough to make her start doubting everything she knew about him. Everything he'd told her.

Far better to not take anyone's word for it.

Kenna was going to have to find the truth for herself.

Chapter Fourteen

Kenna lifted to her tiptoes, one hand on his shoulder, and whispered into Jax's ear. "Found him."

Given the decibel level of the music in the club, she practically had to shout. Jax slid a hand around her waist, over the dress she'd put on. Tight. Long sleeves that hooked over her thumbs. Almost no back to speak of. She'd bought it only a few hours ago at a secondhand shop and thanked God she'd found something that covered the scars on her forearms. An odd thing to thank Him for, but she'd said it anyway.

He looked down to her feet—in her Converse, just in case she had to run—and back up the dress to her hair which she'd fluffed in an attempt to give it more volume. Kenna wasn't sure it worked. "You sure did."

She slid her arms up his chest and linked her fingers

behind his neck. "I didn't mean you." She practically whispered the words against his lips. "I meant Covington Hadley." The current Duke of whatever British town he ruled over. She wasn't going to try and pronounce it correctly.

"Shame." The smile shone in his eyes. "I got you a drink."

She spotted two glasses of something clear and fizzy she figured was what passed for lemonade here, or it was fizzy water. "Thanks." Kenna unfurled herself from him and turned her back to the bar. Took a sip of her drink. Watched the crowd.

The person on her other side backed up, talking animatedly with his arms. Probably in his late twenties. He stepped on the toe of her Converse.

Jax put an arm around her waist and tugged her to his side. The guy didn't even notice what'd happened. Jax leaned close enough so she could hear him say, "Where did you find him holding court?"

"The second room, off the left side." She waved across the main dance floor, a circle surrounded by high tables and stools. Three bars so there was never far to walk to reach refreshments, and an ocean of people all enjoying themselves. Except the guy to her right, all the way over by the wall. He looked like he was about to throw up.

"You think that's the VIP area?"

She shook her head. "Didn't look like it. But if he knows who we are, he'll see us right away if we go in there."

Jax didn't like the sound of that. "But we need to observe more."

"That's usually how surveillance works."

He grinned at her. She liked that she could see micro expressions. He thought she was cute pointing out the obvious just for the sake of humor. He might not always think it was cute, like years from now, but she'd deal with that later. She could also see an edge that darkened his amusement. Worry for Maizie would be there until they heard for sure that she was awake, and that she was going to be okay.

He lifted his other hand and traced a thumb over her cheek.

"Was it that house that tripped her?"

He dipped his head close. "We can't know until she wakes up. All we can do is pray and trust that she'll be okay. She hasn't come this far to be done now."

Kenna wanted to dip her head, stick close for a hug. But that established them as a couple to anyone watching. She'd rather they were taken for two people who'd only just met but planned on having a long night after they left here.

"Dance floor?"

She lifted her gaze to his. "Not the scenario I was thinking of when I imagined you and me dancing."

"Oh?"

She smiled. "Let's try and find a table within eye shot."

The left side, second room, had cutout squares where a window could've been installed. Instead, it was left open so the music could bleed through. So those on this side could see over to the other room, and the odd opportunistic person could hop through the opening instead of using the doorway.

Maybe it let people believe it to be a more "exclusive" space. Though it seemed only to be an unspoken understanding as there were no signs.

The couches and armchairs over there were red velvet and contrasted with the walls and ceiling that had all been painted black. Lights pulsed overhead from the dance floor, flashing across the space. In that room, the constant light illuminated the room but changed colors every few seconds.

"Is it me, or does it smell like a mix of pine trees and balloons in here?" Jax grinned and took a sip of his drink.

She glanced into the room and saw Covington stretched out in the center of a couch with his knees wide. One arm across the back. Shirt unbuttoned almost to the middle of his chest. Hair mussed, but maybe it had been styled that way. His clothes probably fit better twenty pounds ago.

A woman considerably younger than him seemed to be in energetic conversation with a friend, though she knelt on the cushion beside him. One hand on his shoulder and talking across him, she bounced up and down in the seat as if whatever she was saying was hilarious. Another woman stood over the arm of the couch, a couple of feet away. Both were thin and wore tube tops and tiny skirts like they were a uniform.

The two women tipped their heads back, laughing.

Sick of being ignored, Covington grabbed the woman beside him and turned her so she fell into his lap. He stuck his face in her neck, and whatever he was doing, or saying, she erupted into squeals. The contents of her glass went flying in an arc of liquid.

He sat up again, grinning now that he was back as the center of attention.

Across the sitting area, a woman unfolded her legs and stood. She wore white skinny pants, white heels, and a white silk top. Dark hair cascaded down her back. She had to be of either Indian or Pakistani heritage. When she turned and left the area, a tiny gold purse under her arm, Kenna saw a nose ring glint in the light. She also wore a slender watch and plenty of bracelets. A henna tattoo on the back of one hand that was probably real.

She headed away from what Kenna could see, toward the walkway between the room with the dance floor and the side room.

"I'm going to—"

Jax nodded before she could finish. "Go. I'll watch him."

"Watch yourself, too." She left her drink and wove through groups of people around the tables on the perimeter area around the dance floor.

Shouldn't be too hard to spot a woman all in white.

Kenna threaded to the dance floor, then back over toward the wall, using a zig zag. Within a minute or so, she spotted the woman at the bar.

Time for another drink.

Everything they'd dug up on the duke's son said he frequented places like this often. Maybe even most days of the week. He'd been in what the Brits called primary school at the time his father was killed and his family home burned.

The social media accounts he had showed a few posts related to humanitarian work he did. Visiting Africa, where he'd facilitated the building of a well and played soccer for an afternoon with local kids. Most of his posts were pictures from Mediterranean countries where he'd docked his yacht and the days and nights he spent on the blue water with the stars overhead. In the company of a particular woman—or a group of them.

They all fit the stats for the women who had been abducted in height and build, but then, so did millions of women all over the world.

The woman accepted a bottle of water from the bartender and waved off change. She watched the crowd with her back to the bar just like Kenna had.

Kenna eased up next to her and flagged down the bartender, asking for a drink no one would be surprised to hear her order. It wasn't like she drank those anymore. Not for a long time. Tonight wasn't a night to let alcohol affect her judgment. But then, she found she could say that about any night of the week with her job and the way her life often went. It was why Kenna hadn't had alcohol in years.

She glanced at the other woman and didn't take a drink, acting as if she had been surprised. "OMG, you're *her*. You're with the Duke." She tried to channel her inner fangirl. "What's he like? I've heard he's *amazing*." Whatever that meant, Kenna didn't want to think about it, but it was the first thing her mouth came up with.

The woman looked in her purse like she'd suddenly lost something. Probably rolling her eyes at her buried lipstick tube because Kenna was ridiculous—and American. "I work for the duke, if that's what you mean."

"Is he hiring? That would be *ah-mazing*." Kenna grinned. Giggling would be too much, right?

"He's not hiring. Thanks for your interest, but there are currently no open positions."

Good, because that would've been awkward to talk her way out of. "Never mind." She waved her free hand, almost taking another sip. Out the corner of the other woman's eye, it might look like she had. "Are you like...his assistant? Getting his coffee, picking up his dry cleaning. That kind of thing?" She held her hand out. "I'm Mandy."

"Keziya." The handshake was barely a squeeze and then over. "His Grace is wonderful to work for."

Geez, this woman didn't belong in a nightclub. She should be at a fancy party in a penthouse or sipping a cocktail somewhere with Michelin stars. What made her stick around working for Covington Hadley?

Kenna grinned. "I bet every girl wants to be you. Getting to see him every day. Going everywhere he goes. Living the high life."

No doubt with a sordid side. How many times had this woman cleaned up the aftermath of a mess—or a disaster? Not the kind of life Kenna would've chosen, but people made all kinds of choices just trying to live a happy and successful life.

"Are you some kind of reporter, or an influencer trying to get dirt on His Grace?" Keziya stared down her nose at Kenna even though she was not quite equal height. This woman fit the stats, along with half the club.

It wasn't as if Covington didn't already have her right where he wanted her.

Kenna huffed out a breath and set one hand on her hip. "Fine. I work for a magazine in Virginia you've never heard of. Since I was here on a trip anyway, I figured I'd track down Covington and see what I could dig up. Do you *know* how much of a pay raise and a promotion I'd get from an exclusive? It would be insane."

The other woman looked at the ceiling. "No one is going to give you an exclusive. We keep things tight."

Yeah, Kenna already knew that.

"Okay, but his dad was *ca-razy* right?" Hmm. Maybe she'd put too much New York into that. Kenna lifted her hands. "It's not like Covington had anything to do with that. He was little, right? But I heard some stories from my boss, and this lady, Edith. She had my desk before me. Worked there since before NASA, if you know what I'm sayin'." Kenna chuckled to herself. "She told me all kinds of things about how y'all live. Silver spoons and Manolos. Right?"

Keziya took a tiny sip of her water. "It's been lovely

talking to you. Have a good evening." She walked away through the crowd before Kenna could say a thing.

Just enough time to watch her disappear between two sets of tables and into the crowd. Kenna blew out a long breath, left her glass on the bar, and went to find Jax. She eased up to his side and stood with her body pressed against the outside of his arm and her hand on the back of his head. She ran her fingers through his hair.

He glanced at her. "Careful now."

"She's his assistant. Calls him *Your Grace.*"

The skin around his eyes flexed. "Well, he is a duke."

Kenna didn't even know how all that stuff worked. Why would she?

Not royalty. Never would be.

People who grew up in trailers didn't get to be fancy. And besides, she liked who she was. Anyone who could say that was already a step ahead of someone who thought they were better than they really were. Appreciation of the humble state one found oneself in was the road to content-ment. Standing this close to Jax was a road to...something they'd promised to hold off on.

She pushed off him, and he shot her a look as she sat down, one that said *thanks* and also *I didn't want you to go* at the same time.

She checked on Covington and saw the second girl had joined the other on his lap. Kenna looked at Jax, probably showing the displeasure on her face. "Wanna go?"

He checked his watch as he slid off the stool and waited for her to do the same. "Maybe it wasn't a total loss." He glanced down at her dress again.

She slid her arm around his waist. "Not a total loss."

As they walked, she scanned for anyone she recognized,

or anyone in trouble. Maybe they should hang around outside and watch what happened when Covington left. But she felt like she'd gained enough of an impression of him. The likelihood this party guy was the mastermind behind a complex enterprise was doubtful. She'd seen his test scores from school posted on the internet, buried down in the search results. Part of an opinion piece about how the upper class got to skate by while the rest of the country had to work for their living.

Mostly, it was just ranting.

They took a side door that spilled them out onto a brick alley. Jax grunted. "I'm getting Jack the Ripper vibes."

Kenna glanced around. "Apart from that very modern gate at the other end of the alley, I get what you mean. You can almost pretend you're in Victorian times walking around here. Like you just turn a corner, and randomly, it's like going back in time."

"Hotel?"

Kenna sighed. "I feel like something should have come of tonight, but it didn't."

"You do have a tendency to land yourself in the middle of situations at any given moment." He grinned. "But it was nice to just...go out. We haven't done that in a few weeks."

Hmm. Sure. "We were doing surveillance."

"Like when that guy at Outback Steakhouse decided to dine and dash?"

Okay, fine. "I was right, though."

"*I* was on a date. *You* had the guy under surveillance." He chuckled.

She wasn't going to give him the satisfaction of finding that amusing like he seemed to. "Are you insinuating I'm a troublemaker, Special Agent Jaxton?"

"I happen to like your brand of trouble." He chuckled. "Come on. We have to get a taxi or some kind of ride share thing, or we'll end up walking all the way back to the hotel."

Chapter Fifteen

Jax used his key card to let her into the room. She wandered in first, straight to her bed, and flopped down on the covers. At the last second, she remembered to keep it decent with the short dress and just about managed to save the day.

Shoes.

Kenna groaned and shifted enough she could tug at the laces and get her Converse off. The bathroom door closed and locked—Jax. With him out of sight, she changed quickly into sweatpants and a tank top.

She lay back down and stared at the ceiling. Her whole body seemed to want to sink into the bed, but her brain was awake. Maybe it was a good time for her to call her friend, Forrest Crosby. They'd met in Wisconsin nearly a year ago and kept in contact, mostly by email. Right now, she didn't have the energy to type out a whole message. She could call Forrest and gab about being here. Having Jax here.

Most couples worked separately. They kept the personal and professional parts of their lives apart. Jax maybe wanted to merge theirs together. Not that he was inviting her into his FBI business. He was supporting her professional life more than she was supporting his. Because he believed in her, and because he worried about her. At least, that was her guess.

Ugh. Sometimes she felt like a *girl*. But maybe that was normal.

Was being normal even worse?

She looked at her phone screen and saw a text from Maizie's number.

Are you still awake?

Kenna called her back, thanking God that something came up to pull her out of the spiral of worrying if she was *normal*. She shuddered, wondering why Maizie was texting her. Stairns and Ramon must've fallen asleep watching out for her and didn't realize she'd woken enough to text.

"Hey." The teen's voice was quiet, subdued.

"Hey there yourself." Kenna kept her voice soft. "How are you doing, kiddo?"

At some point, the girl was going to turn eighteen and be an adult. Kenna would always see her as the scared youth who'd escaped a horrific situation on her own and sought out Kenna to help her stay free.

Maizie sighed. "I'm still kind of foggy from what Elizabeth gave me."

"The sedative? You know, she did that to give you some relief. So that you could rest."

"I'm not mad or anything."

"You're allowed to be, if you want." They worked hard

to let her feel as if she was free to make her own choices. "Get mad at anyone you like."

Maizie let out a tiny noise of amusement. "I don't have the energy to do that right now. Maybe later."

"I know what you mean." She sighed, long and loud. "Surveillance was a bust."

"Because you didn't get to kick a door in, and you didn't find a dead body?"

"Way to be on Jax's side. He thought it was a *date*."

Maizie chuckled. "It's almost like he wants to spend as much time as possible with you."

Kenna smiled to herself. She needed to shift the conversation back to Maizie and what had set her off. "Wanna talk about it?"

"Not really, but Elizabeth said talking is good."

"Talking is overrated."

"Right," Maizie said, laughing. "Of course you think that. You'd rather drink coffee, sit in a chair outside by the fire, and stare at the sunset. When you're not working a case."

"This one is looking like it'll turn into something big," Kenna said. "But only because people keep *telling* me it's big. No one has actually shown me evidence of a crime other than a few missing persons reports, and those are too widespread and random to cover them all."

"That's what I was trying to do. Get you something concrete to work on."

Kenna wanted to say sorry, but the word didn't come out.

"I have those names that guy, Ian, gave you."

"Did you run his name and pull his history? I'd love to know your impression of whether we can trust him."

Maizie said, "He seems like a good grandpa, but social media isn't a reflection of real life."

"Real life is real enough for me."

The bathroom door opened, and Jax came out along with a cloud of steam because for some reason there was no fan. Just a tiny window that didn't open much without getting stuck.

Real life was a little too real, looking that good in a T-shirt and shorts. Wet hair. The fact she'd discovered he had a small tribal cross tattoo on the back of his shoulder. She'd spotted it during the winter she spent in Phoenix recuperating at his house, and it felt like a secret she wanted to hold close and never tell anyone.

After a few seconds of quiet, Maizie said, "Elizabeth said disassociating isn't bad."

"As long as you have the tools you need to manage it, Maze. It's one of those 'everything in moderation' things. It's not bad until you do it too much."

"Even for me?"

"Even for you." Kenna smiled.

Jax glanced over, tugging on a sweater over his shirt. He wandered to her and set his hands on either side of her before he leaned down so that his face was close. "Hi, Maizie."

"Oh! Hi, Jax."

Kenna smiled. "She says hi."

He kissed her, soft and quick. "I'm going to check on things with Preston."

She nodded and watched him go. When the door had shut, she said, "He's gone."

"I heard."

Kenna rolled over and turned on the lamp between the

two beds. "Do you want to tell me what it was you remembered?"

She waited for Maizie to speak, not wanting to force it out of her. Finally, the teen said, "It was the house." Her exhale was audible over the phone line.

"You've seen it before…or you've been there?"

Despite the barrage of questions that entered her mind, she didn't ask anything or even think about the timing of Maizie being only seventeen. The fire. Her father. Covington Hadley.

Kenna just let Maizie talk.

"I've been there." She paused, and the seconds stretched on. "I went there. I don't think I even realized I was in England."

"First time on a plane?"

"I mean… I think so. Maybe I was drugged or something. It does seem foggy, like I can't quite remember."

Kenna bit the inside of her lip.

"Until I saw a picture of the house."

She stared at the ceiling and felt the touch of the breeze coming from the bathroom window.

"He…" Maizie cleared her throat. "Elizabeth told me to call him Mikey. Something to create some distance and try to diminish him in my mind."

"And he took you to that house?" Michael Rushman had brought her here to this country and made her part of this?

Kenna's father hadn't ended it. Someone had rebuilt the house and continued it under everyone's noses. Maybe not even covertly, since it could be a case of bribes. Everyone agreeing to look the other way so this nightmare could continue.

"Yes." She spoke clearly, strength ringing in her tone. "For medical testing."

Kenna blinked. It hadn't been about abuse. At least not the kind of abuse that she'd grown up with, as the child bride of a disturbed man. "What kind of tests?"

"I know they took my blood. I remember it hurt."

"It does hurt. I don't like doing it." Kenna figured some solidarity would be good for the girl. The knowledge she didn't suffer alone. "Do you want to tell me what else they did?"

Maizie cleared her throat.

Kenna waited.

"Scans. I think. They made me go in this big machine, and it was loud."

Kenna wanted to ask how old she'd been, but so much of her life was a blur of trauma. It wasn't like she'd have known what the date was. And was it relevant? They could narrow the timeline to any year between Maizie being old enough to remember what was happening, and now. So maybe a twelve-year window.

She didn't know for sure if it was the same things her dad had tried to stop. Kidnappings. Births.

Michael Rushman never would have given Maizie up to whoever was operating here. Would he have let her be used by someone else? Perhaps whatever caused those women to have given birth was something he'd have allowed to happen to Maizie.

"Can I ask you a hard question?" She would never have even thought to ask it otherwise. Until now.

Maizie said, "Just do it."

Tear off the bandage. Ask the question. Maizie knew she had the choice of whether to answer because they'd worked on Kenna making requests and Maizie saying no. Over and over, retraining her cognitive functions so that she didn't default to subservience. In small ways, she could take back the power she'd never had.

"Have you ever been pregnant, or had a baby?" Kenna found she was glad Maizie couldn't see her face. She would read too much grief and distress on Kenna's face.

"No."

"That was definitive."

Maizie said, "It's a pretty yes or no question."

"Have you talked to Elizabeth about that stuff?"

"*Mikey* had me take pills every day. We think there might have been birth control in it, but there's no way to know."

Kenna was surprised the man hadn't entirely removed Maizie's ability to have children altogether. But her having a baby meant that in time, he could've tossed her aside and had a new...obsession.

Maizie said, "Most of that is stuff I try not to think about. But I guess it's something I'll have to face eventually."

"Only if you want. Your life is yours. Boys...romance. You've got plenty of time to think about that stuff." And right now, all of it seemed like a giant minefield Kenna didn't have the skills to navigate. Maybe Jax could help by giving the perspective of a healthy man who would be nothing like *Mikey*.

"I found this program online. It puts faces together, like a sketch artist would draw, but it's digital."

"So you find the right eyebrows and put them with the right nose, that kind of thing? Sounds interesting."

Maizie said, "I want to put together faces I think I saw

when I was there, but I can't remember what they looked like. It's just flashes."

If she'd been drugged, it wouldn't be solid testimony. Not that Kenna would doubt it, and they didn't need it to be admissible in any court either, but it could guide them in the right direction. It just wouldn't be definitive.

"Don't force it. Later if you think it'll help you, go for it," Kenna said. "I could use the intel. Plus anything you can get on victims, then and now. Or the Grand Ole Duke of wherever."

Maizie giggled. "I'll run them all."

"And get some sleep."

"Yes, *Mom.*"

"That's right." Kenna chuckled. "I am the boss. Hard as iron. Unyielding. My way or the highway."

Maizie's giggle turned to outright laughter.

"You doubt me?" Kenna grinned. "Put Cabot on the phone. I need a sane opinion of what's happening."

Maizie's laughter got louder. A bang sounded on the other end of the line.

Kenna sat up. "Maze?"

"Ramon, you're here!"

His baritone rang in the background. "Of course I'm here! I thought you were being strangled."

Kenna said, "It's called laughter," smiling at the sound of their voices. They sounded like a comedy sitcom. Relief came, emerging like a long sigh. Maizie was all right. Things in Colorado were good.

"Can I borrow that?" Ramon's question sounded far away. The phone shifted. "Kenna?"

"Hey, Ramon." She sighed. "Things are okay there?"

The door snapped on the other end of the line, and she

figured he'd gone outside. "Long as little *hermana* doesn't lose her mind laughing, it's all good." He sounded like an affectionate older brother.

"Haven't we all done that once or twice?"

Ramon said, "All my marbles are intact but good point. I should let her know I've felt crazy a time or two in my life. How is your case?"

"I'm not sure I even have a case yet. At least not one I can pin down, aside from this mess of thirty years ago." She told him what Maizie had said about the house and listened to him mutter in Spanish. She didn't disagree, or really understand what he said, but that wasn't the point. "Pretty much. Listen, can you and Stairns get everything you can from the list of names I'll be sending Maizie? It's the victims my father was looking for. I want you to piece together his case. I'll work on what's happening here and now."

"Copy that, boss."

Kenna's eyelids drooped. She could feel sleep coming, and Jax wasn't even back yet. "I should go." Then she could text him. Find out when he'd be coming back in here.

"Hit me up if you need anything."

She let her eyes close. "Thanks, Ramon."

"Later." The phone beeped by her ear.

She needed to text Jax.

She needed to...

Kenna blinked against the sunlight streaming through the net curtain, warming the room to where it was nearly uncomfortable. But that wasn't her biggest problem.

A slender blonde woman sat on the velvet chair across the room, looking at her phone. One leg crossed over the other, wearing business casual clothes—black slacks and a white shirt, over which she'd pulled a thin gray jacket that probably came down to the back of her knees.

Kenna sat up, and the woman lifted her head.

She rolled her eyes. *New York.* This was the woman who had been in Wilson Sandhurst's office in NYC. She said, "I thought you were going to sleep forever." Her accent was crisp and British, not unlike the woman from the club, Keziya. The woman they'd had knocked out and left on the floor—who'd been gone before they came out of the hidden office—unfolded her legs and stood. She had the posture of a ballerina and the figure of one.

Kenna's arms couldn't hold her upper body upright like this, so she shifted her hips back and realized someone had put a blanket over her. She glanced over at Jax's bed, which had been slept in but remade afterward.

"Looking for this?" The woman held up a piece of paper. "'Have a good day at the office, dear.' What does that mean?"

Kenna smiled to herself.

"I guess you had to be there." The woman set the paper on the dresser. "We need to talk. I'll be in the dining hall. We can have lunch since you slept all morning."

Sorry to make you wait. Except she wasn't sorry.

Kenna shoved the blankets back. "If I don't show, are you going to break into my room again?"

The woman tore her gaze from Kenna's red, scarred forearms. "As amusing as that would be, I have better things to do. As do you." She headed for the door. "I'll meet you downstairs."

The door shut, and Kenna stared at it.

Looked at the window and the sunshine, then at the clock, which said it was nearly noon.

She sighed. "Good morning to you, too."

Apparently, they were going to talk downstairs whether she liked it or not.

Good thing she wanted answers badly enough to show up.

Chapter Sixteen

Kenna wandered into the dining room and looked around, trying to find the woman who had broken into her hotel room. A handful of people were scattered about, eating lunch or visiting with each other. She wasn't sure they were all hotel guests. Some looked to be locals, office types on their lunch break.

She had hastily showered and pulled on a pair of skinny black jeans, over which she had a long sleeve T-shirt and light blue denim jacket. Phone in her back pocket. She'd opted for boots today instead of Converse.

The hostess wandered over to intercept her.

Kenna pointed at the woman. "I see my friend."

As she approached, she assessed the woman. But it wouldn't be a true reflection, given this was a public place.

This woman was fully aware others could see her, and she would never give away her emotional state so openly.

Kenna stopped by the chair but didn't sit.

The woman held a mug in both hands. She looked up from it slowly, as if she had all the time in the world.

"Why don't we start with what your name is." Kenna dragged out the chair and sat. "We both know who I am. Who are you?"

"It really depends." She lowered the mug and set it on a tiny plate. "In some circles, I'm only a reference number. In others, I was given a name. You can call me Sienna."

"Okay." Whatever that meant about the reference number, Kenna figured she was about to find out.

She had texted Jax while she was getting dressed. He had left before eight in the morning to go to his conference, and he said he'd connected with Maizie as well. He told her not to worry about them and to stay safe through this meeting.

Kenna didn't know how much danger she was in here in a dining hall but knew better than to be surprised.

What she needed to do was get a photo of this woman so that Maizie could run her image and try to get a hit.

"So, Sienna, what did you want to talk to me about?" From the corner of her eye, Kenna spotted a server coming toward her, holding a tray with a mug on it. She shook her head and waved him off.

He seemed a bit confused but complied.

Sienna said, "How much do you know about eugenics?"

Boy, that was out of left field. "Social engineering or the senseless sterilizing of those considered undesirables?"

"Or any permutation of those things." She took a sip of her tea, as if to have a moment to compose herself. "Carefully selected mothers. Carefully crafted DNA. All of it to pass on the traits they want and weed out what they don't. The result is a generation superior to everyone around them."

She certainly did have a slight air of something more. Kenna couldn't help but think about the missing victims thirty years ago, and today supposedly, who were chosen because they were overachievers. Women who had given birth recently.

Kenna said, "Keep talking."

Given what Maizie had told her, she wanted to know everything about these people.

Sienna shifted the cup on the saucer absently. "Artificial insemination. It's all rather civilized. Cold and unfeeling, but the result can't be denied."

"So someone is still on the master race thing? Even after all the destruction it's caused in the world and the lives lost." It almost seemed like something the Rosenbergs would've done. Or at least an endeavor they would've funded. That family was gone now. The Justice Department in the US had taken apart their business and their lives, piece by piece.

Most were in jail. Several family members had taken their own lives before they could be brought before a judge.

"It's best to just keep it quiet these days. Too much publicity on social media to be vocal about your stance—especially when your stance is living above the law."

"How did you get mixed up in it? And how did you get from there to being Wilson Sandhurst's assistant."

Sienna's expression shifted. It almost looked like an eye roll except that she never actually rolled her eyes. "I'm not his assistant. I was assigned to him. Besides, Sandhurst has been dead for months."

"We have a photo of him landing in Barcelona and getting off his plane."

"That was a body double." Sienna sniffed. "It's in their best interests to allow the world to continue believing he's alive. That way Preston Lightwood is kept in line."

Kenna had a million questions but started with, "What do you want with me?"

"Help," Sienna said. "Just like I put in that note."

At the pub. "That was you? Seems like you should have stuck around a minute longer and let me actually help you."

"I couldn't stay. It would have put all of us in danger and not just me." Sienna took a sip of her tea. "Thirty years ago, I was born into this. I didn't ask to be part of it, but I still refuse to put innocent lives in jeopardy just because I want to get out. Those of us who aren't willing to submit do what we can to fight back. To subvert their plans. But their will is powerful."

She seemed genuinely scared of whoever she was talking about. "Who are they? If I don't know where to find them, I can't go up against them."

"That's why I had to talk to you." Sienna shook her head. "They know you're close, and they aren't willing to allow you to get any nearer. You're in danger, and so is everyone you brought with you to the UK."

"Are they the same people that my father went up against when he was here? And my mother?"

Sienna stared at her for a second. Tears burned in her eyes, and she looked away, blinking. "Why dredge up the past? You only get stuck where nothing ever changes."

"Surely you have something to offer that will convince me that what you're saying is true." Or an explanation of why Kenna seemed to make her want to cry.

"The story of Amara Constantine is a cautionary tale

we were told growing up. Of why you don't betray the company."

Kenna bit the inside of her lip. Constantine? "That's easy to say. But how can you prove it? I don't even know who these people are. All I have is intel on one house."

Sienna reached into the inside of her jacket and pulled out two things. One was a postcard and the other looked like an EpiPen. She left the pen on the table beside her empty plate setting and handed the postcard to Kenna.

"What is this?" Kenna took the card.

On one side was a beach scene, a row of tiny sheds all painted different colors. Blue sky and sand with plenty of little pebbles. She flipped it over and saw the addressee's name. Malcom Banbury.

"Your mother wrote that to your father while she was here on business after they married." Sienna paused. "Maybe you can make sense of what she's saying."

The handwritten note on the left side of the back seemed like a boring vacation recap. "The sun is shining. The weather has been good so far. I'm hoping to be home soon. I miss you both so much." Kenna looked up at Sienna. "What's to make sense of?"

Sienna shrugged and glanced out the window.

"You think it's some kind of code? It could just be a postcard."

"In my business, everything is code for something else."

Kenna said, "You mentioned the company. Who are they?"

"I would almost feel bad pulling you into this knowing what you're going to go up against. All because you can't let something go and stay out of it."

But this woman didn't feel bad? Because she wanted out, probably.

"Seems like I'm already in it." Kenna shifted in her seat, keeping herself from getting relaxed so she could leave at any moment if it became necessary. An extra second to get out of her chair could cost her life in the wrong situation. "Maybe even, like you, I was born into it."

"I've thought about that as well," Sienna said. "You are her daughter. Surely something of who she was has been passed on to you. It's likely why you're so good at what you do."

"Then if you tell me who these people are, I'll be sure to track them down and thank them for my keen intellect. They might even be able to do something about the tendons in my forearms."

"I'd advise against that, unless you want to be detained and used as a broodmare for the next generation. After all, that's what this is about."

Thirty years ago. Today. "My dad interrupted the last round, or at least caused some mayhem?"

"Considering I exist, he didn't completely stop it."

Kenna said, "What happens to the mothers?"

If her father had rescued any of those victims thirty years ago, then one or more of them might have been pregnant. And what happened to the ones he never found?

"It's all part of keeping things in the shadows. If there are too many of us, someone will notice."

"So they're killed? Disposed of."

"How else are they supposed to find and correct flaws, except by studying what came before?"

Kenna leaned forward in her seat. "What happened to my mother?"

"Extreme cases require extreme measures. She was not studied. She was simply disposed of so she could never harm the company again."

Kenna said, "Why didn't they kill me and my father at the same time? Surely the two of us represented a liability."

"Maybe they couldn't find you." Sienna stared at her. "But now you've walked right up to their front door and rang the bell."

"And now I'm in danger?" Kenna tucked the postcard in her back pocket.

Sienna handed over the EpiPen. "You will encounter one of my sisters. The ones still loyal. One of them will be sent to kill you."

"And I'm supposed to hit them with epinephrine? Or is that for me?"

"Take it," Sienna said. "But don't actually use it on anyone having an allergic reaction. Or a normal human being. But one of us? It will knock us down long enough for you to get away."

"Thanks, I guess." Kenna put that in her pocket as well. "Anything else you want to give me?"

"Other than advice? Keep your friends safe. They are in as much danger as you are."

"Trust no one? That's all you got. These people need to be taken down, and if you actually help me instead of just kidding yourself that you did, we would have a shot at actually ending this once and for all."

Sienna shook her head before Kenna even finished talking. "I'm not going to lie and say my group doesn't need your help. We have lost two of us in the last few months."

"Your group?" Some kind of sect within the company? Or something else entirely.

"I suppose you would call it some kind of resistance. But that sounds like we actually have a way to fight back. Instead, we merely attempt to subvert their will. We have to do it in a way that doesn't blow back on us."

"Sounds like a worthy fight." Kenna still wasn't sure she believed any of this. It did make a lot of sense, and it seemed to put the pieces together, but the fact her life was right in the middle of it wasn't something she liked at all.

"On the surface, we have to be all about the company. All of us are given jobs. People like Wilson Sandhurst are supposed to carve out a career path that supports the company and its endeavors across the world."

"He was one of you? And his sister, Preston's wife?"

Sienna shrugged. "She was your mother's generation. And if she had done what she was told, she would still be alive."

"And no one has ever spoken up?" It seemed as if her mom and dad might have been planning to do exactly that. Except that it had cost her mother her life, and her dad had spent decades as a wanderer.

Making her question if that hadn't been by design. In order to stay under these people's radar. After leaving the FBI—a career move that might have been designed to try and root out these people and get justice for his wife's death—he'd chosen to lay low.

Her dad seemed to have opted instead to keep her safe and fight crime in the only way he was left with. Because of who these people were, and the threat they'd been?

"Those who do are disposed of. The last surviving member of the previous generation is the one who keeps us in line. She will kill me just for talking to you, but I've decided it might be worth the risk."

"I need a picture of her. So I know who I'm going up against."

"She's nameless. Faceless." Sienna's gaze settled on something distant. Maybe a memory. "She's the monster in the dark, the one we pray to for mercy."

"Which means you've never seen her or you'd know she's probably just one of you." Kenna couldn't help but wonder over the fact it sounded like this woman had been raised in a cult. Maybe, in a way, she had. Considering her whole life had been about being trained to serve the good of the group. Her choice had been taken away. Her mind had been programmed to obey at all costs.

And yet, even with that, free will shone through like a light in the darkness.

An individual's desire to make their own choices. To have autonomy over their own life.

Kenna said, "I'm supposed to warn my friends they're in danger, and then what? You need to give me *something* if I'm going to dig this up and exhume it all."

It certainly might feel like bringing the dead back to the surface.

Dragging darkness into the light.

If she saved a life and stopped these people? The cost would be worth it. But not given what it might cost her friends. If she had her way, Kenna would pay the debt herself so that no one else suffered. The last thing she wanted was for her life and the things she knew she had to do to be the cause of suffering for anyone she cared about.

Kenna said, "I can probably get the State Department to pick up Jax, Preston, Hollace, and Nielson and escort them back to the US so they stay safe."

Sienna said, "Don't trust anyone but each other. Especially not government employees who've been here far longer than necessary, dug in and immovable."

"Why don't you just give me a list of names of people you know are corrupt. That way I don't have to have my people do a deep dive into the background of every single US government employee who lives in the UK?"

Sienna said, "Or Europe."

"So then there's the UK government, police agencies here and in Europe. Governments of individual countries. The European Union. The Hague. Interpol." She was probably forgetting something. "I can't afford the time it will take to cover all of that unless you tell me how to be strategic."

"You know who you trust, and who you don't know." Sienna shrugged. "Start there."

Kenna said, "Unfortunately, that includes you. I don't know you, and I don't trust you."

Sienna tugged out a phone. "I'll text you an address. Go there. It's the home where your mother grew up, and it's a good place to start figuring out who these people are." She paused for a second, then said, "But don't bother calling the number back or tracking it. I'll be disposing of this mobile phone after our conversation is done."

"And if I need to find you?"

Sienna said, "If you need to destroy my life despite the fact that I helped you, then I made the wrong choice." She took another sip of her tea, and then cleared her throat. "So far, five women have been obtained. I don't know where they're keeping them, but I do know they want two more."

Pretty good way to get Kenna's buy in—playing to her emotions and something she would never let go. If someone had listened in on her and Jax's conversation with Ian Birch, they would know this about her.

Kenna tried not to give away that she might've figured out Sienna's game here. She said, "Why not you? Don't they use the previous generation to...birth the next?"

Sienna said, "We're all flawed in our own way. No one wants those things exacerbated when the next group of children are supposed to be even more superior than the last. Why not keep the gene pool fresh?"

Why not indeed. "You took a serious risk finding me."

Sienna said, "If it keeps you alive for a few extra days, there's a chance you might actually succeed in ending this." She coughed. "To me, it was worth the risk." Sienna coughed again.

Kenna frowned. "Are you—"

Sienna reached for the water glass and knocked it over. Liquid spilled across the white tablecloth and onto the floor. Her face reddened. She clutched at her throat and started to lean sideways.

Kenna yelled toward the hostess. "I need some help!"

She got up and try to catch Sienna, but her arms couldn't keep the woman from landing on the floor. She gently set the back of Sienna's head down while the other woman struggled for breath. Fighting to stay alive. Meanwhile, an EpiPen that could subdue one of them was stashed in Kenna's pocket. "Tell me what you need me to do."

Sienna grasped the sides of Kenna's jacket and tugged her down. She whispered a single word. The last word she would ever speak. "Run."

Chapter Seventeen

Kenna raced into her hotel room and straight to the bathroom, where she ran the water and vigorously washed her hands. Then her face. Just in case whatever substance had killed Sienna in front of her had transferred to Kenna's skin.

Run.

She didn't want to ruin it, but she drew out the postcard and wiped it off with a washcloth. Maybe it wouldn't kill any poison and keep it from affecting her, but a little vigilance could save her life. She did the same with the EpiPen, or whatever it technically was, wiping it down with scalding water and praying it didn't get inside and ruin the mechanism.

Outside, she heard police sirens on the street below coalesce in front of the building. That different kind of tone than she was used to, which made it all the more jarring. Even the sound of law enforcement arriving seemed foreign to her ears.

She raced back into the room, and her foot caught on the strap of Jaxton's duffel. She fell to her hands and knees with a cry, and his clothes spilled over. A small velvet box tumbled onto the floor beside her hand.

Kenna froze.

A woman was dead. She had to get out of here. She had to warn her friends that their lives were in danger.

She also had to lift the lid of that box. Take a second and stare at the single diamond on a gold band. She snapped the box shut and stuck it in her pocket without even thinking it through. Not right now. She couldn't do this right now.

Kenna scrambled to her feet and took off her denim jacket, which was way too easily identifiable. She dragged out the raincoat from her duffel and tugged it on, then grabbed her backpack, slinging it over her shoulders as she went to the door.

Look first.

Clear.

She tugged the door shut and hurried to the stairs at the end of the hall. A winding staircase with floral velvet carpet that muffled her steps. Two floors down on what they called the first floor, one up from the ground floor, she ducked out onto the landing where the exit door would take her to a set of metal steps outside. A fire exit.

Kenna pulled the hood of her jacket over her head even though it was cloudy but not raining. She ducked her head and scurried down the fire escape, using the back alley to get away from the front of the hotel. It was now most likely swarming with police officers who would want to talk to the person that had been present when a mysterious woman died.

What Kenna wanted was for them to run the woman's fingerprints and DNA against her ID and come up with some major discrepancies. But people who had been operating for so long that they had multiple generations of children born would know exactly how to cover their tracks. How to make the whole thing seem legitimate.

Most likely, given they probably had influence in powerful circles as well as governments, these people would have her death explained away as natural causes. Or just your everyday drug overdose. Tragic victim of substance abuse.

Two streets away, she dug out her earbuds, stuck them in, and called Jax. It rang a couple of times and then diverted her to voicemail.

Kenna said, "You're in danger. We all are. Call me back."

She hung up and dialed Preston. Immediately after she would warn Jax, she then would need to send Maizie a voice memo. All her friends in Colorado would still be asleep—hopefully—and when they woke up, she wanted them working on getting her new information verified. She wanted the address that Sienna had given her run through any system Maizie had access to, the postcard looked at, and for someone to figure out precisely what this EpiPen thing was and who had made it.

Preston picked up. "Hey."

Whatever else he'd been about to say, she cut him off. "Where are you?"

"Working on something."

She didn't want to rehash the entire conversation. "You're in danger. I'm in danger. Jax is in danger. I know how your wife and her brother are connected to this. I was told he's dead, and he's been dead for a couple of months, and I was warned that we got too close. They might be coming to hit back at us."

"Don't worry. I'm ready." Preston sounded so sure. But then, he had two professional bodyguards with him so maybe he was just dandy.

Kenna turned a corner and wound up in a line of people waiting to take a photo in a red telephone booth. She ducked out of the line and kept walking, skirting around a woman with a huge stroller and extra kids toddling along beside it.

Up ahead, if she kept going straight, she would cross a bridge over the Thames. Every sidewalk was a knot of people, making her only one of the crowd. Easy to never even notice.

Nothing to see here.

"I need you to tell me where you are," she said. "We can touch base in person, and I'll tell you what I've got. Because someone just dumped a whole packet of intel in my lap and told me not to trust anyone I don't know."

From the beginning, he'd been withholding information from her. Allowing her to discover it by herself. Instead, it had been more than frustrating knowing the right answers she didn't have. Miami Security International had done the same thing when they rightfully should have told her a long time ago that they were in possession of her father's journal.

Either way, it was in her backpack now, and she was going to read it as soon as she got some downtime.

Which considering she was on the run, might come sooner rather than later if she needed to hide out for a while. Figure this out. Develop a plan to actually take these people down rather than allow them to continue doing what they were doing.

"Like I said, I'm taking care of something."

Kenna was pretty sure that *wasn't* what he'd said. "You're still going to tell me where you are so I can come and meet you. We need to talk about this."

"I'll send you an address for a park. I'll meet you there in thirty minutes by the little shack where they sell ice creams."

"Assuming I can get there in thirty minutes from where I am." Kenna wasn't entirely sure where she was, but that was what the maps app was for. It would even show her what train to get on if that was an option.

Preston said, "Figure it out."

Kenna ducked into a doorway. Inset into the side of a stone building, the door had been boarded up and was now covered in graffiti. She tugged the edge of her hood down and got on her phone, putting the address Preston sent her into her app and figuring out how to get there.

The underground trains that ran beneath the city would be her best bet, the closest station just around the corner.

She found that red circle sign with the word "underground" in the center above the open entrance. Just inside, the ceiling was low enough to be claustrophobic, along with the ocean of people all walking in the same direction across the tile floor.

Kenna got out of the flow of foot traffic and went to the wall of machines. She used a card she didn't normally use, one that they may not know belonged to her. This way, she might not be tracked buying a pass that allowed her to travel anywhere in the underground system for the day. If she wanted to, she could ride around, back and forth and going in circles, just to wait out the daylight and emerge when the sun had gone down.

She used the same credit card to buy a cup of coffee from a stand and headed for the barriers. Kenna inserted her ticket, and it popped out of the top. When she pulled it free, the barrier opened, and she headed through with everyone else, checking the signs on the walls to make sure she was going the right direction on this line.

Nothing to see.

She was just another commuter with her coffee and somewhere to be. Headphones in—not that people here struck up conversations with those they didn't know. That at least was a blessing. A chatty passenger wasn't about to start a conversation with her here, something that had happened to her in New York. Audrey had been a nice older lady who worked at the library.

One day, Kenna should retire and go work at a library.

She leaned her head back against the window and pushed out some long breaths, trying to steady her racing heart. It seemed right to say a prayer for the dearly departed, but what good would it do Sienna for Kenna to try to help her wherever she was now? It wasn't like she could pray for someone who had passed. Kenna's religious beliefs were new, but she knew a lot of faiths did what they could for those who had gone on ahead.

Can I put in a good word? Maybe it would only make me feel better. She closed her eyes for a second. *Keep my family safe.*

She didn't want what happened to Sienna to happen to anyone else, whether that person was part of her family or not.

Kenna checked her phone, surprised to find she had a little bit of cell signal. Jax hadn't called her back yet, so she sent him a text warning him to be careful because she had reason to believe they were all in danger.

Next, Kenna sent a run down to Maizie, Stairns, and Ramon of everything she needed. Then she looked up the address Sienna had given her for her mother's childhood home, but the maps app refused to load anything. She could look at that later.

She looked up at the map on the wall of the train clattering down the track. Through tunnels. Into the next station. She counted how many more stops she had to go and then pulled out her father's journal.

Flicking through the pages, she just took some time and absorbed her father's handwriting. The fact that he had been here working on the same case made her feel closer to him than she had been in a long time. He'd met her mother here, and they had probably saved lives through whatever they did. But it still meant that whoever these people were —the company—they hadn't been stopped.

Now it was up to her to put an end to it.

Because no one else could.

She flicked more slowly this time, searching for something that would give her a clue as to what leads he'd been following. Eventually, she would have to pay a visit to the house he had burned down. Maybe as soon as she could get everyone safe, they would be able to work the case proactively.

Kenna tucked the journal away as they closed in on her stop. The past didn't need to preoccupy her when there were far too many things happening in the present that she needed to take care of.

As she left the train and headed through the tunnel walkway, up a massive escalator out into the daylight, Kenna tried calling Jax again.

He still didn't answer.

She was a few minutes' walk from the park and tossed the empty coffee cup in the first trash can she could find. This part of the city was quieter. Not as touristy as it was right at the center where all the tourists wanted to be. The maps app indicated there was a museum a couple of streets over, but she avoided that entrance and crossed the street, heading for the couple acres square of green grass in the middle of an intersection.

She went to a bench and sat, giving herself a second to rest. She recalled doing the same thing with Preston not long ago. Sitting on a stone bench, talking to him. Different day. Different park.

After a few minutes, she spotted his car at the far corner of the park, turning onto the street to the left. It pulled up on the side of the road behind some trees, where she couldn't see the occupants inside the vehicle. Kenna got up and headed in that direction, just in case it was them.

A guy on a bicycle rode past her, long scraggly dark hair and long beard. Shorts, sandals, and a vintage band T-shirt.

She could see the car stopped by the curb. Trees on either side of the path arched overhead, creating a covering for the entrance to the park. Trash can beside the low brick wall to the right. Something caused her instincts to spring to life. Made her footsteps falter and slow.

With a great crashing sound, the car jolted with the force of an explosion.

A fireball knocked the vehicle up into the sky and over on the front end, sending a wave of heat and debris in her direction.

Heat flung Kenna back, and she landed on the grass, where she stared up at the sky, blinking. Ringing in her ears.

Preston.

Chapter Eighteen

Malcom followed Amara along the grass beside the road. The blacktop curved, making the water collect at the edge of the road, so he sloshed along getting mud on his boots. They'd opted for casual clothing, so they didn't seem suspicious if someone caught them sneaking around.

The moonlight was enough to show the way, giving a glow to the dark of night. Lighting the trees and the tops of houses on one side of the street. Farms set back from the road. On the other side, to his left, a high brick wall obscured what she'd told him was a hospital.

An owl hooted from a tall, English oak on the far side.

She slowed her pace, and he caught up to her side while she watched a black cat rub against the brick wall. It watched them go, staring as if to assess whether they were the threat or if it was going to attack them first.

"Easy, kitty."

She tugged on his arm. "Shh."

"No one is out here." He kept his voice low, though. It was almost romantic, and definitely would be except for the fact they were out here committing a crime.

He'd decided to simply think of it as reconnaissance.

It wasn't a crime to just look, but he certainly hadn't filled Detective Inspector Birch in on this evening's operation. Anything more than looking around, he was going to take as it came and figure things out as they went along.

Likely, Amara didn't have the same qualms about not ending up on the wrong side of the law here. She could probably talk her way out of any situation involving the police. Meanwhile, his presence meant an international incident. Especially if he was caught red-handed.

His career would be over.

"We're almost to the entrance."

Malcom said, "Are we going to be able to see in?"

Amara looked up at the wall and then at the area around them. There was nothing out here. They were on a country lane in some random town in the middle of nowhere. She'd been positive that this was at least one location where they brought the missing women.

He didn't wonder that she was keeping information from him. Only what that might be, and how much it was going to jump up and bite him when he figured out her secrets.

"The gates aren't locked. We can sneak around. Have a look."

Malcom frowned. "And if we get caught?"

She looked at him. In the dim light of night, he could only barely make out her features. But he'd spent enough time with her that he could picture her face in his mind. She had an amazing ability to compartmentalize. He'd be thinking about how beautiful she was, exotic and striking in a way that took his breath away, and she would mention the case.

He'd given up then and there, realizing she didn't have feelings for him. There was nothing she'd said or done that indicated she was the least bit attracted to him. Meanwhile, he'd flipped head over butt for her, in a way he wasn't sure he was going to recover from.

Malcom pushed all those feelings aside. After all, he was here to do a job and nothing else.

"If we get caught," she whispered, "we fight back. We rescue those helpless women, and we expose what's happening."

"Okay." He could agree with that, at least. They were aligned with each other on something, and none of this would be a waste of time.

She crept to where an arch had been constructed in the high brick wall, blocked with a wrought iron gate. She worked on the padlock for a few seconds and got the gate open.

"You're going to have to teach me your lock-picking skills."

She glanced back, and he saw a flash of smile. "I can teach you a lot of things."

Malcom pressed his lips together so he kept his mouth shut. *I bet you can.*

He said nothing while they moved through the gate to the dark grounds of the hospital. A huge, multi-winged brick building with only two floors. Benches in the fore-ground, bushes that looked to have been planted in a small maze only a couple of feet high, off to the left. To the right were some outbuildings. Sheds.

"We need coverage." He pointed to those storage buildings.

She nodded. "Let's go."

He jogged after her, and they ducked behind one of the buildings. She kept going, skirting around one. He had to step over a shovel leaning against a broom behind the build-ing, where spiderwebs crossed from the siding to the brick wall.

He swiped one away, knowing from personal experi-ence there were far worse things in the world than spiders.

"I hear a car." She stopped at the back corner.

He peered around her shoulder in time to see a car drive in. Looked like a hearse, but he wasn't super familiar with British brands of cars and what all the models looked like.

The car pulled up to the side of the building.

A light came on above the door, and someone stepped out. Two people, one was a man in a lab coat with a shirt and tie and slacks underneath. The other person was female, wearing a light blue, knee-length dress and flat shoes. She had her hair pinned back and a white cap over it on the back of her head—a nurse.

They opened the back of the car and dragged out a stretcher with someone lying on it, a sheet over them.

"Morgue?"

Amara said, "You mean the mortuary. That's what we call it here. And an autopsy is a postmortem. I went to the library and read up on all the police lingo they use here and what's different in the US."

He eased slightly closer to her so he could see more, still looking over her shoulder. A chill in the air made him wrap his jacket tighter over his sweater. Should've brought a wool cap to keep his head warm. "Aren't you cold?"

She only had a light jacket on. "I don't mind it. I hate summer."

He smiled. "Can't say I've ever met anyone who hated summer."

The nurse lady—if that's who was with the doctor—stepped under the light above the door, and they rolled the patient in.

Malcom said, "She looks like a Sunday school teacher I had." He shivered again, and it had nothing to do with the cold. "Used to smack our hands with a ruler if we got the memory verse wrong. I told my mom, and she just said I should get the verse right."

This might not be the time, but he found he wanted to draw her out. Get her to tell him something personal.

"How about you?"

Amara said, "I get all my verses right."

He didn't like the cold way she said it. "You had a hard upbringing?"

"My father was a banker."

When she said nothing else, he offered some personal information of his own. "Mine died in Vietnam. My mom became a schoolteacher to pay the bills. She took me to church on Sundays, and every summer, we drove to a national park."

"I had a nanny. My mother...I never really knew that woman. She wasn't really my mother. Nanny was. Mum spent a lot of time in Monaco with her tennis instructor. One year, she just never came home."

"I'm sorry." He touched her shoulder.

She should've been loved, the way all kids should be. The alternative, as far as he'd seen, was that they grew up cold. Not knowing how to show or receive affection. He'd never met a criminal who had a happy upbringing, but then it also seemed like everyone in the world had their own story of neglect. It was simply to different degrees for each person and depended on how they took onboard their experiences.

What might seem devastating to one child would be a good day for another.

Some people lashed out at others in revenge, and others sought to be better for their sake and everyone else's. Which choice they made dictated the path a person's life went down.

Malcom wanted to find out why people did what they did. He wanted to study human behavior and maybe get in on some research projects. But that would come later, when he was more established in his career.

"I don't need you to be sorry for me," Amara said, her tone flat. "I need you to help me get inside so we can find out what this place is."

"Then what?"

She shook her head. "What do you mean?"

"Are we going to call the police and report a crime? Are we going to set a bomb and blow the place up?" He folded his arms across his chest, which might have seemed odd, considering they were hiding behind a shed, but he needed to make his point. "Which one?"

He knew hardly anything about her. Malcom wanted to trust his instincts, but she made it difficult when she wasn't letting him in. She hadn't told him *why* she was in this. Just that she had the access and intel he needed to work the case.

Things the police had no clue about. That she didn't want them to know she was giving him.

Which meant, at best, she had to be a confidential informant in this.

Amara said, "If I suggest the bomb idea, are you going to walk away and not help me?"

"I just want to know where you're coming from." She either had no emotions on display, or he could see her fighting anger. Aside from that, she didn't seem to feel much at all.

"I have to help these women."

"Try again." She'd said that enough times already it almost seemed like she was trying to convince herself.

"I want to stop these people."

He caught a note of truth in her tone. "Warmer."

She shifted, and he heard an exasperated noise. "*Someone* has to stop them."

"Agreed. Why you?"

"Because I can. Because I might be the only one who can stand up to them."

He touched her shoulder. "But you don't have to do it alone."

That was why he was here, wasn't it? Malcom was so far beyond a sanctioned FBI case that he would likely be suspended for a while as soon as he returned home.

"I can't rely on you." She shook her head. "They'll kill you, and I'll be...upset. I'd rather you just went away if you're going to wind up making me cry after you're dead."

"It's called grief. Not that I'm planning to be killed. I'd rather help you, and we both survive." They could watch each other's backs.

She snorted quietly. "You can't go up against them and live."

"So I'm the sacrificial lamb?" Was he really only here so she could throw him in front of her, and he'd die, but she would live on? Hopefully, even if that happened, she had a plan to finish this that didn't involve her getting killed as well.

"No!" She whispered the word. "I just..."

"Didn't want to be alone anymore?"

He heard the slight exhale. Felt her fingers curl into the front of his shirt.

Malcom said, "Careful now. You'll wind up caring about me."

She shoved him away. "We need to get inside."

"Let's creep around and find an open back door." It was too risky to go in the same one those people had come out of.

Amara said, "Follow me," and raced across the gravel drive to the grass on the other side.

He checked to be sure no one saw her, gave it a second, just in case, and then followed, racing across the gravel to where she crouched behind rose bushes. He eased down beside her. "See a door?"

"No, but at least we know no one is on patrol. Or watching out the windows."

He doubted it was empty inside. A building this big, and with so many windows lit up, had to have resident patients. It was probably busy here in the daylight. Might be a normal hospital, with regular patients, or it could be a mental health facility. A psychiatric hospital. And then whatever they were doing here—these people she was supposed to be taking down—it involved middle of the night patient drop offs?

He needed answers.

"Let's go." She took off.

Around the back, he spotted a nondescript door. Amara picked the lock on that one as well, and they stepped inside. The air in the building was cold and smelled like antiseptic. Sterile.

Quiet.

Too quiet.

Down the hall, from far away, a woman screamed.

Chapter Nineteen

"Miss? Miss, are you okay?"

Someone shook her shoulder enough that Kenna realized she was awake. She blinked up at the gray clouds in the sky. No, that was smoke.

From a bomb.

"Preston." The name sounded like a croak from her mouth.

Sirens pierced the air, multiple discordant tones that fought the ringing in her ears for dominance.

An older woman leaned over her.

Kenna flinched.

"It's okay, Miss. Don't move. Help is coming."

Whatever it was in Kenna's brain that objected to attention, doctors, or help, got her to start sitting up. Like a switch flipped. The urge to run that usually had her moving her into action. Even though, right now, she could barely have said why she felt the need to go just then.

She needed a second to figure this out.

Her head snapped back, which hurt. *Focus.* Sitting up—that's what she was doing. Or trying to.

Kenna set her hand on the gritty pavement beside her. Pain sliced across her palm, and she hissed out a breath.

"You shouldn't move. You need to lie still, Miss." The voice had a terse British accent.

She managed to say, "I'm okay."

The woman's expression shifted to one of disbelief. She had heavy makeup, but it looked good. A nice suit with pants and a blouse, but sneakers on her feet. That was probably her purse on the ground nearby.

"What happened?" Kenna needed to hear someone else say it so her thoughts could have a minute to figure this out.

The woman looked around. Behind her, where the car had been, was nothing but smoke. Farther than Kenna had been from the vehicle when it blew. So, she'd been thrown back? That made sense, considering her back and shoulders hurt, along with her head and...okay, pretty much everything.

The woman started to speak. Her mouth moved, but Kenna couldn't make out what she was saying. Someone to her left screamed. They were through the trees where Kenna couldn't see them.

The woman winced, and her words came into focus, as if her ears figured out how to hear what the woman was saying in all the chaos. "...just flipped over. Another car slammed into it, and another one slammed into that." Tears gathered in her eyes. "I'm sure help will be here soon."

Kenna looked around. Probably half a dozen people lay on the ground.

She let go of the ground and swayed, her backpack still on. She looked at her palms, her hands hanging loose on her lap now. All she could think about was that ring box.

But why now? Maybe the simple fact her mind needed something good. An anchor in this chaos.

She needed Jax, though. Not some inanimate object. A promise, an intention. Those were intangible things. She needed the tangible.

He loved her. They both knew they were in this for the long haul. That was why there had been no rush. There was time.

The woman touched her shoulder.

Kenna flinched.

"Sorry." She lifted her hand. "Just making sure you're okay. Your hands look a bit nasty."

"I'm all right." Kenna wasn't going to admit anything else. She had no idea who this lady was, and she could be with that "company" Sienna mentioned for all she knew. This could be about information gathering. Or she could be about to make sure Kenna didn't survive this.

"You *are* American."

Kenna said, "Last time I checked."

She needed to get up. Get away from this woman, just in case.

Another switch in her flipped, and she knew she had to leave the park now. *Preston.* He and Hollace and Nielson were dead. They'd been in that car. Of course they had.

First, Sienna.

Now them.

She had to get to Jax quick enough to warn him that his life was in danger.

"Are you a tourist? This is going to be a horrible way to spend your holiday." She patted Kenna's shoulder. "Spending a few days in hospital recovering. I hope you have travel insurance. I was in Mallorca once, and I got this ear infection from spending too much time in the sea. It hurt so much, and I was still getting bills months later from their doctors." She shook her head.

"Can you help me up?"

"I really think you should stay there and—"

Kenna shifted her legs and leaned over with her hands on the concrete. If this lady wasn't going to—

"Okay, okay. I'll help."

If she couldn't stand on her own, then she had no business standing up. But having help was a whole lot different from needing it. Jax was a great example of that. Just because he was in her life didn't mean that she couldn't do something without him. His presence was a bonus. She had been fine alone for a long time and hadn't ever considered another relationship after Bradley died.

He had turned out to be the best kind of surprise.

And now he had one of his own, tucked in her backpack.

"You seem a bit out of it. You should probably find a seat and wait to get checked out by the ambulance people."

Focus. Kenna shifted so the woman had to let go of her or it would be weird. She bent one leg, then the other. Rolled her shoulders, moved her arms checking the rotation. Tipped her head left, then right. Her ears started ringing again. She needed a bottle of water to drink and another to pour over her head.

"Thank you for your help." She nodded to the woman. "Really. Thank you."

"Okay." She gathered her purse. "I can see if anyone else was hurt. But you were closest, I think."

Police officers—or whatever they were called here—ran in from the corners of the park. They disbursed, about a half dozen, going from person to person. She saw a couple of EMTs in neon jackets run over to a bleeding man and crouch. One of the pair took a separate bag to another person and knelt.

"I guess I got lucky or something." Kenna didn't know how else to brush it off. She dug out her phone from the jacket and didn't like the gritty sweat on her palms. The woman wandered off, so she dialed Jax's number while she headed for the far side of the park.

An angry tone answered, and a recorded voice told her the network was busy.

She tucked her phone in her bag and spotted a woman with a stroller. The baby inside was crying, and the woman struggled to get the stroller upright. Kenna wasn't going to be much help, but she also wasn't about to walk on and ignore the woman.

"Let me help." Or she would try to, at least.

Kenna gripped the side of the stroller, which looked like one of those old ones that was a bassinet with wheels. Thankfully, the thing was zippered shut, or the child might've rolled out.

They got it muscled upright, and the baby began to cry anew.

The mother swiped tears from her cheeks. "Thank you." She reached for the zipper with a shaky hand. Froze.

Too scared to look?

Kenna said, "Let's make sure they're all right."

The mom hiccupped a sob and nodded, looking relieved.

Kenna lowered the zipper, and the two sides peeled back. "Okay, okay." The kid was beet red, crinkled face, full-blown crying. "That must've been scary, huh." She ran her hands over the child's head, then down his body. She pedaled his legs gently. "You took a tumble, but it's okay. Huh. Mom's okay. You're gonna be all right."

The mom whimpered. "Thank you. I was so scared to look. I didn't want to see blood everywhere."

"Looks like he was pretty protected in that thing."

Relief infused her features. "Thank you."

"You're welcome." She touched the woman's shoulder, ignoring the flash of pain in her forearm. "Looks like he just needs a snuggle now."

So did the mom, but Kenna wasn't offering that service currently. She was going to go find Jax so she could get some of that bonus comfort of her own, while still trying to convince herself she didn't *need* it.

Coming to rely on it, or trust in it, wasn't the same as needing it.

Why her mind felt the need to dwell on this right now was anyone's guess. And a cop was coming her way.

She lifted her chin but turned and started walking the other way. He'd get distracted by the mom and baby, and she could get out of here. Tears gathered in her eyes. So much destruction, and at the center of it were Preston, Hollace, and Nielson. Were they in that car when it blew? There wasn't much by way of other explanations. At least not that she could think of in this state.

Maybe they weren't in the car.

She didn't like coincidences.

Had those people tried to kill her just now? They had technology that made it look like Sandhurst was alive. Was that who had been on the phone with her? Maybe they drew her here to kill her, since she hadn't been poisoned by the tea along with Sienna.

Kenna bit her lip, and twin tears rolled down her face.

A female cop in a black uniform, black, flat top cap, and a neon jacket stepped in front of Kenna with her hands raised. "Whoa there, Missy. I need you to hang on a bit."

Kenna said, "I need to leave."

"And I need you to answer some questions for me. Then we're going to make sure you're all right." The woman's words had an odd, ringing quality to them.

Probably Kenna's ears still recovering from the loud explosion.

"I don't want to stay."

"Well, you can't just run off after an incident like this. I need your information."

"Am I being arrested?"

She lifted her hands again. "Miss, why would I arrest you? Have you committed a crime?"

"Not other than trying to leave." Kenna swiped away the tears.

"You should have someone come here and get you. Just to make sure you're all right. You shouldn't be wandering off on your own if you're possibly injured." She took a slight step toward Kenna. "You could be in shock and not even know you're injured."

"I'll get picked up."

"How about I call someone for you and get them to come here? We can talk while we wait. Make sure you are all right."

Kenna shook her head. "If you aren't arresting me, then I'm free to leave." She took a step away, and said, "I'm okay. I didn't do anything wrong."

She walked away, skirting two other officers and

crossing the street between backed up vehicles who had nowhere to go now that the street was full of wreckage.

Not even sure why she'd added that last part. Maybe she figured they'd be after her with criminal charges waiting, and she'd needed that one second to try and convince *someone* she was legit.

She needed to focus on getting to Jax, who would be at the conference center, right? Or had he heard what happened, and he was on his way here? They could pass each other and not even know it. But then, how would he know she had been involved in this incident? Maybe he'd heard about Sienna dying at the hotel and gone there.

Kenna's shoe caught on an uneven bit of sidewalk, and she stumbled to the low brick wall between the building and the busy street. She leaned against it for a second, trying to get her equilibrium to settle.

She dug out her phone again, half expecting it to be completely shattered from that last stumble. Preston first, just in case he was okay and he answered.

No one picked up. She hung up before she could get sent to voicemail.

She tried Jax, and it rang and rang. Not that there was still a busy network now—just no answer. The maps app said it was a thirty-five-minute walk. She found a coffee shop halfway and bought a bottle of water so she could ask for the code to the restroom.

The mirror told the truth. No wonder everyone she passed looked at her oddly.

Kenna had dirt in her hair and scratches on her face. She washed her hands and face and untied her hair so she could re-tie it back, trying to ignore her arms. Pain pills were in her bag, so she swallowed down three Ibuprofen with a mouthful of lukewarm tap water so she could save the bottle. She stuffed the jacket in her backpack and left wearing just the long-sleeved shirt over her black pants.

Jax didn't answer the phone no matter how many tries she made.

The locator app. She couldn't believe she'd forgotten it. Would it still work?

The map loaded. Jax's phone showed he was at the conference center.

Kenna picked up her pace, energized into walking faster. Certain he was there now. When she got to him, they could figure this out together. She would call Miami Security International and tell them that two of their people had been killed—maybe. That the man they'd been protecting was dead—maybe.

She needed a sounding board.

Her partner.

The man God had given her so she didn't have to be alone.

Kenna finally turned the corner and looked at the conference center. She frowned. The white building with a million windows in rows four high looked more like a hotel. She walked around the building and found the main entrance.

All the strength she had bled from her, and she stumbled. Kenna moved to the side and turned to sit on the white stone steps, leaning against the wall below the handrail. Like anyone else at the conference who needed a break and chose to sit outside.

Focus.

Phone.

Jax.

It rang until the call connected. "Kenna?"

"Yeah." Her voice broke. She wanted to tell him every-thing at once and didn't know where to start.

"I've been trying to call you," he whispered. "Some-thing's going on at this conference. We've all been herded into the main conference auditorium. I think they're going to make an announcement."

She frowned, twisting to look at the front doors. A few people were scattered about, but it did seem quiet. She said, "The car exploded. I think Preston and the guys are dead."

"What—"

A muffled voice cut him off. "Ladies and gentlemen, if I could have your attention!"

Jax said, "That guy has a gun. He's—"

Automatic weapons fire cracked across the phone line, crackling the connection. A series of shots. People screamed.

"Get out of there. Jax!"

"Everyone is running for the doors, but they're locked. We're trapped in here." He sounded like he was moving, and she heard him say, "Careful. Are you okay?" Trying to help someone.

More weapons fire peppered across the phone line.

Kenna flinched, her inhale like a hiss. She squeezed her eyes shut.

Then that voice boomed again, like a loudspeaker announcement. "We cannot be ignored. We stand against corporate greed and police corruption! We stand with Kenna Banbury in the fight for justice!"

She inhaled so fast she had to cough. *What on earth...*

"Go," Jax said. "Kenna, if you're here, go. Get out. Don't get dragged into this."

"You need to come with me." She huddled against the wall and squeezed her eyes shut, wishing she could pull the hood over her face. This place was going to be crawling with armed response cops in minutes. "What is happening?"

She'd gone from that table in the dining room, to the park, and now here. Sienna. Preston and the other two guys. Now Jax. *I found the ring.*

"I don't know what's happening, but everyone is yelling for armed response," he said. "You can't be here. I don't want you caught up in this."

Too late. "Jax—"

He cut her off. "Go, Kenna. Don't wait for me. There's nothing else you can do. Just run."

Chapter Twenty

Kenna ducked into a shop, the first one she'd seen with an ATM sign outside. Rows of convenience foods organized into aisles, a wall of racks of newspapers on one side, and cigarettes tucked on shelves behind the counter.

An older man with middle eastern heritage stood behind the counter, bent forward scrolling on his phone. She swung the backpack off her shoulders and kept her hood pulled low over her forehead, just in case he had cameras—which she would assume he did.

She dug out her wallet and slid the card free.

Two thousand cash was apparently more than the machine currently held. She kept trying and finally came out with a thousand pounds, which might be the transaction limit on her card. Who even knew.

Her thoughts just swirled in her mind. She tried to catch one so she could make sense of what was happening, but it didn't work.

Keep moving. Don't stop.

She barely knew where she was going, cognizant of only a few things for certain. The police would want to talk to her, and she wasn't going to like what they had to say. The sun was still high in the sky. God was still on the throne. Her boyfriend loved her. Her friends were a call away and would do everything they could to help.

And she needed to go.

Kenna shoved the cash in a hidden pocket her pants had. No way was she going to let a pickpocket steal her resources. They could take her phone, no problem. That might actually be a good idea—enough to keep someone off her trail.

She tucked the cell in the side pocket of her backpack, where it was plainly visible to anyone who cared to look.

The jacket had to go. She needed something to cover her hair and face that she hadn't been seen wearing by police. That meant a clothing store, preferably something ethnic so she could cover her hair and at least part of her face. She kept walking, going in the general direction of the train station that would get her out of London and north to the town Sienna had told her that her mother grew up in.

Maybe not the safest place to go right now, but her mind had made the decision, and there was no changing it.

Maizie would know where to find her.

She pushed out thoughts of how tired she was, how achy, and remembered being in the hospital in New Orleans when a bike messenger delivered a phone the teen had sent to her so she could find out for herself if Kenna was okay.

Kenna sniffed. She'd cried enough over the fact these people had murdered her friends. They had destroyed her name with that active shooter incident at the law enforcement conference. Fencing her in because they hadn't been able to kill her—or, more likely given the timing, she was supposed to have been discredited posthumously. They were tarnishing everything she'd ever done and making her the subject of a nationwide manhunt.

If she was detained by the police, they would question her, and she'd have no answers, no evidence she wasn't part of this. No way to talk herself out of prison. She would probably end up spending her life behind bars, if it came to that. Captive with the kind of people she had worked for years to put away.

She couldn't go to the embassy either. Not after Sienna had inferred that Kenna couldn't trust them.

A clothing boutique up ahead looked promising. She slowed to look in the window and saw enough she could make work. Kenna avoided the employee behind the counter and wasn't asked if she needed anything or wanted help. She selected a scarf, a shirt, and a jacket with a hood. The backpack might prove her downfall, so she chose a larger, fancy duffel from the clearance section. The price tag, even on sale, made her wince. This was going to cut down on her cash reserves.

But she didn't have much choice and bought them anyway.

The lady who rang her up didn't smile and didn't make conversation.

Kenna said, "Can you tell me which way I go to the train station?"

She scanned a barcode, her expression completely disinterested. "Up the road, second right. Saint Pancras is about ten minutes' walk."

"Thanks." She had to change first. This city had so many cameras. She'd been seeing them everywhere. She couldn't go into the train station bathroom looking like this and come out in disguise. That would defeat the purpose of the disguise. "Do you have a restroom I could use?"

The woman scrunched up her nose. "You mean the toilet?" When Kenna nodded, she said, "Back there. Don't make a mess, okay? I'm the one that has to clean it up."

"I won't. Thank you so much."

The woman shrugged and went back to her work in the empty shop. In the restroom, Kenna set her backpack down and saw her phone was no longer there. Already? It had been stolen quickly.

She still had the remainder of her cash. It didn't take long to change the shirt, tuck her other clothes in the bag she'd bought. Rip the tag off. Rote things, logical steps she didn't have to think about. A chance to give her brain a rest from the grief, the stress, the endless questions.

Was she doing the right thing?

How close behind her were the police?

Was the situation at the conference resolved?

Was Jax all right?

She cupped her hands and drank from the tap at the sink. Big gulps. Trying to push back down the sickness that wanted to send her to the toilet. She'd barely eaten today and didn't want to have to refill her water bottle already. The nausea was likely from lack of food on top of all the exertion. Nearly getting blown up.

She wanted to laugh hysterically, but how would that help?

Kenna transferred everything to the new bag and pulled

on the jacket. It was a little tight across the back of her shoulders but would work okay. The hood rested on her forehead, covering her hair. Still, she used the scarf to hide her hair, tucking it back in a way that she could use one side to cover her face if she needed to. Could the police ask her to remove it if she had it on for religious reasons? She didn't know how that worked in this country.

All she knew was that they were looking for her—or would be soon enough.

There would be a trap, and she couldn't afford to get caught in it. Otherwise, she would end up like Sienna, twitching on the floor. One breath. Dead.

Kenna braced her hands on either side of the sink and left a blood smear when she pulled them away. She dried off and tucked extra paper towels in her pocket. Her watch...

Could someone track her?

Maizie for sure. But that could be a risk she wasn't able to take.

Kenna dropped the watch in the trash and stuffed the empty backpack in one side of the bag. She was out the door and back in the now-waning daylight. Without her phone and the maps app, she had to ask a couple of people for clarification before she found the train station.

As she approached it, Kenna tucked the scarf across her mouth and nose, leaving only her eyes visible. No one could know where she was going.

Not the police.

Not "the company" Sienna had mentioned.

She bought a ticket that would take her to Nottingham, which involved changing trains in Peterborough, according to the man who sold it to her.

"Departs in twelve minutes from platform eight, so you might want to hurry."

She said, "Thanks."

Evening commuters going home crowded the train station. She kept to the flow of foot traffic and spotted several on duty officers walking in pairs. More than usual? She couldn't be sure.

Her eyes strayed to a screen high on the wall.

Breaking News.

Her face appeared on one side of the screen, on the left was footage of the car. The wreckage of the bomb. Kenna was wanted for questioning regarding the explosion and the incident at the conference.

She eased out of the traffic and leaned against a pillar, reading the words that scrolled across the bottom of the screen. The situation hadn't been resolved yet. There were casualties, but police weren't sure how many. She was believed to be responsible.

Wanted.

The entrance to the platform had a barrier for her to insert the ticket. She chose one farthest from the train employee standing chatting with a security guard. Kenna avoided eye contact and got through with no problems.

She fast-walked to the middle of the train and hit the button. The doors slid open. She found a row of two chairs with not much leg room. Enough space for her to sit with her back to the middle aisle and appear to be preoccupied with what was out the window—or asleep.

Kenna set the bag on her lap and hugged it to her front. Her whole body shuddered. Even with the tension, it didn't take her long to fall asleep. The adrenaline she'd been running on and how far she'd walked today compounded, and she slumped against the window, still holding the bag.

The ring box inside. The one that represented the life she wanted with Jax. A good life. A peaceful life. Everything she didn't have right now, because she'd chosen to come here, not even knowing what was going on. She'd stepped into this case without signing up for it. The result was that she now had a target on her back, and these people were going to destroy her life.

A life that was supposed to include Jax. Partners in solving cases, if he chose to give up what he'd always said he wanted. Or partners in their personal life, and she figured out how to do her job and be static. They couldn't both work with each other, so it had to be a choice they made together.

Either way, the people she'd found herself up against wanted to put all that in jeopardy. They might've killed four people she knew today. Along with the fact they'd killed her mother, maybe even her father too in a way. Had his heart attack actually been that—or something else?

These people had shaped her life and how it began. The way she was raised. And now they were trying to do the same to her future.

In her mind, she held him close...and drifted off to the rumble of the train.

She didn't know how much later the train stopped. Kenna blinked and sucked in a breath, shifting and immediately feeling the burn of all her aches. People stood in the aisle.

The doors beeped and slid open on one side of the train, and they filed out. She waited for the train car to empty, then eased to the edge of the seat and stood. She groaned aloud. *Feels great. So good.*

Every part of her body was stiff, but she made it off the train and bought a sandwich and caffeinated soda for now. The cookie and the chips she tucked in her bag for later.

Half an hour later, she was on another train, and by the time it reached Nottingham, night had fallen. They pulled into the red brick building, and Kenna forced herself to rouse. To push everything out and get where she was going without thinking about what she would do when she got there.

She followed the other commuters to the exit doors, where a line of taxis was parked outside at the curb. An older guy with not much hair leaned on the edge of his hood, reading a newspaper. He looked up as she approached. "Where to, Miss?"

Kenna recited the address from memory.

He frowned. "It'll be about sixty quid."

She dug out the cash and showed him.

"All right. Get in. You look like you're about to drop." He hesitated. "Don't fall asleep in my backseat."

She climbed in. "Thanks for driving me."

"It's not a favor, darlin'. You're paying me."

Kenna chuckled. "It's been a long day."

"You visiting? Holiday. What do they call it...you're on vacation?"

"Something like that." She buckled her seatbelt. "This is where my mother grew up, and where she met my dad."

"Nottingham's nice. Good place to grow up."

Kenna watched out the window as he drove through the city, toward an older part with medieval-era looking buildings she couldn't believe were still standing. All the houses were packed together like a miniature town. Peaked roofs and tiny front doors. Small windows with iron separating the panes.

An old church with gravestones in the grounds outside, all surrounded by a stone wall covered with moss.

The city gave way to winding roads. Plenty of trees. Bigger houses set back from the road.

He said, "The town you want is a little outside the city. It'll be about twenty minutes."

"Thanks."

"Can't say as I know much about it. Their school is pretty elite. You've got to pass a test to get in, and the tuition fees are astronomical. But it's supposed to be the best."

They drove past a brick wall that stretched nearly a mile. She saw the sign for a hospital, but the building looked derelict now.

She'd just about started to drift off in the warmth of the car when he pulled up outside a dark house at the end of a gravel road. A hedge lined the street. Once neat, it was now unkempt and in need of trimming.

"Here we are."

She added a tip to the cost and said, "Thanks," before she shoved the door open.

"Best of luck to you."

He didn't stick around. Soon as she shut the door, he drove away.

Kenna stared at the dark house. One window had been boarded up. There was a lock on the front door, maybe a coded entry like a house for sale. It seemed abandoned.

The grounds were overgrown. The neighbors' houses weren't visible on either side, thanks to the rows of trees blocking the view to the left and right.

She walked to one side and around the back. Through a gate in a wood fence. Into the rear of the property, where a yard stretched back and inclined to a hill. It would have been beautiful once. Probably still was in the light of day, but in an abandoned kind of way. Now the stone tile roof of the out-building had caved in, and the door hung open.

She went to the back door of the house and found it slightly ajar.

No sound came from inside.

Leaves crunched under her feet in the entryway. A tiny room with hooks on the wall on one side.

She closed it behind her and stepped through another door into the house. Bare floors, no furniture. Nothing in the kitchen but empty cupboards and a faint musty smell, along with a space under the counter where some appliance had been installed between two cupboards.

Empty living room.

Bare stairs that led up and a broken handrail.

Her foot slipped off one step, and her shin slammed on the edge of the stair. Kenna didn't bother to hold back her cry. No one was going to hear it.

She got up and limped through the upstairs rooms.

In the last empty one, she stopped. Kenna set the bag down and lay on the floor with her head on it.

Tomorrow, she would find a phone.

She would work out how to finish this, or just what she should do next.

His mercies are new every morning.

She was counting on it.

Chapter Twenty-One

Nottinghamshire

Wednesday 7:13am

Morning obscured the horizon. Dense fog had crept in overnight, and now the sun hung muted behind the clouds. The whole world seemed to have a grayness to it that suited Kenna's mood.

Her stomach rumbled, and water from the tap in the kitchen sink didn't quite quench her thirst. She found a granola bar in her backpack she must've missed before.

Some stretches eased her muscles from sleeping on the floor...and everything else that happened the last few days. *Don't think about it.*

Jax was fine. Preston probably wasn't even dead. Maybe.

The cops would realize she wasn't part of this strange plot, and that she hadn't done anything wrong. If they were even looking for her.

Kenna stood in the open back door of the empty house and stared out at the still morning, absorbing the calm. Giving herself that little bit of rest.

If she had her things, or her phone, she would be able to read her Bible. But those were gone. All she had was what had settled inside her over the past year or so, that she'd been actively trying to walk with God.

The space out the back behind the house was a garden.

She set out into it.

Over soft, wet ground. The air chilled her through the thin sweater and jacket, but she didn't mind. Cold was an old friend she'd lived with for years. She doubted she would ever be fully comfortable with heat.

The sound of a shovel hitting earth cut through the quiet like a sharp *snick*.

Kenna stopped.

When she heard nothing more, she continued on. Walking the ground her mother would have walked as a child, wondering what it must have been like to grow up here.

She heard that snick once more and headed toward the sound, between two rows of earth cut out from the grass. Long beds where flowers or vegetables had once grown. Now there was only dirt and the occasional weed...

And a man digging.

She stopped.

He lifted the shovel and slammed it back down into the dirt, then levered one boot on the top of the blade end and jumped down on it. The metal sank into the earth. He tugged it free and did the same again, softening the soil.

The man had to be in his eighties, at least. He wore brown corduroy pants and a threadbare wool sweater, over which he had pulled a navy-blue wool coat with brass buttons. On his head was a green and brown tartan flat cap. His face was craggy, the whiskers on his cheeks white, the same color as the hair that curled over his ears from under the cap.

He flinched and lifted his chin, staring at her with gray eyes. "'ello."

"Good morning." She tucked her hands in the jacket pockets, trying to seem casual.

"Mornin' to you, Miss." He looked around, and his face shifted to a confused expression for a second before he shook his head and went back to his digging. "Trying to get the potatoes in before the frost, see. Gotta get it done, don't I?"

He seemed more like a lost old man, confused about where he was. Or how to get home.

"Is this your house? I was out walking when I spotted it." Kenna shifted her feet, trying to warm her legs. "It's a lovely place."

"They've certainly let it go, if you ask me." He hammered the shovel into the dirt. "Don't know what they were thinking, leaving it to look like this."

Kenna said, "Do you know how to contact the owners? I might like to buy it."

"Don't know why you would. Nothin' but moths and empty halls now."

"Did something happen here?"

He grunted. "Why'd you say that?"

"It just seems strange that it was left empty." If the owners had moved out, why not sell the place? Was her mother the last family member to have ownership of the house? Maybe after her death, no one had stepped forward to claim it.

"Why would the house be empty?" He glanced in that

direction and frowned. "The girls will be off to school soon. It's still early. They're probably sleeping."

Kenna actually had zero clue what time it was. She had no watch and no phone, and there were no clocks in the house. "What time is it?"

The man shifted the shovel and leaned it against his shoulder. He pulled back his sleeve but wore no watch. "Huh. Must've left it at home."

"Do you live far away?" She shifted the jacket closer around her, colder now than she had been when she left the house.

He glanced one direction, then the other, and finally pointed behind him over his left shoulder. "That direction, at the other end of the property. In the carriage house." He frowned, as if wanting to add, "I think" to the end. "How about a cup of tea?"

He was inviting her over? "That sounds lovely."

"We'll see if Doris has the kettle on, shall we?" The man handed her the shovel and then turned away and started walking.

Kenna brought it with her, not wanting to upset him by leaving it behind. She wasn't quite sure what to make of this man. He was old enough he could have lived and worked here years ago, when her mother was alive. He could know all sorts of things about the family. Or he could be a confused old guy who had no idea where "here" was and didn't know her mother at all.

He wandered between two trees, following a well-worn path.

Thanks to the morning fog, she could barely see more than ten feet in front of her and had to walk fast to keep up with his steady pace. He seemed like he could walk for hours before he tired.

A structure came into view. White stone walls, and a tile roof. The building was barely the size of a garage and had a chimney blowing smoke into the air. A dog with gray hair and white eyebrows lay on the doorstep, on a mat.

"Charlie, did she kick you out again?"

The animal uncurled itself, taller than she'd expected but definitely a mutt. He was scraggly and had to have some Great Dane in him, given the height of his shoulders and hips. He ate, but not much, and he walked stiffly.

The man stopped to pet the dog, who quickly noticed Kenna.

She eased up to them slowly and held her hand out. The dog sniffed a couple of times, then licked her fist. She uncurled her hand and gave him some scratches under his chin. "Hi, Charlie. I'm Kenna." She glanced at the man. "What's your name?"

"I didn't tell you?"

"No, but that's okay. I didn't introduce myself." She straightened and held her hand out. "I'm Kenna. It's nice to meet you."

"It is nice, isn't it. I'm Simon." He shook her hand, gripping way too tightly with his rough palm and squeezing her fingers.

Kenna bit her lip, but he let go before she could bring up the issue.

"Let's go inside." He turned to the door. "It's getting a bit nippy out here."

Inside the house smelled musty. The carpet was worn, and the walls had tiny cracks running up and down that she could see in places. A row of wood-framed photographs depicted Simon and a woman in a long sundress on a pier somewhere, in front of a Ferris wheel. Enough years ago that the photo was black and white, and the color images had begun to fade.

He trailed through to a living room that was not much bigger than her RV kitchen and dining area combined. Just a small, square room with a door. One old armchair and a small couch, facing a tiny square TV and a fireplace. The dog clambered up on the couch and settled in with an exhale. Simon knelt by the fire, and his knee popped. He stoked the embers and added another log. Then two. More newspaper, which he lit with a match and then tossed the thing on top.

The living room warmed, lit by the orange glow.

Out the window, the sky was gray still...and blurred. She realized there was clear plastic over the window to keep the draft out.

Simon said, "Right," as he straightened. "Tea, then."

"Thank you for inviting me in."

He looked at her, and for a split second, he seemed to have no clue who she was. Then he blinked and said, "Right."

He moved past her, into the kitchen, and she could hear him clattering around.

Kenna wandered over to the dog and rubbed both sides of his head, leaning down so her face was close to his. "Does he take care of you, or do you take care of him, huh?"

The dog licked her palm, then laid his head on the cushion with a sigh. She left the animal and went to the kitchen.

Simon pulled out a pan. "See if we've got eggs, will you?"

Kenna looked around for the fridge.

"In there." He pointed to what looked like a bread box. The front rolled up, and she discovered half a dozen brown eggs in a carton. He said, "I collected those yesterday when I fed next door's chickens. They're gone for the winter, down in the South of France somewhere, so they don't mind if I help myself."

"That's nice." Kenna stood beside him as he heated butter in the pan. "How long have you lived here?"

"Oh, Doris and I moved in..." His voice trailed off. After a few seconds' pause, he said, "Go ahead and crack them in there."

"Did you know the family that lived in the house well?" She wondered if he'd think of the neighbors, so she said, "They had a little girl, didn't they? Amara, I think."

"You knew them?" He stared at her with those gray eyes. A bit confused and not sure who she was.

"I haven't met them."

"What are you, some kind of cousin from across the pond?"

"I am related to them." Kenna cracked enough eggs for both of them. "I'm just not sure how yet."

"Shame there's none left to ask."

"What happened?" She tossed the shells in a tiny trash can that had tea bags, vegetable and fruit peelings in it. Compost?

"Things went downhill after Mrs. Constantine never came home. Mr. Constantine was never a warm man, but after that, he got mean. Didn't treat those girls right at all."

Kenna's breath hitched in her throat. "What were the girls' names?"

"Little Anne...and Amanda. Two peas in a pod they were. Used to pick my strawberries and eat them right off the plants. Doris would set the table, and they'd have tea together after school. She always made sure they did their homework."

"Did they grow up and move out?" What was the alternative? She knew her mother had lived to adulthood. What about her sister? And which one later claimed she was the same "Amara Clarke" in her father's journal?

Anne or Amanda?

"After Anne went away, Amanda wasn't ever the same." He shook his head.

Kenna found a wooden spoon and stirred the eggs. "Where did she go?"

"The same boarding school they all go to. Sending children away. It's just not right."

Kenna found salt the same way she seemed to have found these answers. Pointed in the right direction so she discovered what she needed in front of her. "Why didn't Amanda go?"

"She was always sick, that one. Coughs lasting weeks. Bedridden with a fever. Anne ran away from the school more times than I could count. Took bus after bus across two counties to get back here, just to see her sister. Always was spanked and sent back to school." He stared at the eggs until the kettle whistled on the back burner.

Simon jumped into action, turning it off. Two mugs. Tea bags. Sugar in one. He poured, then set the kettle back on the stove.

"What happened to Amanda?"

"They buried her in the church yard the summer of seventy-two. She was twelve years old. Tragic that was. Doris cried for weeks. Anne didn't return for years, and by then, she was a young lady, and she had a new little sister, Allison Constantine. Still, Anne was nothing but a shadow of who she'd been."

Anne Constantine, devoted enough to her sister that she would disobey everyone to see her.

Was this her mother?

The only thing she could figure was that the sister had been one of the babies born. Adopted by the father, raised by the nanny.

Kenna had no way to be sure about much of anything, but it made sense at least. What she wanted to know was how it would help her get out of this mess she'd landed in.

These people had targeted her from every angle, cut her off. Ruined her name so that she had to run. She knew something of what Preston had felt, going to prison for years for a crime he hadn't committed. Again, because of these people. She was sure of that now. His wife had been one of them. For some reason, that warranted her death—possibly in the same way it had for her mother.

Kenna looked in cupboards for two plates and served up the eggs. "What happened to their father?"

"Moved somewhere else, last I heard. Greece or some such place. Far too warm for me." He used a spoon to squeeze the tea bag against the side of the mug and tossed it in a cup on the counter. Added milk. Handed over hers.

"Forks?"

"Cutlery. Right." He dragged open a stiff, heavy drawer and grabbed them, then shoved the drawer back in with a crash and a rattle of silverware. They settled with everything at the table. Stained rings on the surface of it. Rickety chair. Yellowed lace over the kitchen window. Signs of a woman's touch, but she hadn't lived here in a while.

The kitchen door eased open, and Charlie wandered in so he could sniff at the tabletop.

Simon handed him a piece of egg.

"Thank you for breakfast." Kenna tried not to eat like a starving person. Even the tea was good and warmed her from the inside in a way she hadn't known she needed. "I won't stay all day."

He reached over and patted her hand. "You're never a bother, dear. I'm sure Doris will be back soon. She'd love to see you."

Kenna smiled. "I'd love to see her."

Though, she doubted Doris would be back.

Simon slurped his tea. Ate his egg. Tossed another piece at the dog, who snapped it out of the air.

"Do you and Charlie need anything?"

He eyed her. "You're telling me I look more like I'm in need of something than you?" He chuckled, just a shake of his shoulders and no sound. "You look like you've been dragged through a hedge backward."

Kenna enjoyed that mental image. "I am...in some trouble."

"Thought so. You've got that look about you." He pointed his fork at her face.

Kenna bit her lip. "I don't suppose you have a phone, do you? I really need to call a friend who can help me."

"Course I do. Landline in the..." He glanced around. "Bedroom. One in the living room. No, that's not right. That one broke."

"Not to worry." She didn't want him to get stressed out.

"We'll find it." He patted the back of her hand again. "We'll get your friend to help. Don't you worry, Anne. It's never as bad as we think it is in the moment. Once you have a cup of tea, things will seem all right again."

Chapter Twenty-Two

Kenna settled onto the edge of the mattress, which sagged under her. She held the phone to her ear and listened to it ring. After three rings, she set the phone down.

With no idea where Simon had gone after they found the landline in his room, she took a moment in the quiet. Everything he'd told her had to be verified. She didn't think he'd been lying to her, but a confused old man might get his wires crossed and mix up events and people.

The phone started to ring.

She snapped it up. "Hello?"

"Kenna?" Maizie's voice sounded far away. "Is that you?"

"Who else has your super-secret emergencies only number? I just didn't think I'd ever need to use it." Thankfully, there was no way for anyone to trace it. By the time someone realized she'd been here, Kenna would be long gone.

"It's a good thing you did, I was about to dump the hard drive. Someone hacked my whole system, and they're *good*. I barely got the firewalls reinforced before they were breaking the next one down. I've sent them chasing after me over to a dummy server I pay for that I have random cold case files on. They'll figure out soon enough that it's nothing, and the cases relate to episodes of a TV show."

"Do you know who hacked you?" Kenna stared at the old wood dresser, a lace square of tablecloth on top with a pitcher on it made of stone and painted with flowers. A mirror hung on the wall, but someone had settled a pillowcase over it.

On the other side of the room was a tiny sink with a mirrored cabinet above, and next to that a freestanding wardrobe with two drawers at the bottom.

The whole room was maybe ten by ten feet, with barely space to move around the double bed.

"Maizie?"

She came back a couple of seconds later. "I'm here. I think it's them...whoever is doing this."

"The people I'm apparently up against." She didn't want to ask, but she also did, and she knew she had to. "What do you know about Preston and Jax?"

"Jax called me earlier. He got one phone call in the police station. They suspect he had something to do with the active shooter situation at the conference, so they took him in for questioning even though he was right there fighting back. Helping to subdue the shooters."

"You can't be serious. That's insane." Kenna gripped the phone.

"I know that, and you know that. But the British police

don't. Stairns is getting the State Department in on it. Trying to intervene so they can get him released."

"I'm pretty sure the State Department, or someone who works there, is connected to these people. Tell both of them not to trust..." She wanted to say *anyone* but settled on, "Just tell them to be careful."

"Okay."

"Have you heard from Miami Security International?"

Maizie said, "Not since the car bomb. The papers in England are calling it a terror attack, but a lot of people don't care that Preston is dead."

Kenna refused to assume. "Have they confirmed he was inside? And Hollace and Nielson, too?"

"I mean, I haven't seen DNA tests or anything. They have said there were three victims."

"Does that mean three in the car, or was someone nearby killed?"

"Good question."

"Stay on that if you can. I want confirmation." But would she trust it even if she did get proof they were gone? "I don't know who to believe right now."

"Do you know where you are?"

"Do *you*?" Kenna asked her. "Because I'd rather stay off the radar. I need to work this case like it's any other. Get to the bottom of it."

"Stairns did tell me that if you called, I should get him," Maizie said. "He's coming over from the cabin now, and Ramon is with him."

"Thanks, Maze." Kenna didn't feel quite so alone right now. "But don't worry about me. I need you to do whatever you need to do to stay safe."

After all, these people knew who Maizie was and where to find her.

Kenna gripped the phone and waited.

"You're on speaker now," Maizie said. Then to someone else said, "I hear you, okay?" Didn't sound like she agreed and was going to do it, though. "Stairns and Ramon are both here." Her voice had a decidedly teenage tone to it.

"Hey, guys." Kenna squeezed the bridge of her nose. She should go to wherever Jax had been taken and plead his case, but that would only end up with them being separated and questioned. She would wind up in jail.

He was far better off as distanced from her as she could make happen.

Later, they could talk about that ring box.

"Kenna, you okay?" Stairns' tone was almost harsh, which meant he was worried about her.

"I'm good. Kind of." She didn't know what else to say.

"I'm coming there," Ramon said. "ASAP. Maizie is going to get me a flight."

"Do you have a passport?"

"It's gonna take a couple of days."

Kenna said, "This might be over before then. I hope it will be."

"If it isn't, I'll be there to help."

So sweet. "Thanks. But Jax might need more help than me."

"Want me to break him out of British jail? Can't be that hard."

Kenna frowned. "That's not what I meant."

"You said I should help." Ramon's tone almost made her smile. Almost.

She needed to pray for Jax. Implore the Lord to work on his behalf in this situation—the only way she could see he'd get free of being implicated.

She heard Maizie snicker in the background. Stairns

said, "I have another idea. One that might get you help faster than Ramon the Lone Ranger."

Maizie laughed again in the background, then said, "Ack, they're through a firewall. I need to work."

Stairns said, "Kenna, you with me?"

"I'm here." She ducked her head and listened to his voice in her ear.

"I have a buddy nearby. He's on his way. I just need the address, and I can have him pick you up. He's CIA. Or he was. The guy was burned a few years ago. Can't go back to the US. If the Brits find him, they'll lock him up in some off-books prison and find out what he knows. Until his heart stops. Got me?"

"Right. Torture." Not worse than what would happen to her if she was found. "You think I need backup?"

"I want you to have it. So don't argue."

Kenna had trusted Stairns once, and he'd betrayed her. Since then, he'd worked to earn her trust and had proven himself more than once. Mostly where Maizie was concerned.

She gave him the address of the house here. "Have him come get me."

"He'll be there today. I figured you might go there, so I have him already on his way. But I'll confirm that's where he's headed."

"You trust this guy with your life?"

Stairns said, "I'd trust him with Maizie. Until he found out where she came from, and then we'd lose him to a one-man war against the kind of men who do that stuff. Then we'd have a situation to contain."

Before she could respond, Ramon said, "I wanna meet this guy."

Kenna figured they might be two peas in a pod. "Thanks, Stairns."

"As if you have to ask."

She said, "I feel like I should work this case, or it won't ever be over. But I should be helping Jax or working out what happened to Preston and the MSI guys. I shouldn't be out here alone." Tears gathered in her eyes.

She didn't want to be alone at all.

"I'm on my way." Ramon's voice sounded closer now. "And so is this spy. You aren't alone. You have all of us."

"Who does Jax have?"

He and Ramon didn't always see eye to eye. They were never going to be best friends, but she knew they at least respected one another.

She continued, "Or Preston."

Ramon just said, "We'll figure this out."

Stairns commented before she could, "I already called Jax's father. Didn't exactly tell him who I was, but I did say his son needs the best lawyer his money can buy."

"Thanks." Again. Even with nothing, she still had so much to be grateful for.

"Don't get all weepy on me now, girlie. You'll lose your edge."

Ramon said, "Cry all you want. Then get up and work this case."

"I agree with Ramon!" Maizie called from farther away.

Her family. The people who rooted for her. When she got back to the States next, she needed to go and see Javier Ryson, her friend on the Salt Lake City police force, and his wife and their kids. She missed them.

Kenna swiped a tear from her cheek. "I think I'm public enemy number one right now. These people are dead serious. We barely stepped into their world, and they hit back so hard we're spinning out."

Something in her just couldn't quite believe Preston was dead. Maybe it was only foolishness or wishful thinking.

She heard a sound across the other end of the house, like a muffled bark. "I need to go."

Stairns said, "My guy is on his way."

"Thanks." She hung up the phone and went to the hall.

Earlier, on her way back to the bedroom, the floorboard in the hall had creaked. Now Kenna stepped around that spot so she made no sound. She heard the dog bark again. Why did it sound like he was far away, not even in the house?

Where was Simon?

The hall was empty. The kitchen, maybe? Something kept her from calling his name. Too late, she realized the living room was occupied.

Kenna moved to the doorway and eased the door open.

A striking blonde, probably in her forties but who could no doubt pass for much younger, stood there. Simon in front of her, shocked confusion on his face. She had a handful of the front of his jacket, her arm on his shoulder.

Kenna started to lift her hands.

The woman whipped up a knife with her other hand and dragged it across Simon's throat in one lethal swipe, and he fell to the floor choking. Bleeding out in a matter of seconds.

Kenna spun around and ran for the back door. On the way, she saw a dog leash on a hook and grabbed it. Didn't matter if it was part of her plan or not. She might need anything to fight back with. But what she had to get was that EpiPen thing.

She dragged the door open and ran as fast as she could, her arms and legs pumping. Feeling the woman behind her like the breath of a predatory animal on the back of her neck.

At any moment, she would be stabbed in the back, and it would all be over.

Unless she could get to her bag.

Kenna prayed the fog still hung thick enough she could make space between them and maybe lose the woman. She backtracked to the house from memory, praying and running. Each breath another prayer and another push to go as fast as she could.

Victory would only be a dream if she couldn't survive the next few minutes.

Kenna slammed into the back door, shoved it off its broken hinges, and skidded into the house. At the bottom of the stairs, she got a look behind her and saw the woman barely crossing the threshold into the house.

She had seconds.

As she tore up the stairs for the room where she'd left her duffel, she racked her brain to remember which pocket it was in.

Praying.

Running as hard and fast as she could.

She tripped across the threshold into the bedroom, landed on her knees with a cry, and dug into her open bag. *Lord Jesus.*

The woman ran in, brandishing that knife. Running like a banshee at Kenna. It reminded her of Sienna in New York, tackling Ramon.

As she swung down with the blade, Kenna pushed off the floor and launched up. Tackled the woman in her middle and sent her to the floor on her back. *Weren't expecting that, were you?*

She slammed the EpiPen into her midsection and twisted to catch the wrist where she held the knife. Too late. But then, she'd known the cost might be high. The knife didn't slam into her back, though. It was still by her side.

Kenna gripped the woman's wrist, her ability to brace the knife away from her was nearly zero.

Here we go. She knew it was coming. Time seemed to slow so that each second stretched with her heartbeats until they dragged on with great expanses of time between.

The knife touched her jacket sleeve. It came down and embedded in the outside of her shoulder. Pushed in. Pierced skin and sank into the muscle.

Kenna cried out but didn't let go. The EpiPen had already clicked. Whatever was in there needed to work, or she was dead in seconds.

Kenna sucked in a breath. The knife felt like fire in her shoulder.

The woman under her bucked. A surprised expression flashed on her face, and she convulsed again. Anger infused her features. Kenna didn't let go. Didn't stop. She just used the full force of her will to keep the woman still.

Kenna managed to push the knife out, watching it ease out of her. She gasped. The knife clattered to the floor, and the woman convulsed again, shaking hard.

Kenna got off her, falling to the side. Was she dying? Kenna clutched her injured shoulder and watched. After a few more seconds and some violent shakes, the woman stilled.

One long exhale, and she bent forward almost all the way until her forehead touched her knee. She scooted over and pressed two fingers to the woman's neck, feeling for a pulse. It beat low but steadily under her fingers. Wasn't what was in the pen supposed to have killed this woman, or slowed her down? If she was the same kind of person as Sienna, shouldn't she be dead rather than simply incapacitated?

But she wasn't dead. Which meant she needed to be secured.

Whatever part of Kenna's brain had thought the leash was a good idea at the time deserved another cup of tea. She used it now to secure the woman's hands behind her back, which she knotted to her feet so the woman was hog-tied for when she woke up.

Sweat ran down Kenna's back.

Another person dead because of this company. Simon. Kenna winced, and tears rolled down her face. She scrubbed at her cheeks and just let herself cry. Why not. It wasn't as if anyone else was here to see her.

Just Kenna and this woman.

Scratch that.

She checked the woman's pockets and anywhere else that Kenna would have hidden something. No cash. No ID. No wallet or even car keys. In her boot, Kenna found an odd mobile device. It didn't look like any cell phone she'd ever had. The screen on the front was tiny.

She figured out it flipped open. Screen on top and keyboard on the lower half.

Maizie needed to get access to this.

Kenna stuck it in her pocket, trying to ignore the pain in her shoulder. How long was Stairns' CIA friend going to be? He might have an idea what to do with this woman.

Who twitched.

Kenna's head whipped around to look at the bound woman. At the same moment, the woman turned her head and looked over her shoulder.

She smiled.

Chapter Twenty-Three

The flash of teeth that showed when the woman pulled her lips back in a sneer made the tied up killer look like every inch the predator she was. Something like a wolf that had been caught in a trap but was still deadly. In her eyes, Kenna saw the kind of determination that existed in an animal that would gnaw off its own leg just to get free.

Kenna wanted to put space between her and the woman, but backing up right now would be a retreat. The kind of person this woman in front of her was, she would see it as a sign of weakness. As if Kenna was scared.

True or not, they needed to begin on more equal footing.

The woman said, "I thought you were just running. Going into the house didn't make much sense unless you thought there was somewhere to hide. Somewhere I wouldn't find you."

She spoke slowly in a crisp English accent. Her voice had an even tone, and there was almost zero emotion in it. The cold, flat intonation of a killer.

Kenna flexed her fingers, just to remind herself who was tied up and who was in charge right now. The movement made the bleeding wound on her left shoulder flash with pain, but that wasn't a bad thing.

"You were probably hoping the poison would kill Sienna before she could give me that EpiPen." Kenna waved at it on the floor, the substance that had knocked out this woman for only seconds and didn't kill her. "Is that what your company is known for? 'Results may vary' and all that?"

The skin around the woman's eyes tightened as if she didn't like that insinuation. Kenna could only guess how connected to the company she was. Given her age, it seemed she had been born between the generations that were the waves of missing women, if what Kenna could tell from her features was accurate, which it might not be. Likely by design.

"Sienna." The woman chuckled, her voice low and full of mirth.

"You don't like people who break the rules?" Kenna shifted on the floor and tried to adopt a more relaxed stance.

A gleam lit in her eyes. "She's dead, isn't she?"

Kenna said, "Because you didn't like her, or because she broke the rules?"

The woman said, "Yes."

Then she glanced to Kenna's left. Maybe not necessarily so she could see out the window. It might just be that she'd been looking over her shoulder for a while and now her neck ached.

Kenna got up and walked over to the window, looking out there just in case this woman had brought friends with her. "No backup?"

The woman huffed. "That's only an American thing. Something they put in TV shows. I don't need 'backup.'"

Kenna frowned, still scanning the ground outside the window. She didn't see anyone. "You're more like some kind of spy. A secret agent. A hired assassin. You only work alone."

"I'd think you of all people would understand the need to work alone. Why else are you out here by yourself, and not back in London with your friends?"

Ah, a jab at Kenna's emotions. A way to make her feel off-kilter. As though Kenna had done something wrong by running instead of going to jail. Which was where Jax currently sat.

She bit her lip, determined not to let this woman see that her dig had worked. It was only because Kenna's reserves were so low—and she had zero energy right now— that she was feeling it. Any other time, she'd be able to reason her way through this. But when she had just watched a perfectly nice older man have his throat slit right in front of her, she wasn't feeling entirely settled.

This woman knew exactly what her people had done to Kenna and her friends. And the fact they were scattered now meant it had worked. They thought Kenna was off her game, but given she was here in her mother's home, they should think otherwise. It was the best place to start trying to unpack this case and pick it apart, piece by piece.

Kenna turned from the window and leaned against the wall, out of sight of anyone outside. If there was someone out there, she figured they'd have heat-sensing technology, so it didn't matter where she stood. And if they had high-powered weaponry, they could simply take her out through the wall.

She would already be dead. Not standing here with warm blood soaking her left sleeve. But instead, this woman, this precision instrument of death, had been sent to kill her. Quickly. Quietly. Not taken down with a public scandal.

She leveled a steady gaze on the woman. "You didn't need to kill Simon."

A frown creased the woman's brow.

Kenna pointed in the right direction. "The older man in that house. The one whose throat you slit."

"Oh, right. Him." The woman made her shrugging motion, crinkling her nose. "He was in the way."

"So that's what you do."

"We all have skills. You save people, I kill them." She didn't seem concerned either way, which meant she was possibly a sociopath and most likely a brainwashed true believer—a victim of the same "cult."

Unfortunately for Kenna, it was difficult to un-brain-wash a true believer in the space of ten minutes. Which was as long as she wanted this conversation to last. It was highly doubtful this woman would give her any usable informa-tion. Still, what she *did* say would be telling.

Even with the police conducting a manhunt, these people still considered Kenna enough of a threat to be worth sending an assassin to end the problem. Or she had come on her own.

Kenna said, "Tell me something no one knows about you. Something no one has ever asked."

The woman stared at her, then burst out laughing.

"Like my favorite color? Or how I always wanted to have a pet cat, but no one ever let me?"

"We aren't that different, you and I." Just saying that caused nausea to rise in Kenna's stomach. "Raised to do one thing. Cast out in the world alone with the expectation that we get the job done. Nothing more, nothing less."

"I suppose we are sisters, of a fashion."

"Because my mother was one of you?" After all, Sienna had told her that Kenna's mother was a cautionary tale they were told. "Killed because she got out. Because she had the audacity to want a better life than the one they gave her. A life where she was free."

"Freedom is an illusion."

"I assure you, if I were to let you go, you would most definitely be free."

"For a whole five minutes before I have a brain aneurysm, and someone finds me lying in garbage, decomposing."

Kenna said, "Why would you have a brain aneurysm?"

"They engineered us in a lab. You don't think they couldn't add in some kind of failsafe? A way to keep us in line?" She hissed out a breath between clenched teeth. "It took them long enough to perfect it. After me, all the next-gen models received an upgrade."

It sounded like science fiction. Like a TV show that was exciting, but not something that would ever happen in real life.

But that didn't mean it wasn't true.

Kenna said, "Tell me where to find the person in charge. Tell me where they work and the location of every facility they have. Give me bank account numbers. If you tell me what I need to know, I will take this whole thing apart."

The woman on the floor stared at her. "You might not

think I have much of a life, but it's *my* life. Throwing it away gets me nothing."

"So you kill for them, and when you're not on the job, you get to live happily ever after? Is that it?" Kenna shrugged. "You want to keep your personal life, so you don't rock the boat."

She wondered if it was more likely this woman had nothing outside of what she did for the company.

Was she someone like Sienna, who appeared to anyone looking in to be merely the personal assistant to Wilson Sandhurst? In reality, she was living in a tiny room in the office. Sleeping on a cot, using a computer to pretend to be him to keep the ruse going that the man was still alive.

What kind of life did this woman live?

"It's not about your future," Kenna said. "At least not *only* yours. Sometimes, with people like us, it's only about the future someone else can have. Giving them the gift of carrying on, even if it costs you everything you've got."

"Nobility isn't something I was taught. And what's the point, when the person doesn't even care what you did for them? They're too busy being happy and free. They don't give a second thought to the fact you saved their life."

Kenna said, "So instead you resent the people you haven't even saved. You stay in your little bubble. You keep taking lives because they tell you to."

"I take lives because it's what I'm good at. It's the reason they created me."

Kenna heard the squeal of older brakes outside and turned to the window in time to see a car pull up by the gate. The rusty old beater was a dirty yellow color. The door squeaked, and a man uncurled himself from the right-hand driver's side, straightening to look at the house.

She pegged him as American within the first three

seconds, but given he wore a Hawaiian shirt and a pair of cargo shorts with sunglasses on the top of his head, that wasn't difficult. And it was probably entirely on purpose. No one was going to mistake him for a bad guy.

As she watched, he lifted an insulated cup and took a sip.

Kenna glanced at the woman to check she hadn't gone anywhere, and then knocked on the window. When he spotted her, she waved with her uninjured hand.

He lifted his coffee cup in a salute and started walking toward her.

Kenna said, "I guess my ride is here."

The woman stared at her.

"I'm sure the police will be interested to find the person whose fingerprints are on that knife. The one used to kill Simon, an innocent man just trying to live out his life in the house he shared with his wife."

"A sob story? Really?" the woman said. "Am I supposed to be moved with grief over what I've done and try to convince you I've seen the light? I'm a changed woman, hallelujah. Take me with you, and I'll tell you everything. I definitely won't get what I want from you, kill you, and then prove my loyalty to the people I work for by ending this little attempt at uncovering the company myself." She snickered.

"It was really nice talking to you." Kenna shot a fake smile in the woman's direction. "It's been such a lovely visit. We should do it again sometime."

The man appeared in the doorway, his Hawaiian shirt covering a stomach that suggested he appreciated many pints of beer in a row. Two days of stubble on his chin. He couldn't be more than five foot six, but she pegged him as having been military before he'd been in the CIA.

"Bruce Donovan, at your service." He put on a fake English accent that was decidedly terrible.

The woman rolled enough so that she could see him standing in the doorway.

Bruce stared at her. "This looks like it's been fun times."

Kenna knelt by her bag, shifted the handle over her head, and stood without using her hands. The bag bumped against her back. She stuck her fingers in her pockets. "There's a dead man in the house behind the backyard. We should find his dog and make sure it's going to be okay."

Bruce shook his head. "We're not sticking around long enough to find a dog."

"Then you're going to have to explain to me why I would trust someone who wouldn't even try to save a dog."

"That heart of yours is going to get you killed one of these days, Makenna." Bruce pulled a 9mm pistol from his waistband and pointed the attached suppressor at the woman on the floor.

Before Kenna could object, he squeezed the trigger.

The shot wasn't the usual fireworks sound, just a loud snap. The bullet embedded in the back of the woman's head.

Bruce stepped back from the doorway, turning sideways so she could get out. "Let's go get you something for that cut."

She didn't move...or look at the pool of blood on the floorboards. "If I object, are you going to shoot me in the head also?"

"Of course not. If I kill you, Stairns is never going to pay me the money he owes me for our last online poker game." He stuck the gun back out of sight. "Clock is ticking."

She stepped out into the hallway ahead of him.

Bruce followed her to the stairs. "Was she one of them?"

Kenna glanced back over her shoulder as she descended. "You killed her, and you don't even know the answer to that?"

He shrugged. "Why else would she be tied up?"

Kenna frowned and headed for the front door. She kind of hoped they would see the dog outside and be able to take it with them. But as soon as the police found the murder scenes, they would no doubt make sure the dog was taken care of.

She said, "Shouldn't we be removing our DNA from these scenes?"

He stood waiting for her to come with him. "From what I've gathered of these people, it's not like the truth of what happened here is going to come out anyway. Why go to the trouble of trying to fabricate the narrative when they'll just make up whatever they want?" She detected a hint of bitterness in his tone.

Kenna said, "Sore subject?"

"Let's just say I'm not out here because I *chose* to go freelance." He lifted her duffel from across her shoulders and tossed it in the backseat. "Get in."

Kenna buckled up, ignoring the pain in her shoulder. He turned on the engine, and hot air blasted out the vents. It seemed as if he wanted the interior of his beater to be a balmy eighty-five degrees. "Uncle Sam did you dirty?"

"How about we don't talk about how we got here, and we just talk about how we're going to fix the problem?"

He pulled away.

Kenna looked over her shoulder out the back window as the house disappeared from sight. The fog had lifted with the sun, and she spotted that yellow orb behind all the clouds.

"Turns out it's not just one problem," Kenna said. "I've got a whole heap of them."

Bruce hurtled the little car around a corner, going fifty-five on a skinny country road with hedges on either side instead of a shoulder. If a bigger vehicle came at them from the other direction, they were going to find themselves suddenly in a game of chicken.

"Complicated women with problems are my thing." He glanced over at her and grinned. "Or so my therapist tells me."

Kenna needed to talk to Stairns about this guy he'd sent to help her. She also needed Maizie to get into the phone she'd taken from that woman back there—hopefully in a way that wouldn't expose all of them. Again. Had Maizie solved her hacker problem?

Bruce reached over and nudged her knee with the back of his hand. "What's your thing?"

"Tall, blond FBI agents."

Bruce made a choking sound and touched his chest. "You wound me, Makenna Banbury. I'm heartbroken."

"Right now, my thing is coffee." And a way to deal with the wound on her left shoulder. "And Kenna is fine."

He grasped the wheel with both hands and careened around a corner. "Now you're speaking my language."

Chapter Twenty-Four

They drove about forty minutes to the center of a nearby town. Maybe a small city. Kenna was too tired to retain any of the weird names on the road signs. Finally, Bruce pulled out of the flow of traffic on a roundabout and took a sharp right turn onto the gravel that encompassed the front lawn of a two-story house.

"Safe house?" she said, just as soon as she had caught her breath from how quickly he came to a stop.

The parking area was barely big enough for his tiny car, which he had stopped at an angle in front of the house. Just outside her door, she had maybe a foot and a half of clearance before the four-foot-tall red brick wall that separated the car from the street.

"Used to be." Bruce pushed the door open on his side

and climbed out with a groan. He leaned in the back door to grab her duffel. "Now it's just my house. One of them." There was a lilt of Boston in his accent, but it came and went like a tide.

Who knew what kind of work he had done for the CIA. Maybe he hadn't even been retired for very long. Kenna didn't want to sit in the front passenger seat any longer just for the sake of figuring it out.

She reached across her body with her right hand and pushed the door open, so she didn't have to use the injured left one. The pain had intensified through the drive, and now her arm was busy trying to go completely numb.

Hopefully, his idea of medical care for knife wounds didn't involve a fifth of whiskey and a packet of dental floss.

Bruce used a key to open the door and held it wide for her to step in. "Mi casa es tu casa, and all that. Make yourself at home. I'll put some coffee on. Kitchen is through here." He shut the door behind her.

Kenna said, "You should probably lock the door, right?"

"I'll add the deadbolt. But British front doors lock themselves." He turned a latch on the back of the door. "All the windows have to have locks. The house has to have an alarm. Heaven forbid you didn't check all the boxes of what you're supposed to do, and someone breaks in. As if I'd claim on my homeowners insurance if all the stuff I've got stashed away in here actually got stolen." He strode past her, chuckling to himself. "Let's take a look at that arm."

Kenna followed him into a surprisingly modern looking kitchen. "Okay, I have to ask something, because is it just me, or does no one in this country have a refrigerator?"

He glanced over, filling the carafe for the coffee pot in the sink. "You're looking for a giant thing with double doors? Or something with doors at the top and a huge freezer drawer at the bottom?" He lifted one hand and raised it up to the top of his head. "About this high?"

"I live in an RV, but yeah." She looked around. "Where's the fridge?"

"Interesting thing to fixate on, but I guess I'd want to know where the ice cream is as much as the next guy." He turned off the tap and set the carafe full of water on the counter. Then he leaned over and opened what she had thought was the dishwasher, tucked under the counter. "Fridge." He pointed to the other end of the kitchen. "Washing machine behind those doors. Don't ask me why it's in here, but it is."

"Where would you put a dryer?" The room didn't seem big enough.

Bruce shot her a look. "Why would I need one when I can hang my clothes up to dry *outside* in a country where it rains intermittently whenever it feels like it for no reason at all?"

Seemed like he didn't much like living here.

"I know you got burned, but why can't you go back to the US and live a quiet life there?" Kenna dragged out a chair and sat.

He finished making the coffee. "No passport. Only a fake ID, and I don't want to spend two weeks in a shipping container with no cheese puffs. Besides, if I did that, then who would help people like you?"

"If you do help me, and when were done you decide you want to go back to the US... Maybe we can figure it out."

"What if I want to go to Thailand?"

"Let's see if we survive the next week first. Then we can talk about it."

He opened the cupboard under the sink and pulled out

a huge tackle box, which he opened on the table. Inside was all manner of medical supplies. "Gonna take your shirt off?" He waggled his eyebrows.

Kenna stuck her finger in the hole in her shirt and ripped the sleeve down.

"Yeah, I guess that works, too." He opened a couple of packets and wiped the cut with something that made it sting.

Kenna pursed her lips and blew out a breath. "Thanks."

"Are you gonna keep thanking me every time I do anything through this whole thing, or are we gonna keep my ego from exploding my head and maybe just work the problem?"

"I'll say whatever I want to say, and you don't get to tell me if it's okay or not."

Bruce grinned. "Fine, stroke my ego."

"I will not be stroking anything."

He tipped his head back and laughed aloud. "Good to know—if I was interested, which I'm not. I actually dated a woman from that town we were just in. Broke up a couple of weeks ago when things started to get weird. It's been occurring to me since we left there that the whole town is like that. Insulated." He stuck the cut together with tiny pieces of tape and then taped a piece of gauze over the wound. "I'm assuming you don't want me to staple this shut."

"What you did is good. As long as you give me a cup of coffee, too."

"Demanding, aren't you?" He glanced at the clock.

"Only when you have information I probably need about a town I just went to. And the house where my mother grew up."

"Stairns filled me in on the whole thing. In fact, I made a couple of calls on my way over here and found a friend of a friend." He glanced at the clock on the wall. "A friend who should be calling me back anytime now."

He went to the coffee pot and poured two cups, so she gathered all the trash and disposed of it.

That woman had been an assassin there to kill her. She couldn't get the mental image of Simon falling to the floor out of her head.

Kenna sat at the table and put her forehead in her hand, her elbow braced on the top of the table. Her other hand loose in her lap.

She couldn't even find the words to say to start praying about everything. Let alone begin to make sense of it all. Overriding everything was this feeling of *what am I doing here* that she couldn't shake.

A cell phone started to ring. Just a soft vibration, and Bruce tugged it out of his front pocket. "There he is." He answered the call and put the phone to his ear. "Whatcha got for me, Petey?" A second later, he nodded. "Don't worry, I will."

Bruce hit a button on the cell phone and set it on the table. "You're on speaker."

On the other end of the line, Petey said, "I'm gonna get the sack for this," in a thick British accent.

Bruce said, "If you're fired, it's on me. Didn't I say I would make you a rich man? I don't let down my friends. Now can you do it, or not?" He glanced at her and mouthed, *This is why you should trust me.*

"Of course I can do it," the guy on the phone said. "Will told me you're good for it. Just hold on a sec. And don't say anything until he's on."

Kenna frowned.

Through the phone line, she could hear muttered snatches of conversation. Then a buzzer sounded, followed by the clang of a metal door. More muttering, low conversation through the phone line.

"Hey, FBI. Like Bad Boys, right?" He started to sing the song, and it was a pretty terrible attempt at vocals. "Come here. Got a call for you."

A call?

Two seconds later, someone said, "Hello?"

Kenna snatched the phone, took it off speaker, and put the phone to her ear, shoving her hair back from her face with her other hand, even though it hurt her shoulder. "Jax?"

"Kenna?"

Across the kitchen, Bruce mouthed the words, *You owe me.* The guy looked pretty pleased with himself. Then he trailed out of the room and left her to it.

Which was a good thing—the fact that he left—because she started to cry. "Jax, is it really you?"

"I have no idea how you managed this. Maybe I don't want to know. Please don't tell me you have a plan to break me out of British prison. They're just interviewing me. Do not tell me that you're here to bust me out, Kenna."

"I don't know how to get you out." She tried to take a breath. "Stairns said your dad was sending a lawyer." She sniffed, rubbing her nose.

"Are you okay?"

Kenna almost laughed, but there was nothing funny about any of this. "Should I be okay? Because I'm far from it."

She wanted to tell him that two more people were dead. That this case had cost even more lives. But he was facing something that might be worse for him than a quick ending. Not that she wanted him to suffer either. Prison time? She didn't wish that on anyone, let alone someone who didn't deserve it.

"I love you." His voice was soft against her ear.

"I love you, too, but what good does that do us right now?"

He chuckled.

"I'm serious, Jax. These people are way more powerful than us." She took a sip of her coffee, gulping down a couple of mouthfuls. She needed all the caffeine-infused brainpower she could get right now. "How on earth am I going to take them down when we'd barely scratched the surface, and they did this?"

She heard a noise in the background of the call, and he said, "I've got to go."

She wanted to ask him to stay on the line as long as he could, but at the risk of his freedom? Her comfort wasn't worth it.

He said, "You know how to do this, Kenna. Just solve it like any other case."

The phone beeped in her hand, and the line went dead.

Kenna set the cell phone down. She took a couple more mouthfuls of coffee. Picked the phone up again, which thankfully, hadn't locked yet, and dialed Maizie's secure number.

After two rings, someone picked up. "This is Stairns."

"Are you really sure about this Bruce guy? He didn't let me check on the dog."

"Yeah," Stairns cleared his throat. "I can see how you might think he's sketchy. But right around the time the media was telling us that Saddam in fact did *not* have nukes in Iraq, my friends and I were halfway across the world, pinned down and cut off. It had been three days since we made contact, and there was still no sign that anyone even knew where we were. He walked. It was a hundred miles in enemy territory, and the minute he found out we were cut off, he spent those three days we were pinned down making his way to us. He fought his way through with the signal the Navy needed to lock onto in order to scramble jets and give us cover fire for a rescue operation."

"The kind of guy who can get an FBI agent who is in British police custody on the phone?"

Stairns' laughter rang across the phone line. "Yeah, that kind of guy. He never did tell me what operation he was working on in Iraq, but right about the time we were rescued, he disappeared. Turned up later on base, just to make sure we got back okay."

"Thanks," Kenna said. "I actually feel a little better now." Though, that was probably more from talking to Jax and knowing he was okay than it was about whether or not she could trust Bruce Donovan.

"I'm sure you'll feel even better when more reinforcements show up."

Kenna frowned. "What are you talking about?"

"Why don't you get some rest, and when you've slept, we'll figure out how to deal with this?" He was placating her.

Because he didn't want her to understand what he was really saying?

"I don't need to sleep. I need to get Jax out of jail." It might sound selfish, but if he was imprisoned in another country, he could hardly find a good time to propose to her! Maybe that was only one example in a long list of reasons why he should be free to go home, but it was the one she thought of first.

Okay, fine. She needed to sleep.

"I do have an update, though," Stairns said. "MSI got back to me. When I offered condolences for what happened to their people, they said we don't need to worry about the situation. In fact, the guy who answered the phone almost sounded like he was thumping his chest. I had Maizie send a message to Bear, but she hasn't had a reply."

"We don't need to worry about the situation?"

"Yeah," Stairns said. "It was a total 'we got this' thing, where we don't need to worry about anyone they're protecting."

"Which presumes they're still alive, right? But how can they not be dead?" And if not, then where were Preston, Hollace, and Nielson? If they were still alive, she should find them and make sure they were all right.

Stairns said, "If they are still alive, then hopefully, they have the good sense to get as far from this business as they can."

"Apparently, I don't have any sense." That, and she couldn't shake what Jax had said. She should work the case like it was any other investigation. That meant starting with the disappearance of those victims and figuring out where they had been taken.

Or something else she couldn't think of right now.

It would keep her busy, but did she really need to risk everything? The risk was high. She wasn't sure she wanted to see just how far they'd go to stop her.

Stairns said, "You're in England. Eat some baked beans on toast, drink some tea, and when you're done, everything will seem a little bit better."

He hung up the phone about the same time Bruce wandered in and said, "So what's the plan?" He dumped an armful of clothes on the table. "These belonged to my uh... lady friend. She was about your size."

"Thanks." First, she was going to try and take a shower without getting the bandage wet. Then, they needed to pay a visit to the restored Hadley house. "How do you feel about a field trip?"

Bruce grinned. "I thought you'd never ask."

Chapter Twenty-Five

The sign beside a football-field-sized stretch of gravel read, "Car Park." Half full of compact cars and small SUVs, Kenna spotted a handful of older couples on the grass field, some of them with little kids. Toddlers running around the expansive lawn in the sunshine.

Given how foggy the morning had been, it was warm. This was the first sun that Kenna had felt on her face in days. Warm enough that she gave in to the need to lean back against the side of the car and close her eyes, the golden rays touching her skin.

For some reason, stopping to acknowledge it gave her a sense of peace that she hadn't had a moment before. It made her want to thank God for just that little bit of light.

"Now you know why Brits all vacation elsewhere. In

places where it's actually sunny all the time." Bruce used his key to lock the car doors.

Kenna glanced around. "I actually like it here. I like moody, misty mornings and the chill in the air."

Even with the sun, it still wasn't all that warm out here. She zipped up her jacket, aware of the odd sense of being without any kind of weapon. But with her face all over the news and the police actively looking for her, it wasn't worth being caught in possession of a weapon.

Bruce had procured a blonde wig from somewhere.

She wasn't going to ask where he got it from, but even with that, she wouldn't go undiscovered forever. Eventually, cops here would catch up with her. Or the State Department. She just prayed that she had enough evidence to plead her case with some kind of proof when that happened.

They walked across the gravel. Their shoes crunched the shifting stones, and they headed over to a wooden sign that indicated the tea rooms and gift shop were to the left, and the entrance to the house was to the right.

She said, "Are you going to flip out about me thanking you if I say it one more time?"

"I had a guy who owed me a favor."

"So it's no big deal that you got a cell phone all the way into the hands of a guy being questioned in connection with terrorism? I'd hate to see what you *do* think is a big deal."

Bruce grinned. "Not many people would survive that. I'll be okay though, because I'm a little bit more like a cockroach."

"Good to know."

If Stairns said he was a good guy, that was all Kenna needed to know. After all, it wasn't like they were going to become besties. However, if they did resolve all of this and they were still alive at the end, she fully intended to honor her promise to figure out a way to get him back to the US. Or wherever else he wanted to go.

Maizie could probably pull off a solid fake ID. Or Ramon would know who to call for that.

Bruce said, "I went online and bought us tickets already." He turned his phone around and showed her the QR code on the screen.

"If you want me to stop thanking you, then you should probably stop doing things for me." She patted down the side of the blonde wig, under which she had tucked her long dark hair.

She probably looked ridiculous, but hopefully, no one would look too closely at her while she did some recon in this house.

Bruce held out his phone to the older man in a polo shirt at the folding table beside the small path that led around the corner between two hedges. As they passed between the green manicured border, the house came into view.

She'd caught a glimpse of the side view on their way in, but the front of the house was like something from a Victorian era novel. "It's impressive."

She stared up at the weathered stone exterior, tall columns on either side of the front door. Windows in rows on the ground floor and the first floor above it.

"You can't deny that they make things that would stand the test of time," Bruce said. "Or they used to. Seems like nothing lasts these days. Stuff just breaks, and then you have to replace it. Materials are whatever is cheapest."

"Or someone comes along and burns the whole place down, and you have to rebuild it."

He turned to her. "I thought we were just here to look around."

"I was talking about my dad." Like with that pub in London, Kenna found herself in another place where her father had been. Walking in his footsteps, maybe even literally. It was different than knowing her mother had grown up in the house Kenna spent time in last night and that morning.

But she didn't want her thoughts to drift to Simon and his violent death.

She focused on looking at the house.

"Your dad? That's a shame. You were giving me some good ideas." He grinned at her, then headed for the front door.

She followed him into an alcove that looked a whole lot like the vestibule of an old church. Red carpet runners. Stone walls that arched up above her head, where tapestries hung down every few feet like banners.

Another staff member, this one an older woman with curly white hair and the same polo shirt, greeted them. "Lovely day today."

Kenna smiled and turned to look at the long hallway to her right. As if distracted by the inside of the house.

Bruce said, "Yeah, it is," in a thick British accent a lot better than the one he'd butchered earlier.

Kenna stood at one end of the hallway while Bruce spoke to the woman behind her. The woman said, "Feel free to walk through the house, keeping to the designated pathway."

"Thank you." He said ma'am at the end, but it sounded a lot more like "mum." Bruce caught up to her, one hand on the small of her back. "Come along, dear. You're the one who wanted to see the house." He sounded like a disgruntled husband.

Kenna walked with him. "You do that pretty well."

"I've been here long enough. All I watch on TV is British shows, unless I want to watch a movie." His expression made her wonder if he got homesick seeing Hollywood films. "It doesn't take too long to pick up the accent. I just have to think about it when I talk."

The hallway was wide and long, and the walls stretched up two floors. Paintings lined one side, each a portrait of an uptight-looking man starting from what looked like a medieval era, transitioning to more modern times by the last one.

On the other side, between the windows with their tall, heavy-looking drapes, stood a cabinet full of trinkets. Books. Silverware and gold cups. A couple of people milled around, looking at all the things.

The two of them walked slowly as if they actually were here to look at the stuff in this house. At the other end of the hall was a wide staircase that ascended at the sides to meet in the middle at the top. Underneath was a set of doors that had been roped off.

Bruce led her to the right-hand staircase, and their footsteps echoed on the dark wood, polished by years of use. "Can you even imagine living in a house like this?"

"Seems more like the kind of place you would entertain in just to show off to your friends. Or even people you don't like at all. Meanwhile, the nanny is raising your kids—or they're sent to boarding school."

"I walked to school. I wore my older brother's hand-me-down clothes, and for fun, we went to the library and checked out books."

Kenna smiled at him. "I was obsessed with the library when I was a kid. Pretty much homeschooled myself until high school. We settled in Florida, and I graduated from high school in Miami."

"I've always wondered if your dad's books that were made into movies were based on real cases. Or if he sensationalized them."

Kenna rolled her eyes. "I don't know what life he thought he lived, but I wasn't there for any of that."

"But his famous detective had a daughter. He was a single dad, struggling to make ends meet."

"Kicking in doors and taking down bad guys before the police even got there." She stopped to look at a child's dollhouse, all constructed with wood and painted. Worn from years of affection. "Why didn't he ever think that it might affect his credibility that he told lies about what he did for a living? Didn't he ever think about the fact that embellishing makes people wonder what else he didn't tell the truth about?"

"He obviously had a reason to tell those stories like he did. If you read his books, you can see some of who he is peeking through. It's almost like a code. Like solving a mystery, but the mystery is what kind of detective he was. What kind of man."

Kenna glanced over at him and frowned. "They're just books. I think you're reading too much into it if you think there's a code hidden in the pages."

"I mean... It would be cool if there was."

She rolled her eyes. "We have enough problems without you making up stuff about my dad."

"Sometimes fiction is better than reality."

"Maybe it's always better. But it's not always helpful." She was pretty sure there was a verse about that, urging moderation. "When I have some down time, I'll be sure to read one of his books and email you if I have any theories over what he's trying to say."

For now, they needed to find a way into the parts of the

house the public wasn't allowed access to. So far, every room had been staffed, but toward the end of the tour, she spotted a dark staircase.

Visitors were meant to head up to the rooms where family members had bedrooms and sitting rooms. Kenna checked both ways and tried the handle on a side door that read, "employees only."

"Make it fast," Bruce said.

The door wasn't locked. She ducked through, and he followed her, closing it quietly behind him. "Did someone see us?"

"Depends if they have cameras on every inch of this place or just the public areas. Either way our time back here is probably limited."

They headed down the long hallway, doors on either side that said "office" or "storage" on tiny bronze plates. She spotted a bathroom. At the end of the hall, an old stone staircase led down to the ground level. It continued down, but through an open door, she saw a gray-haired woman with a round figure lean back and spot them.

She eyed them, wiping her hands on a towel. She wore black pants and a white shirt with flat black shoes that had rubber soles, a white apron tied around her waist. "Lost?"

Bruce sauntered a couple of steps forward, putting some swagger into his walk. "We paid extra for the *private* tour." This time, his accent was sleazy American, the kind of guy who thought he could get access to anything just because of the color of his passport.

He leaned one elbow up on the frame of the door, which led into the kitchen where she was, effectively blocking Kenna from view. Kenna looked around but didn't see anyone else. Was this woman the only one in there?

"I've been working here more than twenty years. There's no such thing as a private tour."

Her words were as effective as saying, "get back upstairs now." Making Kenna wonder if she had been a nanny—or a prison guard—at some point in her life.

"Twenty years." Bruce shifted his stance, relaxing against the doorway. "Wow, that's impressive. You must know a lot of the history of the house and all the things that've happened over the years."

She said, "I could tell you some stories, that's for sure."

He chuckled, a warm sound that had a low and easy tone to it. Was he turning on the charm?

Kenna wandered to the side and tried a different door, finding only cleaning supplies. There weren't any other doors on this floor. She needed to go down another level, beneath the ground. That had to be where she would find what she was looking for.

She had checked her father's journal before she left, but there had been nothing in it about this house. Only a single entry that indicated the case was closed. No details. No information about the fire or the death of the duke.

She left Bruce to chat up the woman, distracting her from the fact they were trespassing outside of the bounds of the tour. Kenna took the stairs down another level and found a door with a very modern-looking lock. She slid out a bobby pin from under the wig and snapped it into two pieces, using the sharp ends to work the lock.

Probably in view of the camera trained on this door. But she couldn't think about that.

Kenna gave it the time she needed and managed to get the door open. Just in case Bruce followed her, she flipped the lock on the inside of the door to keep the metal bolt out.

It caught on the frame before the door could close. Wedging it open for him to catch up.

Inside the hallway was remarkably different from the world upstairs, which was all opulence and old-world British history. This floor was a more modern structure with recessed lighting and white tile floor down the hallway. Walls on either side that were reinforced glass, maybe translucent plastic. Beyond them on either side, she found laboratory equipment. Testing stations with centrifuges. Cabinets of test tubes.

Past that was a room on the left where the glass wall had been turned opaque so she couldn't see inside. To the right was a bed usually found in a doctor's office.

"Precisely what you expected to find, isn't it?" A slender woman with dark features stepped out of the opaque room. The same woman Kenna had spoken to at the nightclub—Keziya, the duke's assistant. "Proof that we are monsters who experiment on unsuspecting women."

Kenna said, "The kind of people who suffer the loss of one lab in a terrible fire, and then rebuild in exactly the same place so that anyone like little ole me can come down here and find it."

Keziya's face took on a pinched expression. "Of *course*, because our entire operation, which has been in existence for nearly a hundred years now, is entirely about you. It's all here so that you can discover us and expose everything. Right this wrong. Bring justice to the world. Isn't that how it goes?"

"Tell me how kidnapping people isn't wrong," Kenna pointed out. "The last I checked, it was against the law."

"Haven't you kept up with the shifts in culture? We're not victims anymore. It's about consent. It's always about consent."

Kenna said, "You expect me to believe they agreed to this?"

Maizie certainly hadn't. And neither had Kenna's mother, or so she would guess. They both had the misfortune of being born into the wrong family. Victims of other people's display of their own greedy power.

"Of course they agreed. That way you have no case. You're simply harassing us." The woman's dark eyes studied her intently.

"Harassing you?" Kenna huffed. "One of your people tried to kill me." She shook her head. "You can't expect me to believe they agreed to participate in this."

Keziya shrugged one shoulder. "If I do my job correctly, so will you."

Chapter Twenty-Six

Hadley House
Wednesday 2:48pm

"You think I'm going to..."

Kenna's thoughts stuttered to a stop. Everything seemed to shift beneath her. Everything she'd assumed she knew about these people and this case.

"You're delusional if you think I'm going to agree to anything you want. But then, I guess sane people don't do stuff like this."

Before the other woman could respond to that, the door behind Kenna creaked open. She glanced far enough to see Bruce come through. But not so far that she lost sight of the woman. This wasn't quite the same kind of predator she had met in her mother's house. That woman had been a weapon. This one standing in front of her, supposedly the duke's assistant, was an entirely different breed.

More like an empress or a queen.

Kenna wondered if the duke even understood what was going on.

The door clicked shut behind Bruce, and he came to stand beside her, his left shoulder slightly in front of her right one. Standing in a way he could take whatever came at her on himself. The way Kenna did with the people she cared about. She wouldn't even hesitate to give her life if it saved someone in her family.

Still, there was nothing she could do to help Jax right now but this. And it seemed like things just got a lot harder.

"You know who this is?" Bruce asked without even looking at Kenna.

"She's just the duke's assistant. Probably picks up his dry cleaning and fetches his coffee." She just wanted to see the look on the other woman's face as she heard that.

Keziya didn't disappoint. Her expression became decidedly pinched, and she sucked in a breath through her nose.

Bruce said, "I don't think she likes that," dropping his pseudo-British accent and becoming American again—though, with zero trace of Boston in his voice.

"I think you're right."

Keziya took a half step back and motioned to the side door she had emerged through. "If you'll hear me out, I can assure you our offer is quite fair."

She stepped through the door, and Bruce turned to Kenna, one eyebrow raised. Kenna whispered, "They want me to agree to something."

"A fool's bargain or a devil's trap?" He stepped through the door first.

Kenna followed him into a small office with the single white shiny plastic-looking desk that curved to the floor. On top of which was a wide white-backed monitor, the kind with the PC built in. Not the kind Kenna could stick a flash drive in the side without being noticed. Not that she'd brought one with her, though she and Maizie had done something similar at other times.

Could Bruce get Keziya to leave the room long enough for Kenna to type on her computer?

Not likely. This woman seemed entirely too smart to be duped like that. Even for the chance at getting Maizie access—if that helped the teen in the middle of an ongoing cyber-attack.

Keziya eased her chair up to the desk, steepling her fingers on the surface so that her index fingers touched her lips. She studied Kenna and Bruce for a second, then lowered her hands.

"I can assure you that our company is not in the least bit delusional. We haven't been successful for this length of time without knowing exactly what we're doing and executing it with due care and attention."

"Until my father came along and burned this house down."

Keziya's lips twitched just a fraction. Barely visible. "Merely an inconvenience, I assure you. And long before my time."

Kenna said, "Sure, sure. That's why you had my mother murdered."

"You appear to have a terrible impression of us, Ms. Banbury. I'm certain no amount of attempting to convince you of the extensive good we have done for this world will serve to change your mind." She rolled her shoulders, flexing the high neck of her black business dress and making the gold necklace she wore glint in the light from overhead.

Beside her, Bruce said nothing. Acting simply as the muscle? Or cataloguing everything about this place, this woman, and each word that came out of her mouth?

Kenna shifted her weight from one foot to the other, feeling the aches and pains of the last few days. "Let's see. You capture young women, impregnate them. Raise the children and brainwash them into doing everything you asked them to do because you've taught them that even the slightest dissension is rewarded with something out of a nightmare. Did I miss anything?"

"How about our advances in medical science, or the wealth of research we have done and shared?"

Kenna thought she might've heard Bruce snort under his breath, but he didn't move, and his expression didn't shift. Not that she could see much of it from the side view.

"And does that void the harm that you've done? Aren't doctors supposed to vow to help people and not hurt them?"

"It must afford you a simple and straightforward life to believe that everyone in the world is either good or evil," Keziya said to them. "I've discovered things aren't quite so black-and-white. People don't always behave in ways that are expected. Results astound even the most experienced scientist. Take you, for example. The child of two quite different worlds. Two sets of genetic history merging in the person standing before me now. The things you have done should not be taken for granted by the world. The lives you have saved and the killers you have brought to justice."

"What about Bruce?" If Keziya answered Kenna's question, then she would know just how much research they had done. How much they knew about where she'd been the last two days and who this was with her.

Keziya leaned back and slid out a central drawer an inch or two deep that opened on her lap. She pulled out a yellow envelope that thunked when she tossed it onto the table. "Passport, New York State driver's license. Fifteen thousand dollars—a cashier's check payable to your new, completely clean ID. And a one-way ticket home. Welcome to your life, Brian Clauson."

Bruce's body flexed, as if he wanted with everything in him to go over and retrieve it. That envelope likely represented everything he'd been waiting for since he was burned by the CIA.

He hadn't told her really anything about how he'd come to be let go, but once a spy was burned, they could be taken out by anyone from any government at any time. Disposed of by any foreign agency. The CIA and the US government would turn away and do nothing, disavowing any knowledge that he had ever been tied to them.

"I guess you thought of everything," Kenna said. And they'd done it incredibly fast. Blindingly fast, in fact. "And you think sending Bruce back to the US means I'll be alone and cut off from my support system? Maybe I'll be vulnerable enough to agree to whatever insane plan you're going to run by me, thinking I'll go along with it while Oliver Jaxton sits in jail." It was still odd saying his name like that, but she needed it to be more formal, even if they understood how she felt about him.

They weren't in her head.

Kenna needed distance from the things that made her vulnerable. Maizie. Her feelings for Jax. The fact she wouldn't hesitate to die for the sake of those she loved. But what would that achieve? She wouldn't get what she wanted even if she accepted a noble death because she'd been fighting for justice.

What good was making the world a better place if she wasn't here to see it?

Keziya leaned back in her chair. "You aren't willing to listen to what I have to say?"

"I'm sorry, I can't hear you over the sound of the ringing

in my ears. Unfortunately, I was close to a car that exploded a few days ago, and I'm still having hearing trouble."

She heard a tiny snort from Bruce.

Kenna continued, "After that explosion, which killed my friend and two men who were supposed to be protecting him"—she didn't know if Keziya believed Preston was dead or alive—"my name was dragged through the media as being behind an active shooter situation, even though I was nowhere near it."

"I thought you were outside," Keziya said. "Coordinating it all from your cell phone before you made a run for it. Then you disguised yourself and took the train north to Nottinghamshire."

Great, they thought they knew everything.

Kenna said, "Now I'm on the run, hunted by the headmistress. Right? That's who showed up at the house to kill me. I was left to fend for myself against a police manhunt."

"I don't think they call it that here," Bruce said over his shoulder. "Manhunt isn't very politically correct."

"Either way, the result is the same." Kenna shrugged the shoulder that didn't have a knife wound. "You cut me off from the people who care about me, break me down to nothing, and then I'm ready for you to hit me with your sales pitch."

Before Keziya could speak, Bruce said, "It's an advanced tactic. Comes from a whole lot of vicious intention. They want what they want, and the only way they think you'll give it to them is by making you believe you have no other choice. Like I can't find my own way back to the US. I need them to pull all their strings and get me there, only when I arrive, or sometime down the road, I realize there's a price to pay. Some kind of hidden fine print I wasn't aware of when I took the deal. Now I'm stuck working for them. Doing things I never would've done, but they threaten me that I have no choice if I want to keep my freedom."

Keziya lifted her chin. "It's not like there's much you wouldn't do. I've read your file, Bruce."

"And you believe people can't have a change of heart?"

"Like Preston?" She laughed aloud, one single sharp sound. "You've 'seen the light,' I suppose?"

"Why not?" Kenna shrugged that one shoulder again. "I did."

She was so over this conversation. They'd come down here to get intel. It just hadn't been what she'd ever expected it would be. She didn't want to feel like every second she was alive, these people were in hot pursuit of her. Or as if any second, the police would bust in and arrest them all.

Maybe that's all this was.

"You're trying to distract me. Throw me off my game."

Keziya frowned, shaking her head a tiny bit. "I don't know what that means." She said it like her highbrow upbringing couldn't comprehend Kenna's blue-collar phrasing.

"And you expect me to believe you need my DNA or whatever?" She could lean into her dad's way of doing things in a heartbeat, a life that had her unaccustomed to fancy things. Not like Keziya, the kind of woman who lived a monied lifestyle. Wearing fancy, tight clothes and walking across the deck of a million-dollar boat in expensive heels.

Thank You, God. That was not the kind of life Kenna was interested in. But it was the way Jax had been raised.

Was that the problem she had with meeting his mother? That she would in every way not measure up to the kind of woman his mother thought he should be with. Even if it was his choice. Even if Kenna had a sizeable inheritance.

Maybe she just preferred to be who she was without having to feel inferior.

Of course, I have this epiphany right now.

She didn't need to be distracted by random revelations in the middle of this situation, but her mind seemed to want to disassociate from what was happening in front of her. It usually did that by turning her mind to thoughts of Jax.

Nice thoughts.

Very nice ones.

She'd rather he was here, though.

Keziya said, "You are one of us, Ms. Banbury. Whether you choose to acknowledge it or not."

"Great." *So great.* "It's been nice talking to you, but we should go now." She tugged on Bruce's elbow and turned to the door. "I'm sure I'll see you again soon."

"At least think about what I've said. You can't deny the good we've done in the world," Keziya called after them. "The duke vowed to turn things around, and he has done."

"Sure, I'll look into it." Kenna stopped at the door. "Right after you let go of every woman who went missing this time, have Jax released with no charges, and clear my name." She lifted her hand and pointed her index finger at the woman, her thumb up in the air like a gun. "Thanks. Bye."

She put her arm through Bruce's, and they walked to the door at the end of the hall.

"Why are we in a hurry all of a sudden?"

"I don't like it." She paused a second while he opened the door, then stepped through. "It feels wrong. Something is going on."

"Your instincts are going haywire." He caught up with her on the stairs and nodded. "You should listen to them."

"I feel like I can't trust anything right now." She winced. "Maybe you should've grabbed that envelope."

"I don't want anything these people have to give me." Bruce glanced at her as they emerged in the lobby. The staffer in the entryway gave them the side-eye.

Kenna lifted her chin, and the two of them walked outside. She looked around but didn't see anything amiss.

"That's why I'm counting on you, because you don't trust them, and you didn't even think about listening to her sales pitch," he said. "That, and your instincts."

"Right now, they want me to run, fast and far."

"Cars are more efficient for that. Especially when you're injured."

Kenna waited until they were in the parking lot. "We should check it for explosives. Or tracking devices."

"Stay back."

She stopped by the hood of a compact Ford, but not a model she was familiar with. Bruce lay on his back and looked under the car. A light breeze on the air ruffled strands of the blonde wig across her face.

He checked all angles under the car and finally turned the engine on, standing in the space between the door and the seat. Ready to jump out of the way—as if that would save his life.

No explosion.

"Come on." Bruce motioned her over. "Let's get out of here. This place is creepy."

Kenna slid into the passenger seat, and Bruce pulled out, driving slowly to the entrance where a white van pulled in at the same time they slowed to pull out. She glanced at the side window and then grabbed Bruce's arm. "Stop. Stop the car."

She shoved the door open and pulled on the van's passenger side handle. The occupant was a six-foot Hispanic male wearing a dark jacket with a navy beanie over his hair.

"You cannot be serious." She pushed the door wide, wanting to grab his arm and pull him out onto the ground. Kenna knew why the expression was "spitting mad" because that was absolutely how she felt right now.

Ramon didn't even have the decency to look guilty. "I know you don't want to hear it—"

"Don't be mad!" The young, female voice that came from the back sent a bolt of ice hot fear through her. "We had to come!"

Stairns, in the driver's seat, winced. They had to have been on a plane when she spoke to them earlier. Already on their way here, because they thought she needed their help.

Ramon glanced away from her and spoke over his shoulder. "I told you she'd be mad."

Chapter Twenty-Seven

R amon walked into the house first. Maizie stepped in after him, with Kenna right behind her. She left Bruce and Stairns to follow them in. Each of her friends had a small suitcase, the kind that fit in an overhead luggage bin so they wouldn't have had to check it.

Kenna had been attempting to distract herself with mundane thoughts the entire drive over here. Otherwise, she would have started yelling the second she saw all of them.

This wasn't a conversation that needed to be had in front of witnesses. Or in view of any of the cameras that had been positioned around Hadley House.

They congregated in the kitchen, making the small space feel considerably smaller now that it was crowded with people.

Bruce closed the front door and walked into the room. He already knew Stairns, shaking hands with his friend before he turned to assess Ramon. Maybe he knew who the tall Hispanic man was, and maybe he had no idea. Lastly, he looked at Maizie. "Well, don't you look like trouble on two legs."

Ramon pushed off the counter toward the other man. As if he was about to leap over the table and pummel the guy.

Kenna held up a hand to her friend. "He didn't mean it. And you already know if he tries anything, I'll be the first one in line looking for vengeance."

"He won't get that far," Ramon said. "He isn't going to be trying anything."

Across the opposite side of the room, she watched Maizie take in everything that was happening. To her credit, the girl only seemed slightly wary about the situation. But that might be due to the amount of testosterone in the room and the topic of conversation being vengeance.

Ramon glanced at Kenna. "For the record, you do not look good as a blonde."

Right. She was still wearing the wig. Kenna reached up and took the pins out, using only her right hand to slide off the wig and shake out her hair.

Maizie frowned. "Did you hurt your arms again?"

Kenna shook her head. "I got stabbed. But that isn't what we came here to talk about." She glanced around at the four of them, as if Bruce was one of them and had something to answer for. "Why are you all here?"

Stairns had apparently told them that if it came down to this exact situation, he would be the one to talk. They kept their mouths shut while he took a deep breath and said,

"We knew you weren't going to like it, and that's why we didn't say anything to you about our travel plans."

"Because you knew I would tell you not to come," Kenna said.

"We did it safely. No one knows we're here."

He couldn't possibly believe that was true.

She said, "Then you missed who we're up against. I've been with Bruce less than twelve hours, and they already know everything about him." They'd known exactly what he wanted, although maybe it wasn't terribly difficult to figure out. Still, in the time given, they had crafted an entirely new—and clean—identity, and they had put together a packet that they'd been prepared to hand over.

Bruce was probably absolutely correct about them inevitably wanting something in return for it. After all, these were the kind of people for whom nothing was free.

"They know you're all here."

Maizie cleared her throat. "I know you're not happy with this..."

Before she could continue, Kenna clarified, "I'm furious."

Maizie winced. "I had to leave the Airstream at some point."

"Not like this."

The teen stood her ground, staring at Kenna with a steady expression on her face. "I wanted to see the house. I had to know if it was just a nightmare, or if it was a real place, and I'd been there."

Kenna had ridden back in the car with Bruce, neither of them saying much of anything on the drive over. "Did you see it out the window?"

Maizie nodded. "It was the same house."

"Makes sense, since they have suites of medical equipment and testing facilities down in the basement." Kenna lifted her chin. "Now that you've done what you came to do, you should go back to Colorado."

Maizie said, "Don't you want me with you?"

This wasn't the conversation Kenna wanted to have in front of witnesses, or three guys who didn't need to be privy to hers and Maizie's private conversations. But still, she needed to address this. "Not if it puts you at risk. These people are serious."

And not if Maizie was going to manipulate her with the emotional argument.

"These are the kind of people who won't think twice about victimizing any of us."

Maizie lifted her chin, and Kenna was so proud of her that she'd stood up for herself. Kenna just didn't like that it was this situation, where there was so much at stake. Maizie said, "They didn't want me before. Why would they want me now?"

Kenna's eyes burned with unshed tears. She ran a hand through her hair and squeezed the back of her neck.

Stairns said, "I think we're all overtired and in need of some rest. Why don't we get some sleep, and maybe things will look different in the morning?"

Bruce moved around Stairns to the hallway. "I'll grab some more blankets and figure out where everyone can crash. Assuming you're all staying here." He disappeared off down the hall and Stairns followed him.

Kenna glanced at Ramon. "Do *you* think sleep is going to solve all our problems?"

She might be exhausted, but if she lay down right now, was she even going to fall asleep? It would likely only mess up her schedule again when she had just acclimated. With all the issues swirling in her head, she had no idea how she was going to relax. And if she did manage to, that would only welcome thoughts about the ring in her duffel and Jax's intentions.

"It usually works for you. Taking a long nap." Ramon folded his arms across his chest, leaning back against the counter again. He lifted his chin in the direction Bruce had gone. "How well do we really know that guy?"

"He's fine. But it never hurts to keep an eye on someone." She told them about the assassin and how Bruce had rushed her out of there. "He's been with me since."

She stared at Ramon, and she saw on his face that he knew it was because she wanted to know why he had allowed Maizie to come here.

He understood her and what she *wasn't* saying.

She knew it for a fact when he said, "Maizie wasn't going to take no for an answer. Stairns was all in to help her get what she wanted, and I wasn't changing either of their minds. Figured you didn't want me to stay home when they left, so I tagged along."

From what she knew of him, because Kenna understood him—at least to the extent that he allowed it—she knew it was far more complicated than that. He'd felt like he had no choice. His loyalty to them was the reason he was here, not the worry that Kenna would think he slacked on his job.

Rather than tagging along, it was more likely that he had forced his way into the situation in order to keep Maizie safe.

"I feel like you guys are having an entire conversation just looking at each other."

Ramon and Kenna both looked at Maizie.

Both said, "We are" at the exact same time.

"Okay, that was spooky." The girl reached up and pushed hair behind her ear, a nervous action. "Can I be excused? Stairns said Bruce has an entire system set up, and I want to check everything, then get to work."

"Last time I spoke to you, you were dealing with a serious hack to your system. Did you just leave that and come here? Or you left it on the plane?" Kenna tried to keep any accusation out of her tone. Balancing the parenting aspect of this relationship with the fact that they were also coworkers, but Maizie was still a minor.

"Of course not. My laptop is in my backpack." Maizie rolled her eyes. "But I wasn't going to just let you get in trouble without trying to help. I might remember something because I'm here, and it could help."

"So how did you deal with the hack?"

Maizie winced. "I dumped the entire system when we were packing up. I deleted everything. I'll just have to reboot the original operating system from my backup hard drive when I get home."

And that was the crux of why she was worried about Maizie being here. "These people know what you can do. Maybe your genetics isn't what they're after, but do you really think they'll pass up the opportunity to have someone like you working for them?"

"I'm not a scared little kid anymore."

"You haven't been that in a long time." Kenna shook her head. "But it doesn't mean we don't all feel like a scared, trapped kid once in a while. It's just life."

"Then keep me safe." Maizie wandered to the doorway.

Kenna called after her, "If you want me to do that, then we're all on the first plane back to Colorado and as far away from these people as we can possibly manage. But it leaves Jax here, still facing whatever charges they want to bring. And it means we don't figure out what happened with

Preston. Everything gets dropped because we're going home."

Maizie had to understand that she'd pushed Kenna into a corner where she was forced to deal with even more on top of everything else she had in her lap right now.

"That's why we're all here, not just me." Maizie glanced at her, an entreating expression on her face. "So we can help you solve this case."

She went out, leaving Kenna with only Ramon in the room. She let out a long sigh, pushing all the relief and frustration and problems and fatigue away before she inhaled a lungful of fresh oxygen and the chance for new ideas. An exchange that was central to life as a human. Taking in clean air and exhaling toxins.

Such a simple act that it happened unconsciously. Until she felt the need for a second where she just focused on drawing in the one thing that would provide her brain with health and her body with the means to continue.

Ramon said, "You look like you're about to have a panic attack."

"Sometimes you just have to keep breathing because that's all you can do."

"You know I know that. And I know *you* know that." Ramon shifted, but she didn't look at him. "What neither of us knows is what's going to happen next."

"I don't like surprises. And I don't like when things don't make any sense."

He chuckled, a low sound that barely sounded like humor. "Yeah, no kidding. She is right though. With us all here, we can help out, and you'll make sense of this faster."

She turned to him then. "And if I ask you to go to wherever they are holding Jax and break him out of jail?"

"If he hasn't been charged yet, it might not be a good

idea to enact a jailbreak. That's just going to make him look guilty."

"Don't ruin my plan with your logic." She just wanted him here, because it would be one less thing to worry about. And because *she just wanted him here.* "He's in this mess because of me."

"So?"

She straightened. "What do you mean, 'so'? He wouldn't be under suspicion, facing whatever charges—I don't even know because I haven't been there—without the fact that he came here because I was here. Give or take a conference."

"We're all here because of you. Are you gonna get all bent out of shape if something happens to one of us?"

"Of course!" She wanted to grab his shirt and shake him, but they were already barreling to where they'd been in New Orleans. Kenna doing her job and Ramon mad because she wasn't including him.

"That's why we're here." He spoke slowly like she wasn't comprehending.

"I guess because you want me to be more vulnerable." She lifted her arms, then let them fall back to her sides. She pressed her lips together, not wanting to say something that would make him mad.

"Yeah, that must be it." His expression darkened. "Can't be because we think we can help, and we don't like the idea of *you* being alone and vulnerable, so we came all this way. Putting ourselves at risk to—"

Who knew how long he would've gone on for. Kenna waved a hand and cut him off, which, of course, painfully reminded her that she had been stabbed in the shoulder. "Fine. I get it."

"You're gonna have to figure this out. And then get over it."

Kenna pressed her lips together.

He said, "You'll happily go it alone and risk your life to save the people you care about. It's so noble it brings a tear to the eye. But is that how you want to go out? You'd never let someone else do that for you. So why do you get to be the one who always takes the risk? You're not less important or less valuable than the rest of us. We're not worth more than you. Why is it okay when you do it?"

"I'm supposed to stand by and let you put your lives at risk? Dangle Maizie in front of these people and pray they don't snatch her? Or watch Jax's career be destroyed?"

"You think I'm gonna let anything happen to Maizie?" Ramon shifted, his movement stiff. His body radiating lethal intensity.

"That only means you understand where I'm coming from."

"You're trying so hard to keep something bad from happening to one of us that you're tying yourself up in knots and forgetting to find the good because you're so intent on pushing away all the trouble. You can't prevent bad things from happening, Kenna. Not through sheer force of will."

"I'm trusting God."

"Are you?"

She gritted her teeth. He didn't even believe, so what did he know about how it worked? All she could think to say was, "I'm doing the best I can."

"And all we're trying to do is help so you don't have to *do your best* so hard. You deserve to be happy."

She flinched.

"We all know what you've been through, even though

you pretend like you've moved on. Maybe this is part of letting go. Not being so scared that it'll happen to you all over again with Jax—or Maizie. Or any of us. That you'll have to go on without us because you couldn't do enough to save us."

"This is the worst pep talk ever." She tried to smile but it didn't work.

"It's not a pep talk. It's your life. And you're so busy trying to make it free of loss and pain that you're forgetting the good stuff is right in front of you." He walked out of the kitchen then, leaving her alone.

There had been plenty of good in Phoenix, recovering at Jax's house. Quiet days and long talks. She'd been recovering, unable to do much of anything. Maybe that had made it feel safe, because the bad had already happened, and no one close to her had died. Now here they were on the next case. In another country because Preston and MSI had forced her hand. She was back to business as usual.

Pushing people into a spot where they'd be safe.

Even if that was away from her.

Chapter Twenty-Eight

Kenna awoke slowly, aware that someone else was in the room. She opened her eyes and focused enough to see Maizie. Sitting in a gamer chair, the teen typed furiously on a computer keyboard with a bank of three monitors in front of her, one of them turned vertically.

For a second, her mind decided she was in the Airstream, since that was where Maizie stayed almost one hundred percent of the time. But this was a house, not a trailer.

Everything came rushing back. She sucked in a breath and sat up, tangled in the blanket. Lying askew on a small couch that wasn't long enough for her to lie on, but this was where she'd fallen asleep. After all, no one else in this house was doubling up with a teen girl. Bonus, they didn't sleep at the same time, either. So it didn't matter that there was only one couch in the room and no bed.

Maizie stopped typing and spun around. She took one look at Kenna and said, "You're still mad."

Kenna kicked off the blanket and set her feet on the floor, feeling the carpet under her bare toes. "Give me a second to wake up before I have to have a conversation, okay?"

"Fine, because I nearly have something."

Kenna found the hall bathroom where she splashed water on her face, and then the kitchen for coffee, which she drank leaning back against the kitchen counter. Remembering the conversation she'd had with Ramon the night before.

She'd hardly forgotten it even while she had been sleeping, given her dream consisted of her running down hallways. Looking for Jax. Looking for anyone. Knocking on doors, yelling nonsense.

Now that she was awake, she had to admit that some of the things Ramon said were right. Giving your life for someone you cared about was noble. It wasn't like she was using it as a crutch, though. Or trying to control the outcome the only way she knew how. He'd been wrong about one major thing. She wasn't scared.

She was terrified.

Not furious, as she'd told Maizie. At least not in the sense of pure anger. No, this was an ice-cold mess of terrified fury all knotted up in her stomach. They hadn't even given her a heads-up or let her weigh in. They'd taken the choice from her and came anyway.

Which was exactly what she'd have done, but that wasn't the point.

She finished her mug of coffee on that note. The realization that she'd been avoiding exactly this. For years, she'd been determined not to rely on anyone again.

Care.

Love.

Lose.

Grieve.

The cycle went around and around, no matter how hard you tried to stop it. That was just life, and there was no escaping it. Even though she'd tried.

Who would blame her for doing whatever she could to try and mitigate the worst of it?

Compared to how much she wanted Jax here, how much she cared about this company and what they had been doing forever didn't even ping on her radar. Because if she let him swing for her—if she didn't do everything she could to get him back—then what kind of person was she? Not the kind who said she loved him and actually meant it.

Which was the problem with falling in love.

Kenna refilled her mug and went back to Maizie, where she sat back on the couch in the tiny bedroom with just a desk and the seat and nothing else. Just the window and hanging blinds. She took another sip. "Okay, what do you have?"

Maizie didn't turn around. "You sound less mad."

"I'm not mad at you specifically. Just all of you collectively." Because yes, she would rather take the risk alone.

Maybe it was the same reason she'd been going slow with Jax, even though she knew he might want to speed things up a tad. *Hello, ring in a box.* She wanted to dig it out and stare at it, but someone would see, and it wouldn't help her figure this out. *Afterward.* When he was here, then she'd have time.

They'd have time.

And that was the crux of it, wasn't it? The uncertainty of how much time there was left before something happened and whatever you had—a life, a relationship—was over.

Gone.

Like the family she should've had, the one she'd lost.

Now she had a new family, and knowing how it felt to be the sole survivor made everything so much more... desperate? Real?

She didn't even know how to feel about it.

"...even listening?"

Kenna winced and lowered her mug. "Sorry." Her shoulder didn't feel good, and neither did her arms, but what else was new? "Talk. I'm listening."

Maizie glanced over her shoulder, an assessing look on her face.

"I am."

"Okay, fine." She turned back to her computer. "I found a school. They call it a public school because anyone can pay the fees and go."

"They call a private school a public school." Kenna frowned. "Weird, but okay."

"So this one is pretty high-brow, but not like Eton or places like that—the ones everyone knows about because that's where royals go." Maizie typed on her keyboard, and a screen flicked over to the right hand monitor that Kenna could see. "This one is Derringbone College, even though it's a middle and high school, they apparently called it a college. Boys and girls. Separate dormitories."

"So it's a boarding school."

"Right. And that duke guy...Carrington Hadley? He went there. So did the woman Bruce said you talked to, Keziya Shatapathi, she went there. All her sisters."

Kenna took a sip of coffee. "What about Anne Constantine?"

Maizie typed. "Assuming I spelled it correctly, yes. I've got her."

"Simon said she went away."

"Huh?"

Kenna shook her head. "Don't worry about it."

"That's the name of... Hang on." Maizie shifted another window over, one that looked like a news site. "Two bodies found at the house that Sienna gave you the address for. Oh, and a dog."

"They killed the dog!" Kenna jumped out of her seat, nearly spilling her coffee.

"Two murders." Maizie turned to look at her. "It says that they think the dog died of natural causes."

"Really?"

Maizie nodded.

"That's sad. He was a good dog." She set her hand on the teen's shoulder and gently squeezed. "Thanks, Maze."

"So anyway, about this school."

"They all go there." Kenna shifted her stance and drank more coffee. "I should make breakfast."

"Stairns said he was going to." Maizie clicked, and a chat window popped up with messages from Stairns. Another thread, one she couldn't see, was between Maizie and Stairns' wife, Elizabeth, who was a licensed counselor. "He's awake. So the school..."

"I'm not going there." Kenna sipped her coffee. "They'll expect me to do that. If it's where Hadley went, and Keziya, and my mom. They'll be waiting for me to show up, assuming I'm figuring out where all the places are that they operate out of."

Simon had told her one girl went to school. One died.

Another was born later, when the schoolgirl was all grown up. Which one of the two surviving sisters was her mother?

"You aren't even going to consider going there?"

Kenna said, "They might want me to accept an offer to be part of what they do." Whatever that meant. She didn't know if Keziya had been throwing out random ideas, or if it was real. Kenna didn't want Maizie to feel bad that Kenna was being chosen, and Maizie hadn't been. "I don't want to be anywhere near these people."

"Because it puts me in danger?"

"I'm not talking about that." Kenna didn't want to discuss it, and this was about as "mom" as she was willing to get with the teen. "Let's just work the case. That's what Jax said to do, and it's what I'm going to do."

"I hacked into the school database. Want to see Keziya's grades?"

Kenna nearly laughed. "Maybe if you find something internal that sheds light on them, you could...anonymously dump it on the internet for the world to see."

"Oh, I like that idea."

Kenna wandered to the window, listening to Maizie's fingers press keys at an alarming rate she couldn't quite comprehend. She shifted the blinds aside and looked out at the back yard. Just a small square of grass that had grown long enough it was about a foot high and full of weeds and wildflowers.

To the side, beyond a flimsy-looking wood fence, was a perfectly manicured lawn. A stone pedestal in the middle sprayed water in an arc to the other side of the plate that stood on top. Rose bushes lined the back, along the fence. The juxtaposition of the two lawns, one unkempt and wild and the other pristine, reminded her of the difference between her and Jax. At least in the beginning.

She turned back to Maizie. "Tell me Stairns has an idea to get Jax back. I'm going crazy."

"You love him." She dragged out the middle word.

"I'm ill. There's something wrong with me. I can't go five minutes without thinking about him. I'm not a rational person anymore." She wanted to flop on the couch and be all dramatic about it.

"You spent months together over the winter. Why wouldn't you miss him now he's not just...there all the time?"

She made it sound simple. "He went to work. It isn't like we were glued to each other."

"You're supposed to miss him. Think about him all the time. Draw your names on a notebook and put hearts around it. Or so I've heard." Maizie sounded a little wistful.

"It sucks."

Maizie laughed out loud.

Footsteps thundered down the hall, and Ramon appeared in the doorway.

The teen turned to him, and he blinked at the expression on her face. Maizie said, "*Buenos dias, hermano.*"

He stared at her for another second, then wandered off, muttering.

"You speak Spanish now?"

"I downloaded the app that teaches you languages. So far, I'm terrible, but whatever. It's fun." Maizie grinned. "We need to get Jax back before your head explodes."

Kenna had several things she wanted to say to that. Instead, she just opted for, "Yeah, that's probably a good idea."

She wasn't supposed to *need* him. She was supposed to be a strong, independent woman. Only, if that was true, then why did he have to be so darn cute?

It was on the tip of her tongue to tell Maizie about the ring box, but that would only lead to more girl talk.

She finished her coffee, pacing the room while the teen did her thing. Finally, she had an idea. *Thank You, God.* "Okay, I've got it."

Maizie glanced over, still typing. She finished a few keystrokes without looking and then stopped. "What?"

"Find me the person they got to at the State Department in London. Dig into their employment records and everyone's finances. Find the person they turned—or planted—there."

"Don't they vet everyone to make sure they're legit?" Maizie asked.

"Gather all the info and have Bruce and Stairns figure out who has red flags they might not have noticed." She set her mug down by the monitor and went to the doorway. She yelled down the hall, "Ramon! After breakfast, we're going to London."

She heard a distant, "Okay!" from somewhere.

The door across the hall opened, and Bruce appeared. "What's with all the yelling?"

Bruce wore raggedy sweats and a T-shirt with holes in it. With his hair askew, he looked like he'd been on a three-day drinking binge. Or he'd had a fun reunion with an old buddy, and they'd finished the bottle, but because neither was as young as they had been, a three-day bender was a bad idea anytime.

Stairns came out of the bathroom, freshly showered. "Breakfast should be done cooking."

"I'll be there. Maizie needs your help this morning." She looked at Bruce. "Both of you."

They nodded, knowing whatever it was would be important, but that it would also be them protecting Maizie.

Kenna cared about that more than she could vocalize with any eloquence.

Stairns said, "What about the school?"

Maizie had told him about that? "I'm not going anywhere near these people. I'm over it. It's time to get Jax out from under suspicion."

She figured if they wanted her to join them, then they'd make sure she didn't end up in jail. Right? Although, maybe with her in prison, she'd be right where they wanted her—easy access. And wasn't that a terrifying thought?

Someone in the police force here, or the government, or in the US State Department was dirty—or all three. With the number of people connected to them, they might have sympathizers in every part of government. Pulling strings. Working behind the scenes, shifting the tide. Putting together iron-clad cases against federal agents. Making her public enemy number one.

Making her need to process this all over and over.

The last thing they were going to expect her to do was save herself. So it had to look like that was exactly what she was doing.

At least she had until Maizie found the sympathizer to figure out the finer points of her plan.

Then it would be "go" time.

Chapter Twenty-Nine

Richard Laughton, a Harvard graduate who'd spent four years working at the Pentagon, followed by ten years as a State Department attaché, had a gambling problem. One that put him 72,406 pounds sterling in the hole with some unsavory types over in Hackney.

He'd also had too much to drink tonight, something Kenna and Ramon had observed from across the street. He'd stumbled out of the pub just after seven thirty and swayed as he walked two streets over to the train station.

Ramon had insisted he drive, which had nearly resulted in them being killed several times, given he was driving from the wrong side of the car on the wrong side of the street. But Kenna wasn't sure she'd have done any better. They couldn't risk being seen in public until she had enough to make a stand that would result in her being cleared, so she stuck to the shadows and kept her hood low over her face.

Richard fought with the lock on his front door before he dropped his keys and swore loudly. He finally got in the door and closed it behind him without even realizing his alarm had been disabled, or perhaps believing he'd never set it in the first place.

Two steps into his entryway, Ramon was on him.

He slammed Richard back against the door and held him there with one arm across his throat. Richard yelped. "Nigel, I can explain—"

Kenna flipped on the hall light.

Richard frowned at Ramon. "You're not Nigel." He didn't even see Kenna.

"Correct, my friend. Who I am is way worse," Ramon said. "Which is why I'm going to ask questions, and you're going to talk." He tugged Richard away from the door.

The attaché stumbled and then spotted her. He let out a foul expletive.

"I'll respectfully decline." Kenna didn't move from her spot leaning against the wall. "Let's not let this become a vulgar affair. We can keep things civil. If you cooperate."

Richard glanced between them, his eyes flared and glassy. "Why should I listen to the two of you or tell you anything?"

Ramon grabbed his collar, walked him to the tiny living room, and shoved him into a recliner. Kenna closed the living room door and leaned back against it. "Because if you tell us everything we need to know, I'll give you £73,000."

Richard's eyes flared.

"Free and clear. No more worries that Nigel from Hackney will show up to break your legs." Until, of course, Richard went and got himself in the exact same trouble with someone else. That, or he'd take the money and not pay his debt but run and try to hide.

Maybe she should find Nigel and pay the guy directly herself.

Kenna said, "The way this goes is entirely up to you, Mr. Laughton. You know who we are, and you can probably can imagine the position we've found ourselves in. That means we're desperate. And desperate people can be... unpredictable."

"I'm supposed to be scared?" He found some bravado, rolling his shoulders and lifting his chin. "You leave DNA here, everyone will know that you guys were here. That you're the ones who murdered me. Have you seen how the Brits investigate a murder? They wear PPE, and they're *meticulous*. You'll never get away with it."

"Who says anyone will find anything?" Ramon's voice was cold, his tone flat. The epitome of what he'd been for years—a cartel enforcer. Whether he played the part well because he'd done those things before, or he just knew how to talk the talk, she didn't worry about too much. Whatever his past had been, he didn't do that kind of work now. He was the epitome of a changed life, leaving history behind and walking a different path into the future.

Could she do the same thing?

Ramon thought she should alter her course. Figure out how to...what, care a little less that they could be killed? Or not try so hard to keep them alive?

Or was it more about mitigating the risk to herself because they cared about her as much as she cared about them?

Kenna pushed off the wall and went to sit across from Richard, on his couch. "What's the alternative? You keep bouncing around between the rock and the hard place where you live. Playing your bosses, this company, and your creditors against each other so no one knows quite how bad things are for you?"

He didn't have an answer for that.

"This is a simple business transaction. That's all." Kenna lifted a hand and held her palm up, trying to good cop this guy. "You tell me everything you know about Hadley, and eugenics, generations of babies, headmistresses, a public school, and anything else. Dazzle me. In return, I'll hand you every dollar you need to pay off your debts."

Richard leaned his head back and groaned, running his hands down his face.

"This is the best offer you're gonna get." As far as she could see, his alternatives were jail time, getting his legs broken—or whatever crime bosses in the UK did—and the wrath of whoever was behind "the company" Sienna had mentioned.

He groaned. "I don't even know where to start. This whole thing is a giant mess."

"You're the guy they have in the State Department, right? What do they have you do?"

Richard's expression made him look like he was about to throw up what he'd consumed today. Hopefully, not in front of her, though. "I follow people, mostly. I copy reports and send them over. I just keep an eye on things, and some-times, I invite the right people to London."

"Is the ambassador in on it?" She hadn't been entirely sure about that guy, even when he gave her a photo from her mother.

"If he is, he's never said anything to me. These people... they compartmentalize everything. It's how they've gone undetected so long."

"Who is at the top?" Kenna figured it was Hadley. "The duke?"

Richard's expression twisted at that, something like disgust flashing on his face. "That poncey—" He cut himself off with a sound of frustration. "He probably thinks he's the top of the food chain. All those titled guys do. Flashing their money around in front of the rest of us, the ones who have to work for a living. We didn't get Mummy and Daddy to pay for us to go to the fancy school where they surgically implant the stick up your—"

"We get it." Ramon crossed his arms over his chest.

"So Hadley is part of it, but not the big boss." Kenna paused. "An operation like this must have someone at the top. Otherwise, it wouldn't be so organized. Do you know who is in charge?"

"Probably the King of England. Or someone who thinks he is," Richard said.

Super helpful. "Tell me something else I don't know. You want me to spend £73,000 for information, you'd better give me something astounding." Or a whole lot of somethings. She needed someone to explain this entire thing to her, but she wasn't going to admit that to this guy.

Better that he thought she was a serious threat to him.

Richard let out another frustrated sound. "The limo. The one that exploded!"

"What about it?" Kenna asked.

"No one was in it. They drove it around that corner by remote and then blew it." He pushed out a breath. "They claimed there were three people inside, but there weren't."

"To try and kill me. Is that what it was?" Her ears rang just thinking about that explosion. "Where is Preston?" Assuming, of course, that he wasn't dead.

Richard frowned. "They captured him before that, and those two guys. Like, a whole day before."

How was that even possible? Even MSI thought things were fine. "I talked to him on the phone that same day."

Richard shrugged. "Probably that AI program they have. These people have some crazy technology. Hello—they drove a car by remote just to blow it up as near to you as possible."

And whoever had spoken on the phone to MSI confirming they were safe was the same program?

"So they are trying to kill me." Hence, the assassin at her mother's childhood home. But why then would Keziya offer her a place in their operation? Albeit as a victim. It didn't make sense that they'd want her dead and also want her as part of their master plan.

Unless there was dissension in the ranks?

With Hadley wanting to be in charge, or work his way up, maybe Keziya had chosen to strike out on her own and make her own deals. Or one of them was working for whoever was the "boss," and the other was solo.

Richard lifted his hands, then let them fall back to his lap. "How am I supposed to know? I have my orders, and I keep my head down. Every month, they deposit money into my account."

"I'm sure your mother is very proud." Kenna stared at him for a moment. "Where am I supposed to find Preston? You can use your access to them to get me that information."

"Are you going to hold back that money until I get you what you want?"

Kenna said, "Keep talking. We'll see."

She could hardly believe it had been a computer program on the phone with her and not Preston. She still wasn't sure why he was here in the UK. His wife had been one of these people, and she was killed—like Kenna's mother. Meanwhile, he'd also been having an affair with the wife of the president at the time. All of it might be complex, but it didn't give her answers for why he needed to be here.

It certainly wasn't only about her finding out the truth.

Was he trying, in his own way, to finally take them down? To get revenge? The First Lady had been killed in a car accident. If that was what it was, of course. Maybe she was a victim of these people also and could be another thing he wanted justice for.

Which made her wonder...

Was Avery a child of the scientific research these people had done? The connection made sense, and the kind of man a President of the United States could be might also be the kind to pay for his child to be the cream of the crop, as it were. A step above her peers.

Richard leaned forward and put his head between his knees.

Kenna said, "Why was Oliver Jaxton put under suspicion for being connected to me? What do they gain from keeping him detained for questioning?"

"Of course you ask that."

She frowned. "What do you know?"

Richard winced. "You're not going to like it."

"And you're worried it'll jeopardize your payday? Is that it? Too bad for you I care more about people than money. But I'll tell you one thing. I'm not vindictive."

Ramon said, "She might not be, but I am."

Kenna didn't look at her friend. She kept her focus on Richard. "Why is Jax part of this?"

"Because you are." Richard shrugged.

"And?"

He sighed. "Fine. I *might* have heard that Hadley wants Jax so he can use him to lure you out."

"He's already sent assassins to kill me. Why go to so much trouble to draw me out? Jax is in prison." Did they think she was going to try and break him free?

"Who knows what the different cells are supposed to do? These people are organized, but if someone orders one cell to say, offer you part of this, and another is supposed to kill you, then maybe wires just got crossed. Or they want you to be confused and unsure what they want."

Ramon grunted. "Seems ineffective. You've got chaos and not the cold, calculated ambition we've been led to believe this organization has."

Richard said, "There might be rumors there's a sort of rebellion. A resistance. You know, like with the Empire. Someone always disagrees or wants to hinder the plan. Makes sense it would look like chaos because you can't see the global view."

Kenna resisted the urge to roll her eyes. "Do *you* know the global view?"

"I've spent enough time trying to figure it out, but here's what I've come up with." Richard took a breath, looking a little glad to be getting this off his chest. "They're insane. Like, mad-scientist, genocide-of-the-undesirables, bat crap crazy."

"Great." Kenna smiled, and it probably didn't look sweet so much as unhinged. "That's helpful, thanks."

He shrugged. "I call 'em like I see 'em. It's refreshing to get to do that about this."

"Do you know this woman?" Kenna pulled out a phone and showed him a picture of Keziya.

"Stay away from her. She's deadly."

"Why would she offer me a place with them?"

Richard's brows rose. "She did that? Probably so they could lure you in, and then torture you half to death before they use you as an incubator for one of their demon spawn." He shrugged. "I'm just saying."

"Considering I think there's a chance I might *be* one of those 'demon spawn,' I've decided to take offense to that."

"You should." Richard nodded. "These people are offensive. Like you wouldn't believe."

"What's that saying?" Ramon said, "Choose you this day whom you will serve."

Kenna glanced over at him. He'd been reading the Bible? "We all serve something."

Richard said, "I'm not one of their sycophants."

Maybe not, but he was certainly a slave to money. Or his addiction. Kenna said, "You've been working for them… how long?"

Richard thought for a second, then said, "Two years."

"And you have records of the transactions. The orders they gave you. Did you keep a paper trail? Just in case?" *Please.*

He winced. "They make sure the email deletes itself, and there's no record."

"What about the money deposits?" Surely his bank statement showed the money coming in. Even if it was an offshore account or some kind of untraceable online bank.

"They paid cash. I've spent the last bundle they left." Richard waved toward the wall. "They put it through the letter box."

"And you didn't install a camera so you can find out who is pushing money through the slot in the door with your mail?"

Richard shrugged. "I don't want them to stop paying me. They'll probably kill me as well."

"Too big of a risk. I understand." She nodded, like she actually cared. Or sympathized. "But I'm afraid that if you want me to pay off your debt and get you clear of these people—because I *will* take them down, and that can include you going down with them or you can walk away a free man—then you need to give me a whole lot more than Preston being alive with no proof."

Richard stared at her.

"It doesn't matter if you like what I have to say or not. I don't really care at this point. I've been messed around enough. Chased, blown up, stabbed. Everyone I care about is in trouble. So you'd better give me something, or you'll see how fast I can pick apart your life."

Ramon glanced at her.

Kenna looked over and saw his brows rise. He looked impressed. She wanted to roll her eyes, but it would diffuse the fact Richard needed to believe she could do everything she threatened. And that she was desperate enough to go for it.

Richard cleared his throat. "I might have...heard a rumor a few days ago. After the club."

The same club she'd been to when she'd spoken to Keziya for the first time?

He said, "Hadley is trying to take over, and he'll kill anyone who gets in his way. That means you and your friends. But his plan for Preston is a little more elaborate. That guy has been a thorn in their sides ever since he didn't die in prison."

"Why did they let him live this long if he's a problem?"

Richard shifted in his chair. "They figure either people

think he's crazy, or guilty, or both. But now he's here, and that's a problem. His fortune disappeared right before the feds could freeze his assets—before he could hide it elsewhere. When they arrested him, he had nothing."

"How did he afford an expensive lawyer?"

"You tell me. He was friends with your father, right?" Richard shrugged. "This is all hearsay, but when Hadley gets drunk, he's talkative, and Keziya has given up trying to get him to stop blabbing everything to all his adoring fans. Personally, I think she's undermining him and trying to take over."

Now it was all coming out, but not more than what he'd overheard and conveniently couldn't verify. "I thought you were scared of him. You guys are drinking buddies?"

"I just do what I'm told, okay?" Richard said. "He said come to the club, so I went. He was going on about how Preston wanted his money back, but Hadley was laughing his butt off about it. Because he won. I guess they hate each other or whatever."

Preston was here for his fortune. That was the first she was hearing about it.

"He probably promised those fancy security guys that he could pay them when he got the money back."

Kenna said, "People like that usually don't work pro bono."

"Doesn't matter. Hadley will make an example of them one way or another, and more of the company will start to follow him instead of Keziya."

"And my family is caught in the middle."

"It's the way of the world. Those with power do whatever they want, and the rest of us just try to survive the best we can."

Kenna shifted to the edge of the seat and put her forearms on her knees, lacing her fingers together. "If you want money from me, you need to get me Preston's location. If I get him back, alive, then you'll get your seventy-three thousand pounds."

Chapter Thirty

"I know who you really are." Malcom tromped after her down the street from where she'd insisted they leave the car all the way to the big house that belonged to the Hadley family. Where the duke resided.

That snake. That vicious guy who terrorized girls.

A branch from a tree dangled in front of his face. He smacked it away as he walked, wanting to kick the trunk and get out some of his frustration.

He'd seen far too much at the hospital. The woman giving birth that night had screamed loud enough it filled the hallway, waking up other patients. One of the residents had gone into an anxiety-induced episode of screaming and clawing at her face. Pulling out handfuls of hair.

They'd snuck into a room to hide from the staff who ran to attend her.

Malcom would rather have helped her himself, but freedom wasn't always the best a person could have. Sometimes, the best for a person meant constant care. He'd had to walk on, not knowing enough about this to do more than make assumptions about her situation that were based on what *he* wanted. What would make him feel better.

The whole thing had him on edge now.

Amara had insisted they find out who was giving birth. At first, he'd wondered why it was necessary that she know. One of the patients they'd discovered sat up in bed at the sight of her and whispered, "You." Her voice had been full of fear, the dread of seeing Amara.

He'd been out of sight.

Malcom had been putting it together ever since. Adding piece to piece, figuring out who this woman in front of him was and what she really wanted.

"Who am I?" She didn't turn back, just kept walking. Determined to get to Hadley House. And for what? So she could find what she was looking for.

Not the same thing he was after—justice and an end to mysterious kidnappings. No, she was after something different.

Since his conversation with the young man he'd met yesterday, a guy who hadn't wanted to give his name, but Malcom already knew who he was. An up-and-comer in investment banking, a guy making a name for himself. After that conversation? Well, Malcom had a better idea now of what this was.

He only hoped he and Preston could continue to help each other.

Now he said, "You're the one they send in if someone steps out of line. The one the Grand Master sends to take them out." He paused to gauge her reaction to the fact he knew the truth.

He had a far better understanding of everything since Preston had told him all about Derringbone College and how the school fit in. These people waited decades to see the results of their work. They raised and trained assets, then embedded them in every facet of society all across the world. It wasn't enough to change British policy here in the UK, or even other European countries. They wanted to run the world.

To bend an entire globe to their aims. One currency. One leader.

It sounded like the stuff of end times nightmares—like something from the Bible.

Malcom said, "How many people have you killed?"

She spun around then, both hands outstretched, and shoved him in the chest. "You think you know what you're talking about now, then? Think you know everything about me?"

"No, because you haven't told me anything real," he said. "That's why I had to do an end-run around you and find out for myself."

"From your new buddy Preston?" She smirked at him. "He's up to his eyeballs in this, and he knows it. Well, guess what? We all make deals with the devil. I can live with my choices." She slapped a hand on her front. "Can you?"

"I'm trying to. That's pretty much the point here."

"Like why you're following me around like a puppy?"

Anger flared in him. "I'm doing my job. But I guess you don't need my help. Good day to you, then. Bye-bye." He waved at her, putting as much exaggeration into it as he could. "Cheerio."

"I figured you'd leave sooner or later."

Oh, she *wanted* him to walk away. "You'd like that wouldn't you? Because it would mean you can get back up on your high horse and go back to being all superior, lording it over us blue collar folks."

She stalked toward him.

Before she could launch into whatever she was going to say, he spoke first. "What are you looking for?"

"My sister!" She yelled those two words, then clapped her hands over her mouth. After a few seconds of staring at him with wide eyes, she lowered her hands. "Why do you have this effect on me?"

"I got under your skin."

"Well, get out of it. Because I don't need you there, and I don't like it."

He nearly smiled. "Too bad, sweetheart. I got to you whether you like it or not."

She raised her hand, swinging it as if she was going to slap him. He grabbed her wrist and halted it, discovering there hadn't been much strength behind the move. Either way, she wasn't going to hit him.

She flashed gritted teeth at him. "I'm not sweet."

"Right, 'cause you're a killer." He barely paused before he said, "Sweet women don't go looking for a missing sister because nothing else matters but finding her."

He heard her gasp for breath. "Let go of me."

Malcom released her wrist. In the dim light of late evening, she sagged against a tree and looked down the street. He gave her the time she needed to collect her thoughts, but they couldn't stay too long when he was sure there were more women at the house.

He'd brought weapons and even some crude devices he could use to burn the place down. Malcom didn't care that he was so far out of the bounds of his original investigation.

He would face the music as soon as he got home. Take whatever punishment they wanted to give him. He'd been thinking about getting out in a few years anyway, not making a lifetime career of being a fed.

It was far too difficult to toe the line when people like Duke Hadley were affecting the future on a global scale, using people like they were nothing but pawns in his game.

"What is your sister's name?"

She lifted her chin but didn't look at him. "Allison. I've always called her Alice. Not that we ever spent much time together. She's barely sixteen. Why do they have her? She shouldn't be one of the mothers now. It's too soon."

Malcom's stomach flipped over. "If you'd told me some actual answers to my questions, then I'd have understood why it's so important to you that we find her."

She looked at him then. "We?"

He shrugged a shoulder. "I want to take them down. Piece by piece, eventually, we'll have to find her. Otherwise, we didn't get them all."

"You'll really do that?"

She knew what he was really saying. That they would stick together. That he was in this to help her.

"Why?"

He stared at her, even though he couldn't make out her features that well. A night breeze cut through his wool sweater, making him shiver. "Maybe because you got under *my* skin."

"Is that true?"

He took a small step toward her. There wasn't much space between them to begin with, and he ended up standing in front of her.

Malcom braced a hand on the trunk of the tree above her shoulder. He leaned in, not just his face but his whole body. Standing close enough there was barely room for the breeze between them. "I need you to be honest with me."

"Honest about this being a bad idea?"

"Only until you find your sister." After that? Who knew what would come of it.

She tilted her chin up a little. He saw it in the yellow glow of the streetlight between the branches—the hope. "So you're going to stay? Give up your life to be with me."

"I was thinking more like you could quit being an assassin and come with me." She might walk away now, but she'd do it knowing how he felt. That he wanted her to leave and go back to America with him. "I don't want this to be over."

"So what do you think we should do about Hadley and the company? There are pieces of this organization in multiple countries. Assets all over. His reach is extensive. We can't take them all out." She let out a quick breath. "I just want my sister. That's all I've been focusing on. I don't know how to fight them."

"We'll figure it out. You just need to promise me."

She shook her head. "Promise you what?"

Malcom touched her cheek, his thumb on her chin. He saw her eyes flare in the dim light as he said, "Promise me you'll stick with me. No matter what."

"Why are you so quick to toss everything and jump to my side? You barely know me."

"I know enough." He lowered his head to hers, so their lips were close. "So what do you say? You wanna do this together?"

He heard a tiny intake of breath. It felt like the world disappeared around them, until it was only Malcom and Amara tucked together under that tree. Out of sight. Anonymous. He knew then that he'd pack it all in, give it all up, just for her. She was that kind of woman. The force of her pull was powerful enough he'd risk everything he'd built for a chance with her.

Even after everything she'd done, the way she was raised, and who they had bred her to be. At the core of it all, she was just a sister who wanted nothing more than to rescue her family. To save a teen girl victimized by a far more powerful force, led by Duke Hadley.

"Are you sure you know what you're—"

Malcom touched his lips to hers. He kept it gentle, not taking more than she wanted to give. Allowing her the chance to push back. But long enough to get his point across. He was serious. Maybe he was even more serious than he'd been about anything other than a case in a long time.

When he lifted his head, he said, "Help me finish this and then leave with me."

He could hardly believe he'd come this far in just one visit to the UK. He was ready to change his whole life just to be with this woman who had captured his heart. She was a force of nature, with exotic features and a strength like he'd never seen in a person.

"We have to find my sister. If they've impregnated her —" Amara's voice caught.

"We'll take both of them, and we protect them. Always. No matter what."

She nodded. "Okay."

"Yeah?"

She squeezed his shoulders where her hands rested. "Yes. I'll go with you. Even if I think you're crazy, and you have no idea what we're going up against."

"It's all right if you're scared. You're worried for your sister, and they taught you always to fear them." He touched her cheek. "But they have no idea how strong you are."

"I'm glad you think so."

"We're going to figure this out. Together."

"I hope you have a plan." Amara pushed off the tree and picked up his duffel. "But even if you do, we'll probably still get killed."

Malcom eyed the bag. "After we do save your sister and get the evidence to expose Hadley and the entire operation, we're gonna burn it all down."

No trial. No lawyers. No charges.

Only one thing.

His brand of justice.

Chapter Thirty-One

"Are you going to read that journal the whole way back to the house?"

Kenna didn't look over at Ramon to her right, driving the car like a crazy man who'd never driven in this country before. "Better than having to watch you drive," she said. "Besides, I got to an important part."

"Where your dad killed Hadley?"

"No, before that. They were on their way to the house." She cleared her throat, her mind full of every bit of the conversation he'd recounted. On top of the conversation they'd just had with Richard, it all amounted to so much information her head was practically spinning.

Ramon's cell phone, which he'd stuck in the cup holder, started to ring, and the letter M appeared on the screen.

Kenna said, "I've got it." She swiped and put the call on speaker. "Hey, Maze. We're both here." She hit the volume button and raised it.

Maizie's voice came through loud. "Ramon, turn left at the next traffic light."

He changed lanes, indicating at the last minute. The steady stream of traffic around them accommodated his shift, and he said, "What's going on?"

"I guess whatever you said to that guy worked. The email I had you give him to send everything over just got a forward. An internal message from the State Department."

Kenna shifted in her seat to lean her left side on the door and sat up straighter. "What is it?" She bent to tuck the journal in her backpack, pushing thoughts of the past from her mind.

"They're transferring Jax from the main Metropolitan police holding over to the US Embassy. No charges, and whoever wrote the message thinks they don't have enough evidence anyway. They've used up their goodwill with the Americans, and they're giving him back since they haven't found you yet."

"Why pass him to them?" Ramon asked. "If he isn't being arrested."

Kenna said, "They probably want him out of the country, not free. They'll expect the Embassy to get him on the first plane home so they can be done with this."

"Seems like it," Maizie said. "Ramon, take the next left. No, the one after it. I'll send the address. Follow GPS, and it'll take you to the spot they're supposed to be leaving from."

"Got it." The message popped up on the screen, and he tapped to add the route to the car's built-in navigation.

Kenna tapped her fingers on the knee of her black jeans. "I want to make sure he's safe during the handoff."

Ramon glanced over for a second, then looked back at the road in front of them. "You think he won't be?"

"Hadley is out there. Keziya as well. Why would I assume things are going to go smoothly?"

"You just want to micromanage it all because you have no control over what's happening."

She shifted in her chair again to face him a little better. "Will you just drive and try not to kill us, please?"

He hit the gas and turned a tight left corner just as the light went red. Behind them, a camera on top of the traffic light flashed.

"You'll get a ticket in the mail now, or the cops will show up on your tail to pull you over."

"Let them come." He shrugged off her concern.

"I'm wanted for questioning in connection with multiple deaths, a bombing, and an active shooter situation. You really think I need the attention of the police right now?"

Maizie cut off their argument. "Speaking of..."

Kenna glanced at the phone. "What is it?"

"Richard sent some more stuff as well. In fact, he sent a whole lot. Like a copy of admin access to a website. I've got Stairns and Bruce looking at it because it looks like a foundation that provides finances for medical research."

"It's probably connected, so figure out how," Kenna said.

"The foundation is based in France, and their central office is in Paris."

Ramon said, "I've never been." Then glanced at her. "Have you?"

Kenna nodded, then for Maizie's benefit said, "My dad

worked a case for Interpol while I was in high school, over the summer. He signed me up for a coach tour of Paris with stops at all the tourist sights while he picked up a killer who had been torturing and murdering young men across European countries. I think he was a truck driver. Something like that."

"Lovely."

Kenna shrugged. "You asked."

"But it wasn't connected to this?" Maizie asked. "'Cause it seems strange he'd come back after everything that happened here."

"Did you read his journal, Maze?"

"You were asleep. I needed to do something that wasn't looking at my computer."

She sounded as if she expected Kenna to be mad, so Kenna said, "Did you pass the part where they're under the tree?"

Maizie gasped. "He was so sweet with her! I nearly cried."

Kenna kind of agreed, even if it was weird because it was her parents. "He wrote his own version in his own journal. You think he wrote it precisely as it happened? The guy embellished all his novels, and the movies are even worse."

She didn't quite know why she was writing it off as at least partially a fabrication. Sometimes, she wondered why she hadn't found a therapist of her own. Maybe it was time. But then, every time she thought that she never actually followed through with it. Who wanted to get into navel-gazing when the shadows were so dark?

Once Jax was free, she would be able to relax a bit. Until then, she was going to be on edge, okay? It should be understandable, given everything.

Ramon said, "Maizie, why don't you tell us what else Richard sent? Assuming it's seventy-three grand's worth."

"That guy's debt?" Maizie asked. "You know that's like a hundred thousand dollars, US, right?"

"It's fine."

"Because your dad embellished those books," Maizie helpfully pointed out. "So now you have that much money to waste on a guy who I don't think is worth it, but you all know my metric is skewed."

"It's not that skewed, *hermana*. You trust me, don't you?" Ramon looked pretty pleased with his logic.

"Don't answer that." Kenna grinned. "Besides, we need to focus on Jax right now. Make sure he gets where he's going."

"But you can't show your face, or British police are going to arrest you—or detain you, or whatever they call it."

"So we're gonna watch." Kenna didn't want to lose a shot at seeing him. Not when she was on edge and so close to...she wasn't sure yet. She needed to pray for a clear way forward for dealing with this whole thing and working out how to solve this case. Finishing what her parents started. "Maizie, did you read far enough? In the journal. Did they find Allison?"

"Oh, you didn't get to that part?" the teen asked. "That part did make me cry. Are you sure you want me to tell you?"

Kenna sucked in a breath through her nose. "Just tell me."

"They found Allison in the Hadley House. She was one of the girls they couldn't save, but Amara got the baby out. That's why your dad kind of flipped out, and he ended up killing the guy. Because Allison was bleeding out, and Amara did a c-section right there. She took the baby."

Maybe she shouldn't have asked. Kenna swiped a tear from her cheek. "I think Amara isn't my mom."

Ramon glanced over. "What do you mean?"

"Allison had a baby. Maizie just said Amara rescued it. What if that baby was me?"

She felt like the entire foundation of her life had shifted —again. She had questions about so many things, like how Ian Birch had helped and what Preston's role was. But all of it disappeared, and all she could do was try to carry the weight of the shock that caught her breath.

"Would it make a difference if you are that baby? I mean, a difference to what you're going to do next. Or who you are?"

She glanced to the right, at Ramon in the driver's seat.

"We're going to help Jax." He sounded so sure. So steady. "Right now, in this moment, does it make a difference which one of these women was your mother?"

Maizie gasped.

"He's right." Kenna gave herself a second and turned to look out the window. "How will I even figure out where I came from, if I even cared to know? Right now, we need to focus."

Ramon said, "That's not what I meant. You're not unfocused. You're absorbing a lot of deep personal stuff in the middle of a complex case—"

Through the open phone line, Maizie muttered, "So basically, it's a Tuesday."

Ramon smiled a little. "No one thinks you should be fine. No one is expecting you to ignore this. But if you want to work this case, ask yourself, what does this information change? Does it alter who you are?"

Kenna said, "Thanks for keeping me grounded right now. Both of you. Things are moving fast, and I can't focus between the past and the present and everything going on."

"You handled Richard just fine," Ramon said. "Keep doing that, and we'll get out of this okay. Then you can take all the time you need to unpack your history with these people."

"Unless we don't get out of this okay. But I'm not sure I want to worry about all the ways it can go wrong."

Maizie said, "Well, one way is about to hit you guys like a freight train."

Kenna bit her lip.

Ramon said, "What's happening?"

The green traffic light in front of them turned red suddenly. A car at the front of the line braked, and the one behind it slammed into the back.

Someone else pulled suddenly out into the bus lane on the left, driving fast to get past the backed-up traffic.

A police car appeared on the right, coming from the street that intersected this one. The law enforcement vehicle barreled through the intersection at high speed, followed by an armored truck, and then another police vehicle.

A dark-blue paneled van followed the convoy, crossing in front of them. A gun opened fire from the passenger side of the van, taking out the trailing police vehicle. It spun out and hit a parked car at their ten o'clock. The van sped up to catch the armored vehicle, and the whole mess of cars moved out of sight.

Kenna gripped the handle on the door. "Please tell me that isn't the transport that Jax is in."

"Um..." Maizie said nothing more.

Ramon said, "I thought she wasn't supposed to lie."

"Maybe we can pretend we didn't see that and go back

to talking about things that happened nearly thirty years ago, because it might be emotional and heart-wrenching, but it's safer than this right now."

Ramon reached over and squeezed her knee. "You maybe want to go save your boyfriend from that instead?"

Yes. "I have no idea where to even start. And we have no guns, no leverage, and I'm practically a wanted fugitive." But yes, she absolutely wanted to save her boyfriend from that. "At least when he shows up to rescue me, he's got a badge. What do I have to offer that's going to move people out of the way so I can save him?"

"You wanna be equals, but you're not."

Kenna spun to him. After all, they weren't going anywhere in this bumper-to-bumper traffic. "Excuse me?"

"You're not supposed to be equals, Kenna."

"He's not supposed to be in prison."

Ramon made a face. "Duh, but that isn't what I'm talking about. You're so worried about what you don't bring to the table with this relationship you two have that you miss what you *do* bring."

Maizie said, "Preach it."

Kenna shook her head, then turned to look out the left-side window at the now-empty bus lane.

Ramon continued, "You think Jax is worried about you not being a cop, or does he just think you're amazing? You care what he thinks. You help people in ways no one else does. You solve cases."

"And I kick doors in. I've been working on my leg strength." Since her hands were useless at the best of times.

"You think maybe *he* might be worried that he's a fed, and it's a part of your life you left behind a long time ago? So being with him might, for you, feel like going back to something you don't want anymore."

She frowned.

He continued, "So maybe he feels the pull to give it up, so he can move on with you, and you can be happier not having the constant reminder that you're not an agent anymore shoved in your face."

"He doesn't think that." Jax would have said something to her.

Ramon shrugged. "Maybe he doesn't. Maybe he does. But the point is, you guys love each other. You're in this for the long haul, right?"

She thought about the ring in her duffel back at the house.

"Enough said." Ramon glanced at the left side mirror, then the rearview. "Put us all out of our misery already and quit dragging your feet worrying about every tiny little detail. Life is too short to waste it worrying."

"Amen, brother." Maizie gasped. "Oh, I should have said that in Spanish. It would've been better."

Kenna smiled, despite everything. "Fine, I'll shut up. And I'll quit worrying about it."

"I guess, at least in this part..." Ramon hedged, then finally said, "It turns out you're normal, Kenna Banbury. You're officially a *girl*."

She frowned. "That isn't a bad thing. Even if you think I'm being emotional."

"It isn't a bad thing." Ramon grabbed the wheel. "But this traffic is."

She turned to look out the back, which made her injured shoulder hurt. "What is it?"

"Trouble." He pulled left out of the line of traffic, onto the shoulder—a bus lane.

"It's clear in front of us."

"Won't be in a second." He checked the rearview.

"Looks like it's MI5—the Security Service. Like their Homeland Security. Or worse, it's the State Department, and they're going to think you have something to do with this."

"Why would they think that?" Apart from their presence here, what else was she guilty of? Kenna felt like she was racking up charges on top of charges, and she hadn't done anything but come to this country.

Ramon said, "They were on foot approaching our car, and now we're making a run for it, so they have to chase us."

Kenna glanced out the back window and spotted two guys on foot. "I can't say if I've seen them before." Whoever these guys were, she was guilty in their eyes before she'd even met them. "Just get us to Jax."

He cornered so fast, they almost went up on two wheels.

A couple of police cars streamed by, swerving around them and following the convoy heading after the van. The sound of sirens rang, shooting shards of pain through her head.

Ahead of them, a suited man stepped into the street. She barely registered it was Carrington Hadley before he swung up an AR-15 and pointed it at the car. He squeezed the trigger in the same moment. Sprayed the car with a barrage of bullets.

Kenna ducked her head and covered it with her hands. "Ramon!"

The windshield splintered, and the car swerved to the side. They careened across lanes of traffic and slammed into a light pole.

Kenna's head bounced off the dash, and everything went black.

The last thing she heard was Maizie calling their names.

Chapter Thirty-Two

US Embassy, London
Thursday 10:07pm

The yellow penlight flashed in her eye.

Kenna winced. "I don't have a concussion."

The doctor, a heavyset guy with black slacks, a gray shirt, and a white lab coat rolled back from her on his stool. She hadn't climbed up on the examination bed. For this, she'd stayed in the hard chair. Ramon was in the room next door, getting his broken nose looked at because the airbag had exploded in his face.

The doctor said, "As the only one in this room with a medical degree, I'm afraid it's me who will be making that determination. And the truth is, I'm not convinced you don't have a concussion."

She looked at the clock on the wall, relentlessly ticking around while she had no idea where to find Jax. Or how. Or even what had really happened.

Last thing she knew, Hadley had tried to kill her and Ramon.

Then what?

The doctor certainly hadn't been able to tell her.

If Kenna squinted, this could be nearly any doctor's office in the US, but she was still in the UK. She wanted to call Maizie and check in, make sure she knew they were okay, but that would only expose to these people the fact she existed. Too many people knew about her as it was.

"You need to stay here a while so we can monitor you." The doctor glanced at his smart watch. "And while you wait, I believe there's someone here to see you."

Kenna whipped her head around to the door, knowing who she wanted to see more than anything. The door opened, and a suited man she'd never seen before stuck his head in, scanning the room before he moved back and out of the way, disappearing into the hall.

Another man stepped into the room wearing a dark gray suit, white shirt, and red tie. "Ms. Banbury."

She coughed. "Uh." *Get a grip.* "Mr. President." Pain echoed in her head, a result of the crash—and a whole lot of surprise. "Did you come all this way? You could probably have just called. It must've been a logistical nightmare getting you here."

The doctor stared at her like she'd suddenly grown a second head.

President Vaughn chuckled, swiping at the side of his mouth with his thumb. "I was in the neighborhood."

Vaughn had dark brown skin, short, cropped hair, and a staunch policy against drug use among teens that she heartily approved of. However, she'd been in the middle of a case during the last election and miles from anywhere she could've voted, saving an elderly couple from the abuse of their closest neighbor.

"I'll let you two speak." The doctor nodded. "Mr. President."

He nodded in reply. "Doctor."

The doc left the door open. Kenna shifted on her hard seat. "Do you wanna sit? There aren't many options." She kind of waved at the doctor's stool.

"I've been sitting for a while. Feels good to stand."

"I don't mean to be ungrateful that you're here and all, but..." How was she supposed to explain without sounding desperate?

"You'd like to know where SAC Jaxton is? Or your friend who was in the car with you?"

"Ramon is next door. He broke his nose." Which meant he would probably whine like a baby for the next week or two. Though, to be fair, if she had broken her nose, she'd probably make it clear she was miserable for the duration. So she wasn't going to hold it against him.

All the energy she'd had seemed to drain out of her feet.

"SAC Jaxton told me if I was going to speak to you, that I should bring you coffee...as a peace offering."

He'd told the president that about her, seriously? They were gonna talk about that.

Kenna said, "Do you need to give me a peace offering for this conversation? Also, you didn't answer my question about where he is."

"I believe it was my question." His eyes smiled. How the guy managed to be fifty-seven and look it—rather than aging the way every president inevitably seemed to as a result of the stresses of the job—was a nice fluke of great genetics.

"Fine, I'll ask."

Vaughn raised one hand and showed her his palm. "SAC Jaxton has been fully briefed on the situation. He objected strongly to the plan, despite the fact it was coordinated by two of the Joint Chiefs, the Secretary of Defense, and the Director of the CIA. His issue was that he'd have to go alone, and not with you as his backup."

Kenna's body felt like it turned to stone. As if every muscle she had solidified, suddenly frozen. "Alone doing what?"

"SAC Jaxton officially 'escaped' from British police custody, and the cover story is that you helped him."

They should've let her help him.

She wanted to say it, but since she was talking to the president, she kept her mouth shut.

Vaughn continued, "In reality, he's completing a task that has been in the works since my predecessor. Although, the previous president's involvement was merely a cover for the fact he was also part of this organization. One of these trained assets—we still don't know what to call them."

She said, "They're just people."

After all, Kenna was pretty sure she was one of them. The offspring of whatever scientific advancements they'd come up with. Or some cocktail of DNA they'd whipped up in a lab and then used to artificially inseminate her mother.

Still, it wasn't like the babies born had superpowers.

Wouldn't she know by now?

"They have embedded assets into the US Government, the European Union, individual countries, the UN, NATO, everything from local and national law enforcement to things like Australian special forces. Pakistani freedom groups. The Indian delegation to the UN. The Hague. Interpol. If you can name it or imagine it, they thought of it a hundred years ago and worked to get someone in position."

"For what?"

Vaughn kept his true feelings locked tight, which was probably a good thing for a president to be able to do. His expression was nearly completely impassive—and he probably played great poker. "We've been putting together a NOC list of everyone we believe is connected to these people."

"How can you tell who they are?"

"For the most part, you don't want to know. But the essence of it is that we have specially-trained agents on a task force whose job it has been for years to root them out. Identify one of their assets and confirm. We want to know how much of a threat they present and put together an assessment of just how much influence they may have."

Kenna frowned. "What does this have to do with me and Jax?"

"Thanks to Preston Lightwood, you've found yourself in the middle of a multi-year, off book operation."

"My dad might've loved spy stuff, but I really don't."

Vaughn nodded. "That's probably for the best. I'm not sure the world could handle Kenna Banbury, International Woman of Mystery."

"It's been less than a week, and I'm already a wanted fugitive."

"Ah." He shifted his weight so slightly it almost wasn't noticeable. "I needed to speak with you, and it was an efficient way to track you down before someone...unsavory managed it."

"So I was on the run just so you could find me?" As far as Kenna could tell, the plan hadn't worked very well. "And putting Jax in British prison?"

Vaughn waved a hand. "He was only ever in holding, kept for questioning. That was pretty clever, coercing a British prison officer to sneak in a phone. My people aren't sure how you managed it."

As if she was going to tell them about Bruce. "Why keep him for questioning, and where is he now?"

"SAC Jaxton is doing his job."

Kenna pressed her lips closed so she didn't say, *I can find him myself, and I will. Doesn't matter how much information you choose to withhold.* "I get that I walked into your thing. Or at least, I was invited in by Preston. You might not be his biggest fan, but I'm here." She shrugged her good shoulder, though that wasn't what it felt like. "Put me to work."

"This is bigger than you."

"I'm not saying let me solve the problem for you. I'm just saying I want to help."

"To root these people out, or to be there to watch your boyfriend's back?"

Kenna got the overwhelming impression this was a test. "You realize the doctor thinks I have a concussion, right?"

"I figure it's a good time to get a straight answer out of you."

Kenna said, "How about giving me straight answers? My boyfriend was in police custody. For days, I thought Preston and our mutual friends were dead, but a corrupt employee of yours is the one who told me they've been kidnapped." She paused, in lieu of shrugging again, which would hurt despite the pain meds the doctor had given her. "I've been working this case for what...a week? How am I supposed to have figured out more than you when you've had years?"

"There's certainly been more movement since you showed up."

Kenna figured that meant the body count was higher than normal. "We still have missing women, although there's a question of whether they consented to being part of it or whether they were coerced. Or if they were simply abducted."

Vaughn looked at the bad nineties' artwork of a mountain scene on the wall and then back at her. "I understand how close you are to this. How personal the case might be."

"Seems like it's personal to a lot of people." She had no idea if that included the president. "What's Jax's task?"

"I've discovered it's better to compartmentalize information. Especially in situations like this one, although I'd also argue that there are no situations like this one. However, if you'd like to stay in your lane, I do have a job for you."

Kenna clenched her back teeth, but it only made her head hurt. She didn't want to be on the president's bad side. Only, when would that ever be a problem? Her life didn't exactly intersect with powerful Washington D.C. circles. He needed to answer her question.

But he didn't.

He was going to give her an assignment.

"This isn't a pitch to get me to walk away and leave it all alone?" She'd aligned herself with Preston Lightwood, and evidently, that put her in his camp—where they'd get labeled as pariahs. "I don't work for you."

"Believe me, I'm aware."

But he wanted her to? That was interesting.

"So what's the job?"

Vaughn studied her for a few seconds. Finally, he said, "You're right that Preston Lightwood has been missing for days, along with two employees of Miami Security

International. We have intel that they're being held in France, which gets you away from over-eager British police constables trying to impress their chief inspector."

"You're giving me permission to get him back, regardless of who is holding him and what happens to them?"

"I'll give you the file. We know who is holding them, though they're lower level. Get Preston back and lock him down."

Because the US government didn't want him working this on his own? "Why does he need to be 'locked down?'"

Vaughn's impassive expression matched his diplomatic tone. "Mr. Lightwood fails to fly below the radar, despite attempting to travel internationally under an alias. Or using you as a cover story. He's interested in one thing, and that is getting back the money these people stole from him right out of his accounts."

As if that was all he was interested in. "These people destroyed his life. They took his wife from him and cost him years of free living. All because he did what? He wronged them, but it wasn't by killing his wife."

Vaughn's jaw flexed. "Preston Lightwood has inserted himself into this situation for his own gain."

She bit her lip. Arguing wasn't going to change his mind.

"However, for his sake, I'm glad he has friends like you to watch his back. And to go get him out of the situation he got himself into."

Considering Hadley was the one who had shot at her and Ramon on the street, Kenna said, "Who kidnapped him in the first place?"

"A group of four of them, a strike team we believe were ordered by an acquaintance of yours. Keziya Shatapathi."

"Is she in charge?"

Vaughn said, "It seems to be more like factions or splinter cells. All of whom receive orders from some kind of 'Grand Master.'"

"Do you know who that is?" She shifted on the chair and crossed her ankles. At least some of what he'd said aligned with what Richard had told them.

The president said, "If we require your assistance in this matter, I will certainly call you."

"You do that." Kenna nodded, smiling slightly. She might've hit her head pretty hard, but she kind of liked this guy. If it had been anyone else in this embassy telling her these things, she'd have probably questioned whether they were telling her the truth.

Vaughn continued, "Once you have Preston Lightwood and his associates free of the strike team, the government is prepared to reimburse him the money he lost at the hands of these people. In exchange for him signing a non-disclosure agreement, remaining in the United States indefinitely, and refraining from contact with anyone related to this group."

"You're gonna pay him off?" Kenna lifted her brows.

"Yes, because you're going to persuade him it's his only option."

"And the alternative?"

Vaughn shook his head. "Neither of you wants to know the answer to that. And I refuse to stoop to the level of threats."

She would've rather he let slip secret deets about black site prisons. Maybe a floating one in the ocean. Or some kind of underwater impenetrable installation. That could be cool. Still, it would also be a little too science fiction compared to her normal activities.

Not like the rest of this case wasn't a serious leap.

She was spinning out. If her parents weren't directly

involved, she might be inclined to wonder if the whole thing was too hard to believe. Unfortunately, it seemed that the fabric of her life had been sewn into the story of this organization and what they were doing.

She was involved, whether she liked it or not.

"Preston Lightwood will agree to my terms," the president said, "because you will persuade him that he has no other option."

"So I agree to go find him, and we all take your word for it that you're 'taking care of this'?" Kenna shrugged, acting a whole lot more casual than she felt. "What about Jax?"

He couldn't expect her to carry on and potentially leave the man she loved hanging.

Vaughn shifted far enough to pull a phone out of his pocket. "Use this. It's programmed with one number. Call your boyfriend, let him tell you himself that he's fine."

The president didn't hand her the phone, he set it on the counter beside where he stood. Next to the glass jar of cotton balls.

"On a few conditions."

Kenna figured as much. "Of course."

"SAC Jaxton has signed a non-disclosure agreement that aligns with his security clearance level, neither of which apply to you or are available to you. Nor do I plan to change that in the future."

Kenna had to try and not get mad. Though if she was mad about not being included, it was only because she was feeling nosy right now and usually got an explanation when she asked for one. Or at least when she pestered people enough to fill her in.

He continued, "You will not ask him about his task. You will not attempt to interfere with his task. At such time as his task is complete, SAC Jaxton will be free to return to the

US with you, accompanying Mr. Lightwood and the two employees of MSI."

She wasn't sure she liked this agreement.

"Failure to adhere to these stipulations could result in you or SAC Jaxton facing criminal charges and prison time."

"Fine, I get it. Don't play in your sandbox."

Vaughn half-smiled, moving to the side and turning to the door. "Now she gets it."

Chapter Thirty-Three

Kenna gripped the phone, her other hand braced against the wall of the bathroom stall in the airplane Preston had brought them over to the UK on. No sense in it remaining at the airport in England, unused. "Maybe you could just tell me that you aren't going into some crazy dangerous situation all by yourself, with no one to watch your back?"

"Honey, you can watch my back any time."

Kenna shook her head, not because he didn't usually call her by that endearment.

The problem with it was that they had agreed months ago if one of them was ever under duress on the phone, calling each other "honey" was their indicator. Either someone on his end was listening to the conversation, or he believed the president had given her a bugged phone.

Which to be fair, he probably had.

She would have.

Kenna said, "I'm going to take you up on that offer, just as soon as this thing is over."

She didn't bother turning to look at her reflection in the tiny airplane bathroom. She knew she wouldn't like what she saw. Whether that was the state of her right now, or the frustration that was probably on her face.

Jax said, "It's a date. See you soon?"

"I hope so."

"Love you."

She said, "Love you, too." Which might have been the only truthful thing either of them had said this entire conversation.

The whole thing had been just a collection of empty expressions. She hung up the phone, and the plane shifted in the air with a current, creating a jolt of turbulence.

The fasten seatbelt sign came on above the bathroom door, and a chime sounded out of the tiny speaker in the corner.

Kenna stowed the phone the president had given her in her pocket. If it wasn't the only way she had to contact Jax, she might be interested in being pickpocketed again. This time in Paris—or whatever town they were going to.

The president had sent over surveillance photos and papers that were supposed to be where Preston, Hollace, and Nielsen were being kept. Just a few hours' drive from London, and yet in a completely different country. Faster to fly, though. Maizie was looking for connections between people they were trying to uncover in the company and the country beneath the plane. France.

Maizie was going through the whole packet, and Kenna had left Stairns and Bruce working with Ramon on an extraction plan based on the schematics they had for the building, which was an old French countryside mansion. A winery that had been out of business for many years, and before that, had a turbulent history over the last hundred and fifty years.

Talk about an investment property that would keep revealing secrets for years to come.

Kenna shook the random thoughts from her head and tried to focus, but she needed at least another pot of coffee before she could get there.

She washed up, running wet hands through her hair to try and give it some semblance of control. They were about to extract three kidnapped victims, so she tied it back so that it would be out of the way.

In the main body of the airplane, Ramon, Bruce, and Stairns huddled together over a table, their chairs facing each other. Maizie was closer to Kenna, typing on her laptop by herself.

Kenna dropped down into the seat across from her.

Maizie said, "Update?"

Kenna nodded. "Yes, please."

They had all met up at Stanstead airport so they could fly down together, mostly because Kenna wasn't prepared to leave Maizie behind in a different country. She wanted the girl close enough to assist and where they could all work to protect her. The US government might consider it effective to send individual agents out on dangerous jobs that they couldn't tell her about, but her family worked differently. They watched each other's backs.

"I thought you'd be happier after you spoke to Jax."

Kenna shifted in her seat and looked out the tiny side window. "He couldn't really say anything. And how did you know I was calling him from the bathroom, anyway?"

"Because you let me plug that phone into my computer for thirty seconds?" It wasn't really a question, but Maizie hedged like it was one.

Kenna frowned. "You already hacked the phone?"

"If I tell you that I know exactly where Jax is, and I should be able to keep monitoring his location, will that make a difference in what you do next?"

Kenna said, "Depends if you want me to reach over there and give you a kiss on the head. Because you are pure genius."

"You should remember it in the future. I can be helpful." Maizie gave her a pointed look. "Even, and maybe especially, in the field."

Kenna frowned. "Why don't we try and get out of this situation alive, and then we can talk about you going on dangerous missions."

Maizie rolled her eyes, and they drifted over Kenna's chair to where Bruce, Stairns, and Ramon sat. "Fine."

Kenna said, "Do you really want to bring the three of them with you everywhere you go?"

She would rather the teen got a job with a company like Miami Security International, where she could work from the office and be safe, not out in the field.

At this point, Kenna didn't even really want to be out in the field. But that was probably just exhaustion talking.

Here she was, way *way* out in the field.

If Preston wasn't injured to the point he was incapacitated when she found him, Kenna would be having a word with him about bringing her all this way just because he wanted his money back from these people.

Maizie could have just hacked their accounts in the first place and redirected the money if the dollars and cents were such a big deal to him.

"Why don't you just tell me what you want an update on?" Maizie typed on her computer, not really even looking at Kenna now.

"Hadley was shooting at Ramon and me the last time I saw him. But no one told me what happened to him after that."

Maizie nodded. "The police report the Brits filed says that they had no other choice but to use lethal force on him in order to keep him from maiming or killing anyone else."

"So he's dead."

Maizie nodded. "And no one is going to investigate any further than that. As far as they are considered, the threat is neutralized."

"Maybe they'll at least look into his life and why he might have done that," Kenna said. "But I'm not going to hold my breath that it will be the thing which unlocks this entire case. These people have gone undetected for way too long for them to let it slip with one guy's estate."

Ramon came over and sat on the opposite side, his body turned toward them, his feet in the aisle. "I think we have a plan. Bruce and Stairns are going to go with you into the house. I'll stay with Maizie and act as control."

Maizie didn't look up from her computer.

Kenna nodded. "Part of me wants to just call and let MSI take care of it themselves. But it'll take them time to mobilize, and they don't know what we do about the house and the people inside holding our friends."

Bruce came over and sat opposite Ramon. Stairns headed for the bathroom. The pilot got on the intercom and announced that they were twenty minutes from the airport where they would be landing. She looked it up and found it was a smaller rural airport two hundred miles outside of Paris, in the countryside to the northwest.

She had spent far too much time on the short flight over on the real estate website looking at pictures of the house. It might be a clever idea to use an empty place to keep people they'd abducted from being discovered, but they had to know when perspective buyers were coming by. Or the whole thing was a sham, and no one had any intention of selling the house.

Which was a shame, considering it had an in-ground pool that someone could fix up and expansive gardens.

Ramon said, "Is your boyfriend okay?"

"He's fine." As if she was going to get into that with them all listening.

Bruce shifted in his seat. Probably antsy to get on the ground and roll on this operation. "You ever get the feeling no one cares if you live or die? They only care if you're useful."

She glanced at Ramon and saw a stone-cold expression on his face. "No."

Apparently, he simply didn't want to agree with the other man, because she knew he understood exactly how Bruce felt.

Bruce knew it. He looked at Ramon. "We should start our own company. The two of us. Nothing But Our Wits, Inc."

Ramon actually smiled, but only barely.

Maizie said, "Oh."

Kenna leaned forward and set her forearms on the table. "What is it?"

"Richard Laughton was found dead in his house a couple of hours ago. The apparent cause of death is suicide."

"So Hadley isn't a problem anymore, and now Richard is dead as well?"

The president was in London, and his group of people working on taking down every member of this organization was hard at work. She wondered how high the body count was going to get before the day was over.

At least President Vaughn wasn't prepared to allow innocents to be left to die. Unless he didn't much care what happened to Preston and the others. Could be he'd only given Kenna this task in order to keep her busy so she didn't get in the way of whatever else he was doing.

"Things are moving, finally." Bruce bounced one knee up and down.

Stairns emerged from the bathroom in black cargo pants and boots, a faded Metallica T-shirt on his top half. The man looked like the former Marine that he was—if there was a freelance division for retirees.

She didn't plan to ever be in his crosshairs. And she wouldn't want to be.

He buckled in, and the plane landed with only the minimum of bouncing up and down. The president had assured them a car would be waiting for them on the tarmac when they arrived, but Ramon had gotten on the phone and secured a rental van for them to use with the first company whose operator spoke English.

The white van was parked beside a red compact that would barely fit four people, let alone the five of them. Whether there was a tracker on the small car the US government had provided or not, Kenna decided the team should split up. Ramon and Maizie went in the van, and she sat in the back of the compact, in the middle because Bruce and Stairns—in the driver's seat—both had their chairs pushed back so far.

She held onto the shoulders of both their chairs as

Stairns took every corner of the French country roads at top speed.

The house was nestled on the top of the hill, overlooking the valley below. Two outbuildings, one of which was in disrepair, according to the real estate website. Even though the packet of information the president had sent over indicated they were being held in a lower level of the house, some kind of cellar, she decided they should check the outbuildings first and then go inside. Even if it took longer than she wanted, they were going to clear every room on their way to the cellars.

The first contact came as she moved from the last outbuilding toward the back corner of the house, and an armed gunman appeared on the roof. Bruce ran in front of her with his rifle. He lifted it and squeezed off a shot.

The man tumbled off the edge of the roof and hit the ground two floors below.

Kenna winced. "Thanks."

"I shouldn't have to tell you to stay frosty."

"Good." Kenna raced behind him. "Because saying that is a giant cliché now."

Bruce grinned absently, squared up to the door, and kicked his boot beside the handle. The wood splintered. Across the other side of the house, where Stairns made entry, gunfire broke out.

Bruce went in first, but the gunshots were faster than he was. They both ducked to the side, pinned down outside the door.

At the first break in the shots, Bruce stepped inside, already firing. She heard a cry from down the hallway and moved behind him.

Kenna wasn't entirely comfortable with the fact he was risking his life to cover her. But as it was something she had been battling with everyone she cared about, Kenna let herself feel the emotion. Even in the heat of taking shots and scanning for gunmen—or women—she contemplated losing this man and knowing it was because he had given his life to save her.

Not something she wanted. Maybe it was only part of life, the kind she led.

A woman wearing a dark green jacket launched out of a side room, barreling into Kenna. She hit the ground with the woman's weight on her, pinning her gun to the floor. Kenna shifted and brought her legs around. She kicked the woman off her and fired a shot.

The woman rolled to her back and stared at the ceiling with unseeing eyes.

Bruce disappeared around a corner into another hallway up ahead. Kenna scrambled up, using the wall to steady her, and headed forward. The information they received indicated there were at least five abductors watching the three men in the cellar. There should only be a couple left now at this point.

Another gunshot cracked through the house like a firework set off indoors. Someone screamed. Maybe only one left.

She kept going, scanning empty rooms. The next open doorway had a number of items inside within view. She spotted a computer setup with monitors in a row on the table. On screen were a number of images of the captive men, but not video. These were still images. Maybe to send to someone, like updates or proof of life. It could be they wanted Miami Security International, or someone who had received a ransom note, to pay them for Preston and their people.

On one monitor, she found the same computer program

she'd seen in New York, the one that made a fabrication of a person. A way to put words in their mouth—or pretend they were still alive.

Kenna took out the phone and checked the room was still empty while she called Maizie.

The call connected. "What is it? What happened?"

"You need to access this computer system I'm looking at."

Maizie told her where to find the operating system's backend and gave her a series of commands to enter. The whole bank of screens flickered, and the mouse started to move. Windows closed and opened, and someone started typing.

"Is that it?" It looked to her as if Maizie had connected successfully.

Maizie said, "Yes, I'm in."

"Good." Kenna turned to the door, sliding her phone back in her pocket. "I'm going to find Preston."

Chapter Thirty-Four

Kenna followed the route Bruce had taken, down a long hall where at the end, she found stone steps that led down. Gun in front of her, leading the way, she hurried down the staircase as quietly as she could. Aware of people in front of her down in the basement level and someone behind, but not close.

Stairns and Bruce.

Her heart pounded. She knew that even one wrong move here could be the difference between life or death. Whether for her or for anyone she cared about. As she moved, her gun raised in front of her, the knife wound in her shoulder sent shards of pain piercing through the muscle. Her forearms ached.

All it did was help her focus. Keep her mind clear and

allow her to push on, intent on avoiding more pain or allowing someone else to feel it themselves.

The air down at the bottom of the stairs had to be at least ten degrees cooler. The wide landing area looked like it had been carved out of the earth. A set of double doors to the left stood open wide to reveal rows and rows of barrels. The kind that would store alcohol. To the right was another door, one that looked medieval. Made of heavy wood and at least seven feet tall, with iron bars crossed in a tiny opening, a little window to look through about eye-level.

She walked to the side of the gap, keeping her body covered with the uneven earth wall, and looked through. It wasn't latched shut. She could see an inch width and then down the hall, no sound beyond the door.

Kenna eased it open with two fingers and saw a man lying on the floor half out of a door to the right. Looked like a line of cells all in a row. Some hundreds of years ago lord of the manor—or whatever the French called them—with a place under his house for his libations and where he held prisoners who'd wronged him.

The door creaked the last few inches open.

"Who's in the hall?" Bruce's voice came from one of the rooms, out of sight.

"It's me. You clear?" She headed for the open door at the end, passing honest to goodness torches on the wall—though they were plastic and wires now, not the kind that would be lit with fire.

Bruce said, "Get over here." His tone strained, stress in his voice.

She picked up her pace to a run, glanced back at the open doorway. *Clear.* Then stepped inside the room, grateful that the threat seemed to have been neutralized. Her breath caught at the scene.

Chains. Men secured to the wall. The whole place had an odor she didn't want to think about, permeating the cooler air.

Bruce glanced over his shoulder, a man lying in front of him up against the wall. "Get over here and give me that packet in your pant leg."

She unzipped as she went. Wasting no time handing over the military issue gauze with the clotting agent on it, her gun in her off hand. Her body nearly vibrating with adrenaline, which served to reduce her awareness of her aches and pains. Her shoulder. Her head.

There was something to be said for not being dead yet.

Could these men say the same?

Over on the left, Preston had his eyes closed, his head to the side, but she saw the gentle rise of his chest. *Still with us.* He sat with his back to the wall, the farthest over, by the corner of the ten-by-ten room.

A cell. That's what it was.

Bare walls carved out of dirt with no escape. No sun. No air. No chance at life—or hope. Someone had secured hooks to the wall every few feet. Preston's hands were chained, secured to a hook, and it looked like he'd been used for a punching bag. Or worse, given the torn shirt and the burn marks on his chest.

Hollace sat nearer to her, his eyes on her but slightly unfocused. "We need to get them free." She crouched beside Nielson and looked at Hollace. "You good?"

His skin had grayed, his lips cracked. One eye swollen shut. Hollace said, "Just help him. Then get us out of here." His voice was hoarse, either from thirst or from screaming.

Bruce tore the packet open and pushed the gauze pad against Nielson's side, just below his rib cage. Near to where blood had pooled on the ground under him.

She winced. "How bad is it?"

Kenna looked for herself, because she needed to see. Much like the others, he seemed to have been worked over. But Nielson had more cuts on his abdomen. Deeper. Longer. Tortured. And for what? Regardless of the answer, it was over now.

"He got shot. And it wasn't recently." Bruce pressed hard on the gauze. "We need to get him out of here. He needs more help than I can give."

Not recently? If he'd had the wound for a few days, that meant it might have been sustained when they were kidnapped. And he'd been without treatment since.

Gunshots rang through the house.

"We need a bolt cutter for these chains."

Bruce shifted in his crouch and pulled out a hand tool about halfway between the size of a flashlight and a pen. He said, "Hold it close, hit the button. Watch your fingers."

"We need to call MSI." She took the tool to Hollace and used it on the chain. It would leave the bracket around his wrist, but that could be removed later.

Preston started to stir, his head moving, but he didn't wake. Maybe it was for the best that he remained unconscious for now. But how could the two of them haul out three people when her arms didn't work but in a limited way? With her head ducked to her task, cutting Hollace free, she said, "Where is Stairns? We need help to get out of here."

Hollace shifted his legs. Antsy to be free?

"Hold still." She was almost through.

"Give me a phone." The chain fell from his wrist and clinked onto the ground.

Kenna bent to the side so she could ease the phone from her pocket. She put it to her ear. "Maizie, you there?"

"Busy." The teen sounded distracted.

"I'm hanging up. Call back if you get anything." She ended the call and handed the phone to Hollace. "Got it?"

He took the phone and immediately started dialing.

She moved to Preston. "Hey, buddy. You with me?" Kenna patted his cheek and watched him blink, coming back to awareness slowly. He'd started all this, and now she knew for sure it was only about money.

Unless the President of the United States had been lying, or at least withholding the truth. Which, of course, had *never* happened in the history of politics.

"Hold still, okay?" She removed the chains from the cuffs around Preston's wrists. "We need Stairns. Then we can get them upstairs."

She glanced at Bruce. For a second, she saw a look on his face that she wasn't expecting. He seemed...conflicted about something. "You good?"

"This guy isn't going to make it far." The conflicted look was gone, and his expression returned to all business.

She turned to the man between them. "Hollace, can you walk?"

"Copy that," he said into the phone, then hung up. "The chopper is five minutes out."

Kenna blinked. "How did they get here so fast?"

Hollace cleared his throat. He moved one arm across his body and hugged it with the other. "They've been following you. Soon as you landed in France, they called in favors and got down here. There's a chopper waiting. They're scrambling now." His voice broke at the end.

She set her hand on his shoulder. "Let's get you to your people."

Preston stirred. She glanced over and saw that he had

lifted his head, his eyes now somewhat focused. "Hey there, friend."

If she'd been angry at him before for dragging her here because of money, or whatever else, it was gone now. They all had more important things to focus on than hurt feelings. Or withheld intentions.

He managed to say, "Where are we?"

Hollace glanced at him, then said to her, "We had no idea where they took us."

Preston hadn't been awake to hear them talk about being in France. Kenna said, "I'm sure it was a great visit. How about we get out of here?"

Hollace barely smiled, but it was there. "Help me up."

"I'll try." She got his arm over her shoulders and braced his weight before she stood. Teeth gritted. Relying on every bit of strength she had. "I'll have to come back for Preston."

Over by the door, a dark-haired man ran in. Jeans and a tight T-shirt, sleeves of tattoos on his arms. He took one step, raising his gun as he moved.

A gunshot blasted in the hallway, and the man jerked. Surprise washed across his face, and he touched his chest where blood blossomed. He fell to the ground, and his gun skittered across the floor.

Stairns appeared in the doorway. "You guys good?"

She said, "Grab Preston," and turned far enough to see Bruce heft Nielson off the floor. It was slow going, but they got them upstairs and outside, where she led Hollace to a bench beside the front entrance.

Bruce laid Nielson on the stone in front of them.

"How is he doing?" She listened for a helicopter.

Bruce checked the injured man over. "Pulse is weak. He's lost a lot of blood."

Hollace leaned against her shoulder and handed over her phone. She said, "Thanks," just as Stairns walked out with Preston, helping him with each step.

"Kenna, Preston needs to tell you something."

She stood. "Let him sit here."

Hollace caught Preston, helping to steady him. Two guys who had bonded in a high-stress situation and learned to work together.

She set a hand on Hollace's shoulder and crouched in front of them. "Preston?"

He took in a couple of deep breaths. "They…"

She waited, wondering if she should give him some time and let Maizie update her on what she had. Confirm everyone in the building was dead or had been rescued, and they hadn't missed any intel they could've gathered.

But behind her, she heard the steady whir of an approaching helicopter.

"Help is here. If you need to tell me something, do it fast." Soon enough, he'd be whisked away for medical treatment. She prayed Nielson would survive long enough to get to the doctor, and that the three of them would have favor with the medical professionals. They didn't need any difficulties getting help.

Preston found her, his gaze settling on her. "Kenna…"

"Can it wait?"

He shook his head. "They were talking. About an operation." His eyes shifted and became unfocused.

She looked at Hollace who shook his head and said, "They didn't say anything in front of me."

Preston must have overheard something. She touched his arm, enough to get him to focus on her again. "What did they say?"

It could be anything, but it could also have something to do with the job that Jax had been sent on. But was that only wishful thinking? Just because she wanted to be where he was and watch his back.

Preston winced. "Publisher. They said something about a publisher." He leaned over to the side, away from her, and spit on the ground a mix of blood and saliva. Swallowed and said, "Enduring Flame."

Kenna frowned because she received checks from them into her trust fund account regularly. Still, even to this day. Enduring Flame Entertainment was the name of the publisher her father's books had come out through. "An operation at the publisher?"

That didn't make any sense. How could they be connected to this? His books had come out years later.

Preston's head dipped to the side, and his eyes closed. Stairns pressed two fingers to his throat. "He's out cold. Let's get them out of here."

The helicopter touched down on the grass lawn in front of the house. The door slid open, and two men jumped out with a backboard and duffels. No insignia, no uniforms. MSI people who had medical training.

Some of the tension in her eased. "We need to find out what this publisher thing is."

No one heard her statement.

She helped Hollace to the open door, then stepped back. When the three of them were loaded on, she turned to Bruce and Stairns. The chopper lifted off, and they moved back toward the gravel drive, stepping off the grass. She shielded her eyes and watched it leave. "We need to get out of here before local police show up."

"Do you have everything you need from inside?" Bruce asked.

"I don't know." She had only found that one room. "Do I?"

Bruce looked at Stairns, who said, "You got Maizie in the system?" When she nodded, he said, "The rest of the house was clear. Let's go."

They moved back to the car and drove to where Ramon had left the van. Tucked beside a tree on the side of the single lane country road, a sweeping field on one side. About as out of sight as they could get it.

As they climbed out of the car, Ramon slid the door open and stepped out. "She's on the case. No disturbances."

Kenna said, "What's going on?"

"Maizie is sifting through their system, connecting dots." Ramon folded his arms. "You got them?"

"On a chopper, headed to the hospital."

"Where are we going?" Ramon asked. "Otherwise, you'd have gone with them, right?" He glanced over at Bruce and Stairns, talking together quietly.

"They're being taken care of." She told him what Preston said about a publisher. "The company that published every single one of my dad's books. All of them."

Ramon frowned and shook his head. "What does that have to do with this?"

"I have no idea." She rolled her shoulders, trying to brush off some of the adrenaline coursing through her. When it was done, she was going to crash hard. But they needed answers before that happened.

She moved around him and looked in the door.

Maizie let out a frustrated sound, slammed her hands down on the keys, and slid the rolling stool back slightly.

"Talk to me, Maze." Not just that, but she had questions about this publisher. Anything to keep this operation rolling. After all, Jax was out there somewhere on his own, doing a job for the US government with no backup.

She might not be able to interfere, but if she just happened to be in the same place on an unrelated matter? She would argue that in court all day long.

Fighting for freedom was always worth it.

Chapter Thirty-Five

Kenna waited until the van had barely come to a stop outside a closed down two-story brick building on the corner of *Rue* whatever-street-this-was. All she knew was that the publishing house, Enduring Flame Entertainment, halfway down the block, was about to be the target of an attack.

She shoved the door open and jumped out.

"Kenna!" Stairns called after her, but she wasn't going to stop.

She raced down the sidewalk, the sides of her jacket open. Her skin slick with sweat. Adrenaline still coursing through her, and it wouldn't stop until she got what she wanted. Jax. People safe. Keziya in handcuffs, hauled away by the police.

Any of it.

All of it.

As she ran to the building, she yelled, "Talk to me."

Maizie's voice came back, through the earpiece the teen had scrounged up. "The GPS signal puts Jax in the building. If I had a little more time, I could hack the cellular networks and figure out how many other people are in the building, or surveillance for the area to see if I can see who came and went from the building this morning so far."

"Don't worry about it. I'll get them out." She ran as fast as she could toward the front door. "Any way to warn them?"

She heard people running behind her and figured it was some combination of Ramon, Stairns, and Bruce—whoever hadn't opted to stay in the van with Maizie.

The teen said, "No one is answering the business phone line."

"Got it." She hurtled up to the front door and yanked on the handle. Nothing happened. The door rocked but didn't open. It was locked. Kenna found a buzzer to the side, like a doorbell with a tiny speaker. Hopefully, they had a camera.

She hammered her finger on the button, laying on it. Then she lifted her finger and tapped it a few times. S-O-S. Good idea. She pressed out the audio tones that made up morse code anyone should recognize. It was an international standard, right?

Ramon came up beside her, breathing hard.

"Come on, come on." She pounded her fist on the door. "Open up!"

Ramon hit the buzzer, inciting angry tones that she hoped someone heard.

The building was old, red brick, and looked like it had been abandoned years ago. Why had her father gone with a publisher all the way in Paris? Maybe they were the only ones who had offered to put his book out. She had no idea, and if this place was destroyed, it wouldn't matter much.

"Hello? Is anyone inside?" She waited a few seconds, then backed up. "Stay clear. I'm gonna get this door open."

Kenna slammed the sole of her boot beside the lock. The door split a little but didn't open. She hammered her foot again.

It swung open at the last second, and she stumbled forward. More than one person stood behind the door, but all she saw was Jax.

He reached out and caught her, swinging her around so she didn't fall.

"Hey, babe."

Ramon started to laugh behind her. "No time for that. We need to get these people out."

A woman just inside the door said something in French.

Kenna held on to Jax. She slid her hands up to his cheeks and kissed him quickly. "There's a bomb. Or some kind of attack. We don't know what, but it's coming, and we need to get everyone out of here."

Jax turned to the woman and the man standing beside her and said something in French.

Kenna frowned. "Are you telling them to evacuate?" And since when did he speak French? "Tell them to hurry. How many people are inside?"

Jax squeezed her hand.

The man said, "I will tell everyone," with a thick French accent. He turned away and jogged down the hall.

The woman looked at Kenna as if she recognized her. She nodded and did the same, jogging away.

Jax said, "You both should come in."

Ramon squeezed past them. "I'll get people to clear out. How many are inside?"

"Maybe six. But they'll want to wipe the computers and clear out any evidence first. They aren't going to leave anything behind."

She frowned. When Jax turned to her, Kenna said, "This is your mission? A publishing house?"

"It's the home of the resistance. The people who are double agents within the organization and work to subvert their efforts. They feed information back to intelligence agencies and law enforcement worldwide. It always has a specific tag, so people know it comes from them. They've spent decades building up credibility so that their intel is trusted."

"You're not supposed to tell me this."

He said, "That part wasn't covered in the nondisclosure. Only my mission here and who sent me."

"He was persuasive."

Jax's eyebrows rose.

"He gave me Preston's location, and we got him, Hollace, and Nielson back. They're safe and receiving medical treatment."

Now she needed to fill in a few gaps in her knowledge. Namely, how her father's books connected to the publishing house. Had he known when he sent the manuscripts in that it was to the resistance? That meant it could be a cover story—and a solid one. She wasn't sure about codes, but she liked the idea he might have knowingly written in order to fund their operation. And to set up Kenna for the future.

She needed to give Maizie more time to look into them. But in a way where the people behind the threat didn't find out anything more than they already knew. Since this location was at risk, they already knew geographically where to find them.

Did that mean they knew what she didn't about this

publisher and how the whole thing—and her dad's books—might simply be a front for...what? Funding the resistance?

She felt like she'd fallen into a spy movie. On the run in Europe. Fighting a shadowy global organization with double agents. The whole thing made her head spin. Plus the teensy chance she might have a concussion.

Jax nodded. "That's good they're safe."

"And you?" He looked all right, but she didn't know how it had gone being in custody for days. "Does your nondisclosure mean I can't ask you how you are?"

"You can ask whatever you want. I'll answer what I can."

Speaking of international people of mystery... "Are you gonna be a spy now?" She lowered her voice at the end so no one overheard.

Someone appeared in the hall, coming down like that opening was the bottom of a staircase. Backpack in hand. The young man rushed to the door. He said something in French to Jax and ran past them outside.

"You speak French?" She shook her head. "Tell me later. We need to *go*."

Jax said, "Let's go downstairs and make sure they're getting the women out. They might need help."

Ramon came out a door to one side, carrying a young woman. A pregnant young woman.

She said, "You good?"

He nodded. "She speaks Spanish, so we're good."

"Get to the van."

Ramon passed them. Kenna glanced at Jax as they hurried down the hall, her following him. She said, "They have pregnant women here?"

"They protect a few people who were impregnated and don't want their babies taken and placed with a couple to be raised by them. They've seen too much of the lives some of the children lead, and it's not just having cold and unloving parents who are too busy being rich to take care of them."

Kenna winced. "I'm glad I'm here to help."

He stopped by the open door and nodded. "I'm glad you are, too."

"Wish I knew what the threat was." She followed him through a doorway to a long hall. "Could be a bomb already planted in the building, and it's about to blow at any second."

"A bomb squad would make everyone evacuate, so these people might as well take their evidence with them."

She bit her lip and stepped into an office after him. Jax went to the computer, where the woman from the front door stood, bent over and typing on the keys. "Okay." She said something in French, which Jax responded to, and then she straightened. "Let's go."

She understood English? Kenna said, "How long will it take to get everyone out?"

"Just a few minutes," the woman said. "Then we can talk."

Kenna nodded. "I'd like that." She had a distinct feeling that she and this woman were sisters of a kind. Turned out, Kenna had more family than she knew what to do with. More than she'd ever expected she would have in her life, given everything she'd lost.

The woman opened a safe on the wall and took out two packets. One, she handed to Jax. "Keep this safe."

"I will." He held onto it.

The other envelope, she slid into a backpack, which she slipped on her shoulders and headed for the door.

Jax and Kenna followed her, Kenna first and him behind. Someone came out of a sliding door to one side—a woman in scrubs, helping an older man walk—behind which was an elevator car. Two people came down the staircase from the floor above, skidding around the corner.

"Antoine!" A woman ran to the older man and held his other arm, saying something in French.

They all seemed so...ordinary. Like everyday people.

Not in the least what she'd have expected from a group determined to fight against a powerful force. A sophisticated group who had been operating for years in the shadows. These people didn't seem like they had the resources to do much.

But maybe that was the beauty of it. And the reason they'd been undiscovered for so long.

Everyone rushed to the door, to the daylight.

Kenna pushed all the disparate thoughts from her mind and focused on moving as fast as she could. They caught up to the older man at the door, squeezing through the smaller opening. A choke point.

Before she could object to the fact they were boxed in right here, making them easier targets, an explosion rocked the building behind them.

She turned back and looked.

No explosion. Just a rumble under the ground, the steady pulse of small charges.

"Go. Go. Move!" Jax shoved everyone out the door.

The floor of the hallway cracked and started to cave in. Kenna turned and raced out of the building after them. The ground rumbled like an earthquake—the kind that took out a whole street. She stumbled and went down on one knee, her hands landing in the gravel. Ramon was across the street, his arm around the pregnant woman.

People gathered around them, watching the door—where the older man was helped across the road. Everyone stumbled. The asphalt started to split in the center of the street.

"Run!" Kenna screamed the word.

Jax said something in French, equally as loud.

She grabbed his arm and pulled him toward the van, because they wouldn't make it across the road. A crack opened in front of them. She let go of his arm, and they both ran, jumping over the crack, even while it widened.

Was this it for them?

The earthquake turned to thunder.

Ramon and everyone with him raced down the street, where people were gathering. The smell of burning and sewage wafted through the air, along with a cloud of smoke.

She looked back and saw a fireball erupt through the crack, an odd color. Chemicals igniting? Hopefully, only a small quantity.

How far away were they supposed to run?

Up ahead, the van shifted sideways off balance. Stairns jumped out of the driver's side, onto the curb, then reached for the sliding door.

The van fell away from his hand, tipping sideways into the hole.

Inside the van, Maizie screamed.

Chapter Thirty-Six

PARIS, FRANCE
FRIDAY 9:32AM

Kenna ran for the van, shoved Stairns out of the way, and jumped.

Jax yelled, "Kenna!"

She landed on the door and moved sideways to grab the handle and haul it open. She got it about an inch back, toward the rear of the van. Sliding it. Pushing. Shoving.

The van shifted farther into the hole.

She couldn't get the door open.

"I'm coming!" Jax shifted his weight, standing at the edge of the crack in the asphalt. The part the van had been on had torn away from the stable edge, leaving layers of asphalt in view along with pipes and tubes under the street. Sharp ends of rebar poked out under where he stood.

"Stay there!" She could get the door open.

"Kenna, help me!" Maizie cried out from inside the van.

Everything inside Kenna screamed, and the sound burst from between her lips as she shoved at the door. It opened maybe a foot, and then slid back toward her. Kenna's fingers caught between the door and the frame. She screamed.

Jax slammed into the door behind her. "Let me help."

She gritted her teeth, tears running down her face. He pushed at the door, far stronger and more capable than her, while she was immobilized by what she couldn't do. Incapable. Not strong enough. Not able.

This man God had sent her would have to do it. He'd have to be the one to save Maizie while she stood by.

The ground shuddered, and the van slipped lower into the ground. Maizie screamed. Maybe Kenna did as well, but she needed to pray, not let the fear swallow her.

God, help us.

Jax eased around her, pushing the door as he went. He braced on the edge of the floor and the roof, let go with one hand and held it out. "Maizie, take my hand."

The teen huddled on the far side of the van, her face pale with fear. Unable to do anything. Frozen where she was.

"Maizie." Kenna leaned around Jax so she could see the girl. "Look at me, honey."

The teen's gaze flicked to her, wide eyed. In shock.

"Reach out your hand."

No way could Kenna grab it. She couldn't pull Maizie out or help her get from the van back to the street level. Why had she jumped down in the first place? Kenna shouldn't have done that. Now they were going to have to rescue both of them, because she couldn't even pull herself out.

Kenna said, "Come on, Maze. We've gotta go."

The girl moved gingerly, pushing off the side of the van.

"That's it. Keep going." *Ignore the van slipping deeper into this hole.* If it fell farther, who knew how deep they would go. Trapped under Paris. In a catacomb—didn't they have those here? Or a sewer line, which was more likely, given the smell down here.

Smoke drifted between debris below them, surrounding them in the cloud of dust.

Kenna turned and spotted Stairns and Ramon by the edge, knotting a rope. Intensity on both their faces. She was the liability here. The rest of them could pull themselves out. She couldn't even grab a hand and let herself be pulled up. Not if she wanted to use her arms ever for the rest of her life.

Shouldn't have jumped.

But instinct had driven her to do whatever it took to save Maizie. She'd have done the same for any of them, which wasn't the point. It just made her reckless in a way she didn't like. Ramon might just be correct in his assessment of her and the way her instincts drove her. Not that she'd ever admit that to him.

Kenna would lose something just to save someone else.

If it meant they lived, or that they were safe, she would jeopardize her arms without thinking about it. She would give her life without a hesitation.

But the cost?

She didn't like the idea of living without her arms. There would be future times when she would need to save one of them, or all of them, and she'd have no way to do it because she'd destroyed her arms here.

Or if she lost her life saving them once, who would save them next time?

It might sound like a good idea in the moment. Giving of herself for someone she loved wasn't ever a bad thing. But with the high cost, it only solved that one problem. It wouldn't help any time after that.

And there would be times after.

But if she lived, and she had at least some use of her arms, then she would always be around, no matter what. She'd be able to do what she could, over and over, in situations where they had to fight for survival, for years to come.

The van shifted.

Jax grabbed Maizie around the waist.

Fear washed over the girl's face.

Kenna said, "Look at me." Who knew what she was thinking about.

When Maizie's gaze tracked over to her, Kenna said, "We're gonna get out of here."

Maizie nodded. Jax turned her around, leaning his back against the van. "Ramon!"

"Got her." Ramon lay on the ground, his head and shoulders over the edge. He reached down. "Grab my hand, *hermana.*"

Jax gave Maizie a boost so she could grab Ramon's hand, and he pulled her up. Stairns and Ramon tugged the teen over the edge.

Jax said, "Ready?"

There was no time to wait—and no reason to. "How am I going to...?" She didn't even know how to ask. She just lifted her hands.

He held out his hand. "Come this way."

Stairns lowered the rope over the edge, close to the rear corner of the van. Kenna just had to step over the door.

She looked at the opening.

The van shifted.

Kenna took a step onto the lip of the van, at the open

door, all her momentum going toward Jax. She grabbed his hand, then around his waist.

"I've got you."

"I know." She knew how it sounded, and there was no time to explain. But guilt still suffused every inch of her. If it wasn't for her, he would be out of this hole. But she'd jumped in after Maizie so he had to rescue both of them.

She might've helped Maizie settle, so maybe she hadn't been completely useless.

Jax grabbed the rope. "This is gonna hurt whatever way I do it." He wound it under her arms and tied it off, high on her chest.

She tried to breathe around it but ended up just thanking God this would only be a few seconds. She looked up and saw Ramon and Stairns at the edge of the hole. More people, the ones they'd helped evacuate from the building, had gathered at the edges.

Her face heated.

"Go!" Jax yelled.

Stairns and Ramon pulled on the rope. She lifted off the van, out of Jax's arms. "Get up here!" She wasn't leaving him down there. She wasn't going to be up on street level if he was down in the van when it broke through another layer underground and disappeared. She wasn't going to lose him like this!

Fear caught the breath in her throat.

Jax grabbed rebar, then the edge. Working his way up, hand-over-hand, like he was rock climbing. His shirt snagged on a jagged piece of metal, but he only grunted.

Her friends slid her over the edge, hauling her onto the asphalt where they dragged her back from the edge.

She pushed them away and watched Jax climb. The French people they'd helped gathered around and pulled him up the rest of the way. He spoke to them and even shook a couple of hands.

Maizie slammed into Kenna, winding her arms around Kenna's waist.

The rope loosened.

Kenna wrapped her arms around the teen and laid her cheek on Maizie's hair. She let out a long sigh, pure relief. No words in her mouth to speak how grateful she was that they'd made it out.

Jax came over, speaking to Ramon and Stairns. She couldn't make out what they were saying. Then he was winding his arms around her and Maizie. The girl stiffened for a second, then let go of it.

Kenna lifted her chin, and he kissed her, quick and gentle. She smiled. "Ask me now."

Maizie didn't move. "Is this about the ring in the box?"

Jax's brows rose. "Does everyone know about that?"

"I don't know what you mean. I don't know anything." Maizie eased back, then got up from between them and went over to Ramon and Stairns. Police sirens filled the air. The building behind them was toast. It looked like the whole thing had collapsed in on itself and fallen into the hole in the ground.

Someone must have set charges under the building. Maybe in basement rooms or another spot under it, like tunnels or pipes.

"Did we get what we came here for?"

Jax touched her cheek. "I think so."

"I'm not talking about us. I mean your mission."

He touched his lips to hers. "Time will tell."

Kenna leaned against him. "This isn't over. I know that because it never really is."

"Sounds like you've settled something, though."

"It's not that I *want* to give my life for you guys. It's that we get into a lot of situations where that could happen. Where it would be the right thing."

"But…"

She said, "I'm gonna try and live instead. And not make myself another victim like I just did. I'll try not to make a habit of jumping without thinking."

"I like saving you."

Which meant he'd have to be with her in order to do that. Did Jax really want to quit his job and work with her? She'd never asked, and he hadn't told her.

Something else they should talk about.

A police car rounded the corner, followed by an ambulance.

Jax said, "To be continued," and kissed her again. Yeah, she was hoping there would be more of that to come. Jax helped her stand, holding her steady while she found her balance.

Whoever these people were, Kenna felt like she'd barely scratched the surface. They might believe they'd won here today, destroying the publisher that just might be a front.

Keziya was still out there.

Who knew where they would find the leader, the one who called the shots of their whole organization. It might be the woman she'd met, Keziya, and it might be someone else entirely.

In time, she wanted to pick the entire "company" apart, piece by piece. Or persuade the president that she should have a part in the operation. Cover the home front and any operation they had going there, while others moved across the world and fought on other fronts.

Kenna looked at her family.

She had plenty to stay home for. Lots of reasons to stick

close and work with the team she had now. Live her life, rather than let it get swallowed up by a mission that was all instinct.

Contentment would be in the balance between those two.

The future and her brand of justice.

Chapter Thirty-Seven

Rodanthe, North Carolina
June 1991

Wind whipped her hair across her face, snagging on her ice cream. Malcom leaned over and tucked the hair behind her ear.

She smiled, bouncing baby Kenna on her knees. Precocious kid was making a mess of the tiny cone she had, smearing it everywhere. Amara said, "How did the takedown go?"

"We got 'im." Malcom ate his own ice cream cone. "I have a few days off."

She glanced around, watching the boardwalk around them rather than reacting to what he'd said.

"Thought maybe we could get a cabin for the weekend. Take Kenna and spend some time together, the three of us."

Amara looked over. "That would be nice. But I don't think I'll be able to come."

Malcom frowned. "What do you mean?"

She'd been increasingly antsy lately. He figured it was because he'd had a handful of back-to-back cases, where he'd been gone for days at a time. Or weeks.

He was going to leave the FBI at some point, but not yet. He had to put in his time first, or he'd leave no better off than when he started. They'd have no way to support themselves. And it wasn't like he'd ever learned how to do anything else.

Malcom reached over and helped Kenna with her ice cream. The kid was intent on putting the whole thing in her mouth at once.

"I got a call from Paris."

He frowned.

"They think it's a good idea we don't go back there or do anything to help out." She hesitated. "Now I'm worried someone betrayed us."

"You think there's a mole in the resistance?"

Amara shrugged. "It's so hard to know who to trust. We're all trained to deceive everyone. It's why I never went all in with them, because they wouldn't trust me any more than I would trust them."

"We promised this was about keeping Kenna out of that life."

She nodded. "You know I wanted to help. For Allison. And Anne. Both of them are dead because of this." She cleared her throat. "My sisters."

Malcom didn't say anything because there was no point debating it over again. They'd had that conversation plenty of times.

"Raising Kenna isn't nothing. But I still don't feel like I'm doing anything."

"So what do you want to do?"

Amara said, "First, I'm going to figure out why it feels like someone has been watching us all day."

In a moment, she went from a mother, a woman who grieved what she'd lost, to a focused agent. A highly-trained asset. As if the years away from that life hadn't diminished one bit of who she really was.

It almost made Malcom regret taking her away from that life. Forcing her to diminish who she was into simply a woman with a child to care for. A wife and mother. As if that was all she could be.

But she'd made the decision before he had that her role in this world was about raising her niece as her child. Keeping her safe, every day.

Making some good come from everything that had happened.

He tossed his cone in the nearest trash can and came back to where she was wiping Kenna's hands and face with a napkin. "You're certain we've been betrayed."

"I can feel them watching."

Malcom didn't look around, even though he wanted to. "Then we should get out of Dodge. Go dark for a few days and try to shake them."

She stood and handed Kenna to him. "Promise me something?"

Malcom frowned. "What is it?" Hadn't he made enough promises to her already? He'd said "till death do us part" and all of that. They'd chosen each other—love and forever.

A family.

She kissed him softly. "No matter what happens, promise me you'll look after her."

Before he could do that, she was gone.

Kenna shifted in his arms, leaning her head on his shoulder. He touched the child's back, echoing his promise to her mother in his mind. He searched the boardwalk. The street.

Turned around and looked for her.

Worry turned to dread. Was she going to come back?

Malcom prayed for the first time in a long time, pouring all his fear into silent words to God.

And then he heard it.

A single gunshot.

His whole body flinched, and Kenna started to cry. "Amara!"

Chapter Thirty-Eight

Kenna knocked on the teal front door, the sun beating down on the back of her shoulders. One white painted house in a row of similar houses, all along the hillside. Overlooking the water between this island and the smaller ones around it. Haze hung in the air, which the driver had told them was sand, blown up from Egypt with the air current.

She'd opted for khaki shorts and a white shirt, under which she had a white tank top. Sunglasses tucked in the front, and a straw sunhat on her head. It was hot out, and Jax had commented that it felt like California heat.

He waited behind her. Just the two of them, because she'd insisted the others go back to Colorado. She was heading there tomorrow, and Jax was flying with her to Atlanta before he went back to Phoenix.

They would part ways again. But not for long.

Or so she hoped.

She knocked again, and the door opened. A tanned woman with caramel highlights in her dark hair stared up at her. Black slacks and a white button-down but tucked in, unlike Kenna's. She wore it like a uniform. The woman couldn't be more than five-two and was at least sixty years old. She said something in Greek.

Kenna said, "Do you speak English?"

The woman frowned. "Yes. What do you want?"

Jax touched her shoulder, giving her a little solidarity. The strength to say, "I'm looking for Andreas Constantine."

"They said someone might come and visit him." She stepped back, holding the door open.

The entryway was tile, and a pile of shoes by the door told Kenna to slip her flipflops off. The cold floor helped her center herself as she followed the small woman through rooms of the house, to the rear, and a bedroom.

An elderly man lay in a hospital bed.

Machines beeped in a steady rhythm, standing watch by the bed. His chest rose and fell steadily.

The woman moved to the other side of the bed and smoothed down the covers. "It won't be long now."

Kenna took in every inch of the man, trying to imprint the sight of him so she would always remember what he looked like. At the same time, her mind wondered what he would've been like at full strength, in his younger years.

"Did you know him?"

Kenna didn't take her eyes from the man. "He's my grandfather."

The woman said nothing.

Kenna touched her grandfather's forearm and looked at

the woman. "My name is Kenna Banbury. I believe Allison Constantine was my mother."

The last week had been about finishing her father's journal. Finding out what happened to her mother and confirming she'd died giving birth to Kenna. Amara had rescued her, and they'd married so they could raise her together.

Ramon had been right that, in the moment, it didn't change the need to solve the case in front of her. But this was so much more. Now that they'd done what they came to Europe to do, they'd taken some downtime and figured out the answers to her questions. They had done the research, met with Ian Birch one more time. Gone to the British government and requested information about her mother.

Some of it gave them answers.

Other questions were met only with silence.

Maizie had found Kenna's last surviving family member, the man who had adopted Amara and her sisters, here on the island of Crete where he'd moved years ago after all his children passed.

Sure, there was plenty to do uncovering more agents of the people who had caused all this. Kenna wanted to help every double agent, support whatever the president had going on, and make sure no one else was victimized. People with that insidious kind of power shouldn't be allowed to force global change just to suit their own ends.

But before she got to work, she'd needed to come here and meet this man.

For herself.

The woman across the bed said, "Makenna Banbury?"

"Yes." Kenna nodded.

She turned away, moving out of the room.

Jax came over and touched her shoulder. "You okay?"

She wasn't sure. "I guess I should say it was good I got to see him." Kenna didn't know what to say to an unconscious man she didn't know. They were relatives. He'd sounded like not a nice person but could've had a change of heart in the years since.

The woman came back into the room holding an envelope like the one that French woman had given Jax. It had been information for him to pass back to the president. Ways they could help the resistance, a signed agreement between two parties that they would work together. Trust each other.

She held out the envelope to Kenna. "This is for you."

Kenna grasped it. "Thank you."

"Actually, it's you that I need to thank, as I will no longer have to worry that no one will ever come." She looked at the man in the bed. "That he will be forgotten, and no one will ever hear the truth."

Don't believe anything they say. That was what had been written on the back of the photo.

Even the Bible said to test all things, though in context that wasn't about being cautious about who you trusted. Just that a believer had to be careful to measure truth against the Word.

Kenna looked at the front of the envelope, where three words had been written across the otherwise blank surface.

The Constantine Initiative.

"I believe what you'll find in there is the one book your father never published. The last novel he ever wrote."

Half an hour later, they left the house.

The driver waited at the curb in a shiny silver

Mercedes, keeping the air conditioning on. Ready to take them back to the airport for their later flight back to Paris.

Jax snagged her hand. "You okay?"

"Not really."

The driver jumped out, coming around to open the door for them.

She slid in, and Jax followed her. "How about dinner? There's a place in Elounda. We don't need a reservation."

Kenna nodded, buckling her seatbelt so she could watch out the window.

"Wanna come back here sometime?"

She half-smiled. "Maybe. This trip has been a lot."

He squeezed her hand. "And it isn't over. Almost feels like it's the beginning."

"I don't even know if I want to get in the middle of it. The whole thing is above my paygrade."

"I know the feeling."

The dinner place turned out to be a restaurant with seating outside under a canopy. Wrought iron chairs and tables and a full menu of smoothies. She needed something to settle her stomach after everything. Including injuries and jet lag. She'd booked her own hotel room after Maizie, Stairns, Preston, Hollace, and Nielson all returned to the US, and slept plenty.

No one had seen Bruce since they'd shown up at the publishers in Paris.

Stairns tried to find him but hadn't made any progress. The police in Paris had asked them about Bruce—though, under a different name. He was evidently a wanted man there.

"Are you okay?"

She glanced over at Jax, whose burger had been delivered along with her smoothie. Cars passed on the street.

Tourists and locals wandered around. Beyond all that was a dock with rows of boats. Water. Sun.

She said, "I'm good. This is great."

Jax leaned over and kissed her, tasting of burger. "Mmm."

He chuckled. "Sorry."

"Don't worry about it." She nudged his shoulder.

Jax wiped his hands and tossed his napkin on the table. He shifted on the seat and faced her. "You said to ask you."

She eyed him, a million things running through her mind.

"I had a plan. It was a whole thing in London. Maizie helped me set it up."

"Guess you won't be getting your deposits back."

"I definitely didn't plan to be in the custody of British police. But it did give me time to think." He took her hand. "There's always a case. Other people's actions mean things don't go how we plan. We get swept along with a case. Or manipulated into a situation, and we go off in a direction we hadn't been planning to go."

She looked at their fingers, entwined together. "Seems like that happens a lot."

"But then we get this. We protect each other, and when it's over, we get to spend time together."

"But you want more?"

Jax was quiet for a second, then said, "Do you?"

She lifted her gaze. "Of course. I'm not just stringing you along because you're good looking."

He smiled. "Glad to hear it."

"I also like your house."

Jax chuckled. "Maybe it could be a more permanent home base for you. Until something changes."

"Thanks for not asking me to change everything. Or

announcing you're going to quit your job and work with me."

"Too much change at once?" He stared at her. "Things will change, just not yet. I am working out when the best time is to exit the bureau."

"You should stay there if it's what you want to do."

"It was, for a long time," he said. "Then I met you, and now I've found my priorities have shifted. I'd rather be with you."

"I'll try and not be too much of a pain in the neck."

Jax chuckled and leaned over to kiss her. When he leaned back, he said, "I wouldn't have it any other way." He shifted and dug the ring box out of his pocket. She didn't know when he'd taken it back from her. It had just been gone from her stuff. "Will you marry me?"

He continued, "Not today or next week. But also not two years from now. I meant what I said about Florida and getting married on the beach. And—"

She touched her fingers to his lips.

He stopped talking.

"Yes." Kenna lowered her hand. "Whenever. Wherever. However. I'll be there. In a dress." She winced. "I guess."

He laughed again. He slid the ring on her finger and kissed her again. "Like I said, I wouldn't have it any other way."

She was about to speak when instinct flared in her awareness.

Kenna glanced around, trying to figure out what was wrong.

Jax shifted in his seat. "What is—"

The cup on the table in front of her exploded, sending smoothie and shards of glass at her and Jax almost at the same time as she heard the crack of a bullet.

Jax shoved her back, and both of them toppled onto the ground behind them. Kenna's head glanced off a table, and she hit the ground on top of the chair.

Another gunshot rang across the street.

She looked in that direction, blinking at what she saw. Looked like a woman tumbled over the edge of a roof onto the sidewalk below. Kenna rubbed her face, and her fingers came away smeared with blood. Jax had blood on him from tiny cuts as well but had turned away. Already moving. Responding to the threat.

Someone screamed.

A car slammed into something, but she didn't see it. She only heard the sound of metal crunching.

Jax had his gun out when Bruce strode onto the restaurant patio.

"You guys okay?"

Jax turned far enough to grab her elbow and help her up. She stuck close to him. "What's going on?"

"Keziya." Bruce sniffed. "She's dead. You're welcome."

He turned and walked away, leaving them standing there in the middle of chaos. A second later, he called over his shoulder, "I'll be back to collect on that favor you owe me."

Bruce disappeared into the crowd as quickly as he'd shown up.

She sagged against Jax and wound her arms around him from behind. "Give me a second. I think my heart is in my throat."

"I was trying to take your breath away, but I didn't mean like that." He laid his hand on hers, running his hand along her forearm.

"Don't ask me if I'm okay. I'm sick of not being okay, and now I'm covered in blood."

"You need RV time."

She smiled against the back of his shirt. "I thought you'd never ask."

"If we get married today, I could go with you."

"Thought you had to get back to work. Don't you have an office to run?" She felt him chuckle under her cheek, but he said nothing. "And I guess I have a novel to read."

Sirens split the air.

Another day, another country. Another case. It was enough to make her wonder if trouble just followed her wherever she went.

All the while, she did what she could. Walking the path God had put in front of her, with the people she loved. One step at a time. One day at a time.

With Jax by her side.

Keep Reading For...

- Where to find more great Lisa Phillips books.

- How to sign up for Lisa's newsletter and get a FREE book.

- Where to find Lisa on social media.

About the Author

Find out more about Lisa Phillips at her website, where you'll discover more romantic suspense fan-favorite series and heart-pounding thriller novels.
https://authorlisaphillips.com/

If you loved this book, please consider sharing about it on social media. Or leave a review at your book retailer website, on Goodreads, or on Bookbub. Your review will help others find great books to entertain and encourage them!

Signup for Lisa's newsletter by scanning the QR code below
to stay updated on sales, new releases, and
recommendations for your TBR pile. New Subscribers even
get a FREE book!

Find Lisa on Social Media!

facebook.com/authorlisaphillips

instagram.com/lisaphillipsbks

bookbub.com/authors/lisa-phillips

Also by Lisa Phillips

Find out more about Brand of Justice at my website:

https://authorlisaphillips.com/product-tag/brand-of-justice/

Book 1: Cold Dead Night

Book 2: Burn the Dawn

Book 3: Quick and Dead

Book 4: Over the Limit

Book 5: Skin and Bone

Book 6: Dust and Ashes

Book 7: Long Road Home

Book 8 : Dead to Rights

Book 9: Fear No Evil

Book 10: Out of Time

Book 11: Every Which Way (April 2025)

———

Other series by Lisa:

Last Chance Downrange

Chevalier Protection Specialists

Last Chance County

Northwest Counter-Terrorism Taskforce

Double Down

WITSEC Town (Sanctuary)

Numerous other titles including several with *Love Inspired Suspense,* find the complete list here (or scan the QR code):

https://authorlisaphillips.com/all-books/